The Jamerican Anomaly

ISBN: 978-1-998315-35-2
         978-1-998315-39-0
         978-1-998315-38-3

Published by Inicio Press
iniciopress.com

The Jamerican Anomaly

Dedication

To my lovely daughters, Krisi and Stephanie, I appreciate your abundance of love and support for my daring adventures. You've inspired and embraced me as I've evolved into a globetrotting photographer and as I acquire this recognition as a novelist.

My love for you is never-ending.

The Jamerican Anomaly

CLAUDETTE J. DEVEREAUX

Contents

The ICU Patient

Beep......Beep......Beep.

The audible, rhythmic sound startled me, yet it was familiar. Somehow, I could not open my eyes; the lids were so heavy. I attempted to raise my arms, but my movements were restricted. I was restrained to the bed.

I tried to scream for help, but I couldn't make a sound. I had a tube in my mouth! Oh my God, I'm a patient in a hospital and on a ventilator.

I'm an emergency room physician! What happened to me?

Beep…Beep…Beep…Beep.

The rhythmic sound hastened. I was connected to a cardiac monitor, and its sophistication transcribed my heartbeat into an audio frequency. In anguish, my body thrashed around. Suddenly, there was a soft-spoken female voice.

"Hello! My name is Bette, and I'm your nurse. You're in the ICU, Intensive Care Unit. There's a tube in your throat, so you're unable to speak right now. The tube is connected to a ventilator, which is breathing for you. I need you to remain calm. We are working hard to get you well."

Beep…Beep…Beep…Beep…Beep.

The rapid series of beeps were continually getting faster, indicating that my heart was racing. In the medical field, we call this tachycardia—a heart rate greater than 100 beats per minute. An average heartbeat is 60-90. My current rate was 130. This experience was overwhelming.

Bette, there is no way I can remain calm.

She directed simple tasks for me to perform. "Can you open your eyes?"

No response.

"Can you squeeze my hand?"

I failed again.

Reassuring me with a gentle touch to my right arm, she said, "I'm going to give you medication so that you can relax." She connected a syringe to my intravenous line, then steadily injected a sedative. Becoming more agitated, I objected to her unilateral decision to sedate me. I didn't want to rest. I wanted someone to explain why I was in this condition, but I couldn't communicate with her. If she could only hear my thoughts.

Beep…Beep…Beep.

My heart rate decreased to seventy-two beats per minute. My arms became heavy, actually flaccid. My thought process slowed down and became cloudy.

The Graduate

7 a.m. After lying awake for two hours and staring into the darkness, I quickly rolled over to turn off the blaring alarm clock. This was a special day, a milestone. Today, I will graduate from medical school in Albany, New York. A new chapter in my life was beginning, and I looked forward to new challenges.

During the past four years, I portrayed myself as just another starving student who dined on salads, tacos, and pizza. Fortunately, I'm an elite mountaineer who can burn the carbs off. Hopefully, my classmates wouldn't recognize the extravagant designer attire I planned to wear to the ceremony. As I pondered about the day's event, my cell phone rang.

"Hey, girl," I answered jokingly.

"What's up, Dr. Johnston? I'm sure you've been awake for hours," insinuated Jewel.

She and I have been best friends and neighbors since we were nine. Laughing, I responded, "How did you know?"

"I know you more than you know yourself."

"Well, do you know that I'm famished?"

"Yes, actually. That's why I called. Let's get breakfast."

"Sure, but I don't want to go to a greasy spoon diner. We're almost physicians, and we need to splurge on a nice restaurant."

"Ditto," she replied.

"Let's go to the Walton restaurant."

"Meet you out front in thirty minutes."

Just the thought of having a nice Walton breakfast made me energetic. I quickly showered, placed a dab of foundation on my face, and gathered my dreadlocks in a scrunchie. Dressed in a white button-down work shirt, torn jeans, and sandals, I was all ready. Jewel was tardy. I waited out front for her for over ten minutes before she made her entrance.

"Dr. Greenebaum has arrived!"

"Oy vey!" I said with disgust.

"You say that better than me, and I'm the one who's Jewish."

"Dr. Greenebaum needs to hurry the hell up! What part of me being hungry don't you understand, girl?"

She did a little dance while belting out the lyrics to my favorite Bob Marley song.

"You are so annoying!" I complained, laughing at her awful rendition. "Let's go, fool!"

Jewel drove. We bobbed our heads to nostalgic reggae tunes blaring from the car stereo.

It was such a beautiful day—a beautiful day to graduate from medical school.

Breakfast was fulfilling. I ordered eggs Benedict Florentine and orange juice. Jewel had the same but with coffee. When we were teenagers, she would comment that we couldn't be friends if I didn't indulge in a cup of joe.

Sadness suddenly infiltrated my beautiful day as I thought about how happy my parents would be if they were alive. In my dorm, I curled my body into the fetal position on my bed and wept as my mind jumped back to that fateful day in 1992 when I became an orphan at the age of nine.

My parents, Wilbur and Inez Johnston, arrived in New York City from Kingston, Jamaica, in 1982. During that era, America represented a beacon of opportunities, a land that turned dreams into reality, the proverbial welcome mat. Many Jamaicans flocked to New York, known as the goose that laid the golden egg. An array of jobs was available for those willing to work hard.

I was born the following year. My parents were strict but loving. I was raised in a Christian upbringing and taught to respect others. My extracurricular activities consisted of church functions, children's religious groups, and the Brownie and Girl Scout organizations. My parents splurged and purchased a baby grand piano. I was a mere child the day it was delivered. Reminiscing, I remember how I expressed the biggest smile ever, especially when Daddy said that it was for me. It was distinctively displayed, accentuating the living room. I received private lessons at my house from Mr. Dowell every Thursday afternoon.

My father attentively listened to me play the piano. I possessed an "ear" for music, able to reproduce the sounds just by hearing the tune once. As I practiced, he would sit on the sofa with his eyes closed, waving his arms about as if he were conducting an orchestra. Mom would peek into the living room, watching the production and smiling proudly. He frequently referred to me as a prodigy, expressing his vision of seeing me as a pianist with the New York Philharmonic, the most prestigious orchestra in America.

One afternoon, my parents left home to purchase groceries and a metro bus blew through a red light, colliding with their vehicle and killing them instantly. Fortunately, I was at my Aunt Birdie's house, playing with my cousin Genesis, who is five years younger than me. Uncle Herbert and Aunt Bernadette became my guardians and won a multimillion-dollar settlement on my behalf. Losing my loving parents at a tender age was devastating.

I never played the piano again.

Besides my parents' desire for me to be a pianist, they also had their heart set on me becoming a physician. Their dream became my dream, and today, that dream was coming true. Posthumously, this degree was for them.

My phone rang, catapulting me into the present. I mustered up a cheerful tone. "Hello, Auntie."

"Hello, dear."

"I really wish Mom and Dad were here," I whispered.

"I know." She paused. "I feel the same way. They're so proud of you from heaven, my dear child."

"Thanks, Auntie."

"We will be arriving early so that we get good seats."

"Okay, but don't forget that we'll meet at the flagpole after the commencement."

"We love you, Chanel! Again, we're so proud of you, ya know."

"I love you too, Auntie. See you later."

My spirits lifted slightly. She and Uncle Herbert showered me with love, raising me as their own.

Time flew by. Adorned with my new Vera Wang dress and Jimmy Choo shoes, I admired myself in the mirror and smiled. The graduation ceremony was a tad long but pleasant. So much love filled the auditorium. I met my family at the flagpole and was immediately embraced with their hugs, flowers, and balloons.

My family and Jewel's held a surprise dinner party for us at an elegant Caribbean restaurant. The food was succulent, and the ambiance was superb. My aunt and uncle presented me with a gorgeous Cartier watch.

Kicking my shoes off as I entered my dorm that night, I sat on my chair thinking about my life. I reminisced about the bullying I'd endured as far back as I could remember. My haters would flip out seeing me now, a twenty-two-year-old medical school graduate.

From an early age, I knew I was different from the other kids. I wasn't particularly interested in what everyone else did. By the time I was a teenager, my interests were the polar opposite of what teens of color enjoyed. I was on the volleyball team and possessed a killer serve. I excelled in racquetball and mountaineering and dabbled in the sport of parkour, the art of gracefully jumping and climbing obstacles through acrobatic precision. My volleyball teammates' boyfriends taught me their outrageous moves. By the time I was thirteen, I would dream about climbing Mount Everest, the world's tallest mountain. Wanting to avoid being taunted by my peers, I hid my desire to climb.

Proud to be Jamaican-American, known as a Jamerican, I march to the beat of my own drum. I chose my path in life regardless of who would disapprove. I was frequently ridiculed for sounding "white." Unbeknownst to my peers, I spoke Patois, a Jamaican dialect of rapidly spoken, broken English, as a child. It was the household vernacular, so by speaking it, I was emulating my parents and extended family.

When I entered the first grade, my teachers insisted that I attend speech tutoring sessions so that they could understand me. Actually, it was so that I would sound more like them—white.

During my freshman year in high school, I remember getting into Jewel's mother's car for a ride home. A girl yelled out to me.

"Chanel, are you white?"

I was dumbfounded! The entire student body was outside and heard her obnoxious question. It couldn't get more embarrassing than that. I silently entered the vehicle, remaining speechless for the duration of the ride home. Looking back, I don't know how I survived the harassment.

While I was in high school, the difference between me and my peers grew. I appeared well-adjusted on the outside but was actually lost and didn't quite fit in. Fortunately, I graduated at fifteen and didn't have to deal with them anymore. I was mature for my age, and people frequently referred to me as having an old soul. By the time I left school, I no longer cared about fitting in. I accepted being an anomaly—someone or something that deviated from what is standard, typical, or expected—someone like me.

In my late teens, the anomaly trait continued. Being a daredevil, I rode a motorcycle, became a scuba diver and an elite mountaineer, and possessed a modified helicopter pilot certificate that I obtained on vacation in Hawaii when I was twenty. I was proud of myself, proud to be an anomaly.

Flooded with these thoughts on the night of my graduation, I took my exhausted self to bed. Finally, I fell asleep.

I awakened early and had a protein shake for breakfast. Jewel dropped by around noon. "I can't believe that you're going into the Army."

"This country has given me so much. It's the least I can do."

"Well, I'll be waiting for you in California. USC-USC-USC," she chanted as she did a little dance.

"You're too silly. Sit your skinny butt down. Use some of that energy to help me pack."

"Oh, hell no! I need to pack my own crap."

"You really have a lot of stuff. Glad I started taking things home two weeks ago."

"I can't believe you're going to climb Mount Everest, where you could die. And join the Army, where you could die. You're going to have so much fun." She saluted me. "Oorah!"

"The Army's battle cry is Hooah. Oorah is the Marines."

"Well, it's not too late to back out."

"Actually, it is. I paid a lot of money to Everest's climbing consultant. And since the Army paid for my medical school, they own me. So yes, it's too late. It doesn't matter because I'm eager and ready for both."

"You are so different from anyone I know."

"I've told you a million times that I'm an anomaly, remember?"

"Yah, mon!"

Laughing, I threw a pillow at her. Exiting my room while walking backward, she chanted, "USC-USC-USC!"

"Remember that you're going to LA for your medical internship and residency, not to become a party animal," I shouted.

"Yes, mother," she responded in a child's voice.

That night, a group of us went clubbing. We had a great time dancing the night away. Even though we were headed in different directions for our internships and residency, we vowed to keep in touch.

In the morning, I rented a trailer to transport my motorcycle. After hitching it to my jeep, I drove home and found myself back in my old bedroom again.

Over the next three months, I studied for the medical boards and exercised diligently in preparation for Everest. Jewel's family lived next door, so we studied together.

Everest was my first goal, actually an obsession that I'd had throughout my teenage years. Thoughts of me at the summit infiltrated my daydreams and night dreams. In fact, instead of immediately leaving for the Army, I took a six-month deferment so that I could climb the tallest mountain in the world. I'd waited my entire life for this moment to achieve this ultimate challenge. Once I started working as a physician, I wouldn't have the time or opportunity to attempt such an elite climb. I envisioned myself posting American and Jamaican flags on the summit, 29,000 feet above sea level. I might be the first Jamerican to do so.

Mount Everest

Jewel and I passed the medical boards, so my celebratory trip was right on cue. I landed safely at the Tenzing-Hillary Airport in Lukla, Nepal. The airport is named after the pioneers of 1953 when Sir Edmund Hillary, a New Zealand mountaineer, and Sherpa Tenzing Norvay of Nepal were the first to conquer the summit of Mount Everest. This small airport, with an even smaller runway—only 1,729 feet long—trails directly into a mountain. It's notably known as the most dangerous airport in the world. A typical runway length is 8,000 to 13,000 feet.

Lukla is a small town surrounding the airport at 9,383 feet above sea level. Catering to trekkers, it provides hotels, stores, cafés, and not much else.

That afternoon, I arrived at the prearranged lodge to check in. The room was comfortable. At 4 p.m., I met my group in the lodge's conference room. Willard Duncan, our lead and organizer for Altitude Advantage, welcomed us. I became part of a group of eight: two women and six men. Seated around the table, we introduced ourselves. I was first. Smiling, I began my introduction.

"Hello, I'm Chanel Johnston. I've been a mountaineer since I was a young teenager. I've climbed Kilimanjaro in Africa, Denali in Alaska, and alpine climbing in Alberta, Canada. I've always dreamed of conquering Mount Everest."

"Food for thought," interrupted Willard, "memories always last longer than dreams."

"So true! Oh, I just graduated from medical school. This is my graduation adventure."

Everyone applauded.

"American?" asked the female sitting next to me.

"Yes, I am."

"Such an achievement!" she added with a British accent. "Congratulations!"

"Thank you."

She was next.

"Hiya! I'm Shelley Burgess from London. I, too, climbed Kilimanjaro along with K2 and Denali. K2 was brutal. Rumor has it that Everest is less challenging."

"Glad to have you," said Willard. "Well, you know what they say about rumors."

Everyone chuckled.

Rounding out the remainder of the group was Morgan Hunter from Cornwall, England; Hans Vogel and Helmut Krüger from Frankfurt, Germany; Paolo Branchi from Sicily, Italy; and Oliver Taylor and Lucas Ferguson from New Zealand. After everyone spoke, Willard gave us a tentative itinerary.

"Our trip to Base Camp is 38.5 miles; it's at a level of 17,598 feet, from which it will take us nine days to reach the top. Our biggest obstacle will be to acclimatize as we climb the tallest mountain in the world at 29,035 feet. We're going to take our time and let our bodies adjust to the altitudes. We'll start tomorrow. It's a scenic route trekking from village to village. Colorful rhododendrons line the trails.

"English-speaking Sherpas and bovine yaks will transport our equipment and supplies. You'll be assigned a Sherpa from Base

Camp to the summit and back. They will be your personal guide, climbing coach, and friend. They are multitasking mountaineers born and raised in the region as farmers and herders. Their most dangerous source of income is their employment with an expedition company. They not only give guidance and support but also secure ladders over ice crevasses, attach railing ropes, strategically place oxygen tanks on the mountain, and assist in carrying your load. They are not just cooks and porters. Sherpas risk their lives by helping you achieve your summit goal."

Willard sternly emphasized that he wouldn't hesitate to stop any of us from ascending the summit if our health was in jeopardy.

He proclaimed, "It's imperative to have enough energy to climb to the summit and return to Base Camp." Reviewing the levels of Everest, he continued: "We will begin at Base Camp, 17,700 feet, then go on to Khumba Falls, 18,000 feet; Camp 1, 20,000 feet; Camp 2, 21,000 feet; Camp 3, 22,300 feet; Camp 4, 26,000 feet; Hillary Step; and then the summit at 29,035 feet. With acclimatizing and training, we should be ready to reach the summit in sixty days."

That night in Lukla, the group relaxed and kicked back with a couple of beers before settling in for the night. I was exhausted and jetlagged. I turned in early and woke up rejuvenated. We were going to begin our adventure that morning. Trekking to Base Camp wouldn't be a walk in the park. It consisted of rugged terrain with constant elevation challenges.

During the nine-day journey to Base Camp, I was cordial but mainly kept to myself. I took the time to reflect on my life—past, present, and future. Engaging only in small talk, I wanted my thoughts to run free. Ascending this part of the mountain proved to be cathartic.

We walked along the paths, through rustic villages, farms, mountains, and even the forest. The multicolored petals of rhododendrons lined our trail, elevating nature's natural beauty.

The air was fresh, cool, and clear. Due to the rise in elevation, the days were long and tiresome. Each nightfall, we were tucked into one of the cobblestone guest houses, known as tea houses, that were built along the route. They were old abodes with basic accommodations that met our needs.

The locals were gregarious and hospitable. Over the years, they'd witnessed hundreds of international tourists eager to climb their infamous mountain. We gladly shared the trail with residents, Sherpas, and what I called the yak animal train.

A yak is a long-haired breed of cattle indigenous to the Himalayan region. Females weigh 500–560 pounds, and males can weigh up to 1,300 pounds. The yak convoy was impressive. The yaks hauled heavy bags on their backs without missing a step.

With our group of Sherpas as porters and the procession of yaks to lug our gear, we were grateful. Watching the porters haul our packs, food, supplies, and equipment on their backs was nothing less than impressive. Sherpas carried around 200 pounds each, yet they trekked with ease. They were superheroes, making it look so easy. Without the Sherpas and yaks, we wouldn't have had the luxury of camping in comfort at Base Camp.

Our trail was scenic as we trekked from village to village, stopping at ancient sacred monasteries to receive blessings on our journey. The road to the camp was more than trails. There were numerous suspended pedestrian bridges, all varying in height and length, able to produce vertigo for the faint of heart. The mammoth of them all was the Giyadi suspension bridge. It was unnerving to some, towering at 384 feet high above the Modi River and 1,128 feet long. Local pedestrians, motorbikes, and farm animals audaciously strutted across, but foreigners crossed with trepidation. We remained silent as we traversed a quarter of a mile on a minimally stable wooden lattice flooring bordered by a chain-link fence on each side. The anxiety heightened with the sound of rushing water below. I paused briefly at the bridge's center, admiring the scenery from such a unique vantage point.

Mount Everest, the tallest mountain on earth, is the ultimate challenge for a mountaineer. The path to the summit, a height of 29,035 feet, isn't hampered by just the treacherous icy terrain and intense weather; there's the risk of deadly avalanches and earthquakes. Hypothermia, cerebral and pulmonary edema, and death are among the nemeses that raise their ugly heads in an attempt to dissuade climbers from achieving their goals.

Our arrival at the Base Camp initiated a flurry of emotions. It's a continuously growing international community, a melting pot of mountaineers with an array of colorful tents. We bonded as a family, a camaraderie that comes from speaking the same language—climbing.

For the next eight weeks, Mount Everest was my residence. A typical mountaineering tent had become my humble home. Shelley pitched hers right next to mine, and the remainder of our group placed their tents in the same vicinity.

Shelley and I bonded as we hung out in her two-person tent, listening to music and sharing stories about ourselves. At twenty-four years old, she was an accomplished mountaineer. She usually climbed with her girlfriend. This expedition was a solo feat. A year prior, her girlfriend, Annice, was killed in a cycling accident. They had been together for four years. I loved her accent. I could listen to it all day. As a Jamerican, I have been intrigued by British culture, especially the royal family.

Sharing my admiration with her, I asked, "Have you ever met Queen Elizabeth II?"

"Yes, I met Queenie."

"No way! Sorry, I mean no disrespect. It's an American phrase."

"None taken. I've heard that saying before," she chuckled. "Last year, I was honored as the recipient of the Queen's Gallantry Medal for bravery at an investiture at Buckingham Palace."

"Congrats! What brave act did you do?"

"I just happened to be at the right place at the right time. A small boat was transporting school children on a tour when it took in water and sank. I was on a pier, and without hesitation, I jumped into the water. I swam children ashore one by one. After I retrieved the third child, another bystander from the pier jumped in to help. No way could I stand by and watch them drown."

"Amazing! You rock, girl," I said while clapping.

"Thanks! So, what's your story, Chanel?"

"Well, I just completed medical school six weeks ago and passed my boards. I am officially a licensed physician."

"How old are you?"

"Twenty-two."

"I'm gobsmacked! Such an achievement at a young age."

"Thank you! From the time I was thirteen, I fell in love with Everest. I would literally dream of climbing this colossal mountain. My dream has finally come true."

"So, do you have a boyfriend, girlfriend, pet?" We laughed. Her spunky personality reminded me of Jewel.

"I date men, but I'm a free-spirited woman, so anything is possible," I said jokingly as I winked at her. We laughed again. I continued: "During college and medical school, I dated men casually. I didn't want to be in a serious relationship. I'm obligated to enter the Army as an officer in three months."

"Bloody hell! Aren't you Americans fighting in Afghanistan?"

"Yep, so are the Brits."

"Not this Brit," she proclaimed.

It was snowing steadily when we joined the others in the mess tent. The flakes dusted my dreadlocks with a white hue. We were offered Sherpa's stew. It wasn't the greatest meal, but it was hot, and it was good. After dinner, my group hung out together to socialize as we listened to music. We were each given a glass as a bottle of an unknown alcoholic beverage was passed around.

"Yuck! This tastes like toe jam," Shelley complained.

"It can't be that bad." As I took a sip of the concoction, my face suddenly contorted.

"I told you!" she griped.

"Well, I don't need alcohol to enjoy music."

Noticing Hans bobbing his head and tapping his feet, I approached him. His smile was inviting, so I gestured for him to join me on the makeshift dance floor. Wearing bulky arctic clothing, I did my best sexy salsa. The evening was festive. Shelley danced solo.

The night was frigid, but I bundled up and slept pretty well. By morning, our tents were encased in a fresh, thick blanket of snow. I awakened to the sound of shoveling. Separating the Velcro storm flaps and unzipping the outer vinyl door, I was greeted with the chill of the mountain. Hans was shoveling a path in front of my tent.

"Guten morgen (Good morning)," he said. "My English not too good."

"Guten Morgen und danke, dass du mir den Weg geebnet hast. Dein Englisch ist hervorragend. (Good morning and thank you for shoveling a path for me.Your English is just fine.)," I replied. We smiled at each other as I continued, "Bei dir kann ich mein Deutsch auffrischen. (I can brush up on my German with you.)"

"Perfekt! Ich kann unsere erste Sitzung kaum erwarten. (Perfect! I can't wait for us to have our first session.)"

Giggling, I was shocked that I was actually flirting. He moved to Shelley's tent, shoveling a path for her. *Such an attractive Afro-German Black man,* I thought. From his hazel eyes and soft, curly afro to the broad shoulders of his bodybuilder physique on a five-foot-ten-inch frame, he was distracting me.

"Damn," I whispered to myself as I watched him shoveling.

Just then, Shelley exited her tent, saying, "Wow! I've heard Everest called many things but never matchmaker."

"Oh, be quiet! Can we get breakfast, please?"

"It's incredible. We traveled an entire week and a half to get here and nothing but a nod from him. Now that we're on the mighty mountain, he is, um—what do you Americans say—he's a Chatty Cathy."

I cracked up. "He's being friendly. You're the only Chatty Cathy that I see."

In a mocking voice, she said, "Oh, Hans, I speak German. Blah, blah, blah. You're such a hunk!"

I laughed uncontrollably while playfully hitting her on the shoulder as we entered the mess tent. The area was cold, but the food was hot. Everyone had coffee with their meals except me. I brought my own tea bags for this trip. Drinking hot mint tea reminded me of Morocco. I found solace there. I sat between Shelley and another female climber from a different team.

As I sat down, I said, "Hello, I'm Chanel." Pointing to my new friend to my right, I said, "And she's Shelley."

Shelley greeted her with a wave.

"Top of the morning to you! I'm Siobhan," she said with an accent.

"You're from Ireland. Your name is spelled S-I-O-B-H-A-N, although it is pronounced Shi-vawn, right?"

"You're right, Chanel," she said, surprised. "Most people botch the spelling and enunciation of my name."

"Chanel, are you some kind of linguist?" asked a puzzled Shelley.

"Actually, I am fluent in several languages: seven, but who's counting."

"Bloody hell, girl, you're incredible."

After eating, Shelley and I walked around the camp. The scenery was breathtaking, and we found ourselves staring at the summit as it taunted us.

Shelley, Hans, and I quickly became friends, but it was obvious that Hans and I were attracted to each other. Shelley would sometimes stay away from us, never wanting to be a third wheel.

As it turned out, Hans and I actually dated on Everest. As we acclimatized over the initial three days, we walked, talked, and laughed constantly. He loved playing with my locs. Hans, a biracial man born to a Kenyan mother and a German father, followed in his father's footsteps and became a firefighter in his hometown of Hamburg. He spent his free time hiking in southwest Germany's iconic Black Forest region. He expressed his love for that place.

"Es ist wunderschön. (It is beautiful.)," he said with the broadest smile.

"Guess I need to go to Germany."

"Ja, das tust du. (Yes, you do.)"

I shared my Jamaican-American background with him. Stating my love for both countries, I told him I planned on leaving both flags on the summit, displaying them forever. He, too, was impressed that I was a physician at twenty-two. I told him I had dreamed of being a doctor my entire life. I went on to tell him how I enjoyed mountaineering and felt most free in nature. I even apologized for isolating myself during the trek to camps. I expressed that I felt the need for solitude as I decluttered my head.

He laughed when I said that I was a lousy cook. He promised to teach me. Shocked that I was a yoga fanatic, he suggested I teach a class at the camp.

"Put up list. I sign up," he eagerly stated in broken English.

I nodded, saying, "It sounds like a great idea." We high-fived.

I discussed the idea with our team physician, Dr. Ziron and Willard. They thought it would be ideal. Within an hour, the sign-up sheet was posted. Hans was the first in line.

The following morning, Shelley and I met in the mess tent at dawn. While drinking hot tea, she asked, "How's Mr. Wonderful?"

"He's just wonderful," I gloated.

We giggled like schoolgirls.

My first Everest yoga class consisted of ten participants, and we held it in the medical tent. Hans positioned himself right up front. I focused on relaxation and stretching techniques. Whenever I looked in his direction, he smiled and winked at me.

An hour after yoga, my group prepared for our initial training day in the infamous Khumba Icefall, the perilous icy gateway to the summit that was a mandatory step in our climb. We had all heard of this intimidating frozen landscape. From that day forward, we wore crampons—an attachment of steel tooth spikes—over our mountain boots. This enabled us to grip the ice surface as we walked, crunching the ice with each step. Approaching the icefall that first day, I gave an audible sigh.

In contrast to its reputation, its beauty emitted a calmness—it was a visual nirvana! This area consisted of bright white ice hills with layers of a distinctive azure-colored hue below. Though this fantastic land harbored such beauty, danger lurked around every corner. The vastness of the area and its multitude of crevasses, as well as wide and deep cracks in the ground, elevated this scene to a deadly level.

Before training day, our Sherpas explored the territory, planned our route, and secured basic aluminum eight-step ladders vertically to ice walls and horizontally over crevasses. Varying in size and depth, these crevasses were the largest craters I'd ever seen. A couple of years ago, during an arduous trek in Hawaii, I searched for an active lava flow, crossing many dangerous crevasses in the pitch-black darkness of the night. Lava was actually flowing right under my feet. I consider that adventure tame compared to this.

During the next two days, Willard taught us the ladder-crossing technique. It was challenging traversing the ladder with crampons. Depending on the size of the crevasse, up to three ladders were overlapped at the ends and secured together with rope to provide the length required to traverse the massive gap in the earth, creating an unstable pedestrian bridge. Fixed ropes were aligned parallel to the ladder, serving as a railing, but mainly offering a false sense of security. Willard emphasized that we must advance on the ladder slowly and methodically by placing our boot arch and the crampon overlapping the linking bar on the rung as we stepped. To maintain our footing, we had to avoid stepping on the spikes on the ladder rungs at all costs.

Twenty to thirty ladders were strategically positioned throughout the area. Even as elite mountaineers, we needed to train how to cross and climb the ladders repeatedly. Our trek to Base Camp had been challenging due to the sudden elevation in altitude, but the Khumba Icefall was by far the most dangerous terrain we'd encountered. Aside from the blustery cold atmosphere and inclement weather, the icefall proved to be a unique challenge for most of us. It tested our weaknesses and strengths, our fears and competence. We practiced day and night.

It was our seventh night on Everest. Hand in hand, Hans and I walked to my tent. Pulling me closer, he gently caressed my neck. Leaning in, we parted our lips ever so slightly as we kissed. The Milky Way shone radiantly over us, appearing large and close against the jet-black backdrop.

The ambiance was magical.

Our body heat thwarted off the frigid evening temperature. In a romantic tone, he said, "I'm a lucky man on Everest. I'm kissing a beautiful woman on a beautiful night."

I smiled at him, then softly said, "Good night, Hans."

"Good night, Chanel." He headed to his tent.

I looked up to the canopy of stars before entering my canvas abode. Smiling, I cozied up in my sleeping bag and dozed off to sleep.

The following morning, I met Hans and Shelley in the mess tent for breakfast. We were informed that the glacier field had shifted during the night, causing the Sherpas to reroute our path. Previously crossed crevasses were no longer passable, so the Sherpas were required to navigate another route. Training was canceled today. After yoga, the three of us hung out in my tent, listening to music and playing cards.

The following day, I awoke fully rested and full of vigor, ready to set out for another day of icefall training. Ice axes in hand, we spent the morning conquering ice walls. Some had ladders affixed to them. Wearing crampons, one by one, we awkwardly ascended the ladders attached to the vertical sheets of ice, descended, and then repeated the process. Other walls required intense upper body strength as we ascended: We used an ice axe in each hand to penetrate the wall and pull ourselves up, using the spikes on our boots to assist with the climb.

The agenda for the afternoon was tackling the crevasses on the new route. Most of the passages were double-ladder crossings: two ladders would be tied together at the ends, with a rung or two overlapping across the center of the crevasse. We all crossed with ease. However, I was in awe as we approached the most enormous crevasse I'd ever seen. It was a quadruple-ladder crossing. I couldn't fathom how the Sherpas had managed to place four ladders across that vast gap. Willard crossed over first, followed by Sherpa Norbu, Sherpa Wangchu, and Hans.

Then it was my turn. As I prepared for my horizontal crossing, a loud crashing sound resonated from the other side of the crevasse. Hans left the area to investigate. I held the flimsy rope in each hand as I traversed, consciously deciding to focus on the immediate rung ahead as I stepped. Approaching the third ladder in the center of the makeshift bridge, I felt vulnerable. It was unsteady and unstable. Curiosity got the best of me as I took my eyes off the rung and looked straight down into the ice gully. Unable to visualize the bottom, I realized that it was the entrance into the abyss. What I did see was a corpse in neon yellow clothing that adhered to the ice wall about forty feet down. The face was cyanotic, blue from death.

Disturbed by such a morbid sight, I kept walking and misstepped, missing the rung. Losing my balance, I veered to the right, shifting my body as I slid off the ladder. Clinging onto the rope, I wedged my boots between the ladder railing and the rung in a desperate attempt to keep from plunging to my death. I was upside down, hanging headfirst into the mouth of that colossal crater.

"SHIT!" I yelled.

"Bloody hell! Somebody, help her!" shrieked Shelley.

Everyone scrambled to the edge of the crevasse, trying to avoid falling in. Tossing his backpack down, Sherpa Tashi was already in action, crossing the ladder at an amazing pace. Hearing the commotion behind him on the other side of the crevasse, Hans turned around and witnessed the catastrophic event.

Bolting toward the ladder to rescue me, he yelled, "VERDAMMT! (DAMN IT!)"

Willard blocked his path, physically restraining him from stepping onto the ladder.

Holding him back, he yelled, "It can barely hold two people. Tashi will help her. Hold the rope. Please! Bitte! (Please!)"

Against his will, Hans retreated. He grabbed the rope and assisted the other Sherpas. With his eyes filled with tears, his cracked voice shouted, "Chanel, hold on, baby!"

Nervously, I yelled back, "I'm trying!"

It was a dire situation. Although I was usually passionate about Everest, I hated it that day. I said a prayer. I kept my arms crossed on my chest to prevent my pack from slipping off my back. Tashi was precariously standing over me. He knelt and secured my feet.

"Let go of the rope and slowly slide the pack off, then throw it up to me," he ordered.

I did.

The wind was picking up as we were suspended over this cavernous ice field. The ladders were swaying, elevating the level of danger a few more notches. Placing my pack beside him, Tashi continued to interject instructions.

"Now, I need you up here."

"I can swing my upper body up and grab the rail as you release my feet. Then, help me climb onto the ladder."

"Ok, on the count of three!"

In unison, we said, "One, two, three!"

I thrust my torso upward and grabbed the railing as Tashi released my feet and then held my arms. Swinging my right leg up and over the railing allowed me to pull my body onto the ladder. Tashi held my waist as I rolled over on my back. Catching my breath, I lay supine on the rungs for about ten seconds. Then, he assisted me to the standing position. I was glad to be back on my feet—literally.

Before I could hazard the rest of the bridge crossing, Tashi had to trek back across because his additional weight jeopardized our safety. Regaining my composure, I completed the task of crossing over. Running into Hans' arms, I felt him embrace me tightly and then kiss me. He removed his gloves, and as quickly as my tears fell, he wiped them away with his bare hands. He was the most lovable and gentle man that I'd ever met.

Shelley and the rest of the team crossed over without incident. Giving me the biggest hug, she said, "That was bloody frightening! I was so damn scared for you!"

"I was scared, too! I've done a lot of courageous and outrageous things, but this was the scariest by far."

As Tashi disembarked the bridge, I gave him a prolonged hug. I repeatedly thanked him for his support and bravery.

He blushed.

Hans also hugged Tashi and thanked him. Shyly, he smiled and nodded. Before we moved forward, Willard hugged me.

"Are you alright? Do you want to continue?"

Hans turned to me. Speaking German, he said, "Lass dich davon nicht entmutigen, Babe. Du musst wieder ins Spiel kommen. (Don't let this discourage you, babe. You've got to get back into the game.)"

"Einverstanden, Schatz. (Alrightt, honey.)"

Turning to Willard, I said, "Yes, I'm ready."

Our journey continued. Luckily, the next crevasse to cross was a single ladder. I would not admit this to anyone, but I had become a little gun-shy of the ladder bridges. There wasn't stability or safety crossing them. As I stepped on the first rung, Shelley yelled, "Chanel, don't fall!"

I stopped abruptly, turned around, and gave her a stern look.

"Oh, too soon?" she said jokingly.

"Yup!" I replied.

"Sorry," she said while laughing.

Hans turned his head away as he began to chuckle as well. Crossing my arms, I gave him "the look" too. I proceeded to cross with confidence, grace, and poise.

Everyone clapped once I successfully crossed over. I smiled and bowed. The remainder of the day was uneventful.

During the next couple of weeks, the relationship between Hans and I grew stronger. We couldn't be apart for more than thirty minutes. The training steadily grew more intense. We continued to trek through the icefalls, then climbed upward and onwards to Camp 1. We would eventually make it back to Base Camp. The days were long and hard due to the altitude and frigid weather. The temperature frequently fell below zero degrees Fahrenheit.

One day, as we traveled across the icefall heading to Camp 1, a dark eeriness sped across the sky, enveloping us with moody clouds and a significant drop in temperature. The weather suddenly turned to blizzard-like conditions, with what seemed like 100-mph winds descending upon us with a vengeance.

Training was aborted.

We hastily returned to Base Camp, where our tents were tossed about like rag dolls. We huddled together, warding off the inclement terror. A few hours later, it was over. The clouds dissipated, allowing the sun to emerge and illuminate the summit in a goldenrod glow. Its intrinsic beauty enthralled me. We spent the remainder of the day cleaning up after the calamity.

The weeks passed quickly. We trained tirelessly, ate, slept, and repeated the routine the following day. We rotated between Camps 1 and 2, then 3. At the beginning of week eight, we were at Camp 4, preparing mentally and physically to summit within twenty-four hours. We were 26,000 feet above sea level. As soon as we passed Camp 4, we would enter the infamous "Death Zone." Our bodies would actually start to decay at that level. The plan was to minimize our time there and avoid gridlock. We needed to move methodically yet swiftly. Well, as swiftly as we could under arctic weather conditions and climbing in a single line to the height of an airborne jetliner.

It was 9 p.m., time to ascend the last 3,000 feet. Just 9–12 hours to reach the summit. I was excited and anxious. Finally, the moment that I'd been waiting for came to fruition. I planned on pushing my body to the limit and a bit more, if necessary. With headlamps illuminating the steep, narrow, icy path and breathing supplemental oxygen, we traversed single file through the Death Zone. Tethered to the rope with carabiners, we forged upward. Step by step, we silently penetrated the darkness as we advanced closer to our goal. A group behind us broke the silence. Some of my team heard chatter, but I heard the sound of someone in distress. Concerned, I turned to find a climber hunched over, gasping for air. Breaking away from my group, I told Hans and Shelley I would catch up. Assisting the anonymous male and his Sherpa, I offered, then administered, an injection of dexamethasone, a steroid, to help ease his shortness of breath. Dr. Ziron, the team physician, had supplied me with a few syringe-filled doses to help those in need. I strongly advised the climber to descend immediately to improve his breathing. Initially stubborn, he then complied. Leaving them, I eventually caught up with my group.

The group of nine that had trailed us was now reduced to seven. The mountain was practically bare. Climbing through this region surrounded by the thinnest air known to mankind was tricky. At this altitude, there's only a third of the oxygen compared to sea level. It was like playing Russian roulette: We could be fine one minute, then be struck down with acute shortness of breath or even death the next. The majority of the deaths on Everest occurred in this zone. Camp 4 to the summit is an extremely steep incline, a trek that requires endurance.

At almost 29,000 feet, we cautiously approached the bottom of the Hillary Step, the last obstacle before reaching the summit. Even though we were tethered to the fixed ropes, it was another white-knuckle experience to trail through the snow- and ice-packed narrow ledge of this jagged rock cliff. There was an 8,000–10,000 foot drop on either side.

We've all heard stories about gridlock on the Hillary Step. I couldn't imagine being precariously positioned on this narrow ledge for over an hour or more. Luckily, we were gridlock-free. Evidence of the ice-cold temperature was adhered to our clothing. We were all covered with rime, a white ice residue resembling frost.

Reaching the summit at dawn was the epitome of this adventure. The view was majestic. I had only dreamed of what it would be like, and now I know it's ethereal. A palette of colors beamed off the low-lying clouds, accentuating the scenery of neighboring mountain peaks as the sun slowly rose above the horizon, creating a naturally soothing ambiance. I briefly slid the hood from my head, exposing the tips of my frozen dreadlocks. Cautiously removing my oxygen mask, I inhaled deeply, breathing the air that circulated near heaven. I was elated that I had embraced the challenge of climbing to the roof of the world.

I climbed Mount Everest!

Replacing my hood, I tearfully said a silent prayer, thanking God and my parents for giving me the endurance to accomplish this journey. Hans approached me, grinning from ear to ear. We engaged in a brief ten-second celebratory dance while laughing, aware that we needed to reserve our energy. We looked deeply into each other's eyes, then I moved closer. I cupped my hands around his face, and we kissed passionately. Everything went silent. As far as we were concerned, we were the only ones on the summit. Shelley's sarcasm abruptly interrupted our imaginary solitude.

"Oh my word, this is not a bloody summit lovefest!"

Everyone laughed.

I whispered to Hans, "I think she's jealous."

Limiting our time on the summit to just a few minutes, we took pictures for keepsake memories. In the first picture, Shelley and I were touching the summit peak with one hand and holding our national flags in the other. I held both Jamaican and American flags, and she held the British. The second, third, and fourth photos were of me, Hans and I embracing, and Hans, respectively. The last was a group photo. I was so glad that my ultimate sports camera survived the subzero temperatures. The wind chill factor felt more like subarctic temperatures.

We had succeeded as a team, comrades, friends, and family. Our lead, eight climbers, eight climbing Sherpas, and two guides were elated. We congratulated each other with hugs and tears of joy.

After a brief, euphoric encounter on the summit, it was time to leave. We aligned in a single file for the descent. Traversing back down the Hillary Step was more challenging as fierce wind crept upon us. Although it was a harrowing experience, we came through without incident.

Trekking back through the infamous Death Zone, we continued on to Camp 4 to rest. The next day, we proceeded to Camp 3 to rest. As we continued to descend, we suddenly heard a rumbling sound above us.

Hans yelled, "AVALANCHE!"

He quickly unclipped his carabiner from the fixed rope, then unclipped mine and Shelley's. Peeking over the side of the cliff, he told us to jump onto the ledge below, squat down, and place our backpacks over our faces to protect ourselves from the falling debris. Shelley and I acknowledged with a nod. I briefly watched him assist others as Shelley and I prepared to evacuate the avalanche path. Shelley leaped first.

Before taking the plunge, I called out to him, "Hans, be careful!"

He winked at me, and then I jumped.

Somehow, I awakened in a dark, cold atmosphere; I found myself buried in the snow. My pack was wedged above my head, providing an air pocket. I turned my headlamp on and began to dig my way out. I was successfully released from the ice tomb and realized I was precariously positioned on the ledge.

It was a little past midnight, which meant I'd been there for several hours. Removing my oxygen mask, I yelled for Shelley. No response. I frantically looked around to find her. I saw her legs, clad in neon-orange-colored mountain pants. Digging further, I found her alive but unconscious. I repeatedly patted her face until she opened her eyes. I took a deep breath in relief.

"Are you okay?"

Weakly, she said, "I think so."

Performing a little neurological test on her, I asked, "Who am I?"

Staring at me for a minute, she softly said, "Chanel."

Looking around, she became aware that we were alone. No one else was in sight. "Let's stay here," she pleaded. "They'll find us in the morning."

Vigorously shaking my head no, I responded, "I don't think it's wise for us to stay immobile during the night. We could be dead by sunrise. I'm not dying here—not today- and neither are you! Open your eyes, Shelley!"

She did.

Her breathing was becoming labored. She was mildly short of breath. Her oxygen tank was empty. With plenty of oxygen in my tank, I exchanged her tank with mine. My respirations were slower than hers because I focused on my breathing, keeping it moderately steady. She was weak, but we had to get off that ledge.

"My hands are so cold. I can't turn my torch on."

"Your what?"

"My torch—er, headlamp," she replied.

"No problem. I'll turn it on for you."

The packed snow created a small hill on the ledge. It was sturdy enough for us to climb up and access the path. I went first so that I could assist Shelley. Grabbing her arm, I assisted her and got her to stand.

"C'mon, I got you. We're walking out of here. Just place one foot in front of the other." Arm in arm and alone, we began our descent as we held each other up.

The weather became wicked. The wind was loud and fierce, penetrating right through us. Walking was challenging. Making matters worse, frozen snow blew around intensely, battering our exposed faces. It felt like shards of glass were attacking us. The stinging was unbearable, even with goggles protecting my eyes and a balaclava covering most of my face. I had sustained multiple wounds from the wind-blown ice particles, and the seeping serum flowed down my face. I kept tasting blood. The subzero chill was no joke, but we had to keep moving. Making our prolonged descent, we noticed a body partially submerged in a snowbank, face up. I didn't recognize him from our group or even remember him from our ascent to the summit. He looked like he had passed away some time ago. Now, he was frozen in time. Due to the constant freezing temperatures, the deceased don't decompose. His body must have relocated during the avalanche.

"Don't look at him, Shelley."

After seeing him, our spirits plummeted. Without saying a word, we realized that our future was grim. With our lives at stake, we continued inching our way down the mountain. Along with saying prayers, it was the best we could do.

Shelley broke the silence. "Are we almost at the summit?"

"We already summitted, Shel." I was really worried about her. "I even have the pictures to prove it." I couldn't tell if her confusion was from hypoxia, a brain injury from her jumping onto the ledge and possibly hitting her head, or worse, a cerebral edema.

Just then, she said, "Oh, yeah, I remember. It was a beautiful sight."

"Yes, it was, girl. Yes, it was."

"My hands and toes are so cold."

"Are they numb?"

"Yes, and they hurt too."

"Mine too! Keep wiggling them to keep the circulation flowing."

I knew we were experiencing the first stage of frostbite, known as frostnip. The injuries sustained to our ears, fingers, and toes produced unbearable pain with constant stinging and numbness. I prayed that we didn't have permanent damage. Shelley developed episodes of coughing. Within thirty minutes, she had hemoptysis. I found refuge from the wind between two massive ice boulders. This protective barrier enabled me to give her an injection of dex since she was coughing up blood.

After resting for a few minutes, we continued our journey—slowly. Giving every ounce of strength we had, we mustered up the energy to move forward, pushing through our fear. It was as if we were walking forever, taking short rest breaks. I was feeling overwhelmed and despondent, and my eyes welled up. Visibility was practically nonexistent. We were lost on a frozen mountain.

"Are you still hanging on, Shel?"

Her weakened voice simply said, "Yes."

The oxygen tank was going to be depleted at any moment. I didn't tell her, and instead, I prayed.

Beyond the howling wind was a high-pitched noise, a clanging sound. "Do you hear that?"

"Yes, but—I thought—I imagined it," she said slowly, periodically gasping for air.

I removed her mask. The tank was empty, and I tossed it aside. Reassuring her, I said, "That's not a hallucination. It's an auditory breadcrumb to lead the way."

"Huh?" She was perplexed.

"That's the Sherpas guiding us! The closer we get, the louder it will become."

"Are—you—sure?"

"Yes," I said with confidence. I hoped I was right. "C'mon girl! One f-foot in front of the other."

My breathing became compromised. I needed oxygen, too. I was violently shivering, barely able to walk. Hypothermia consumed my body. I could no longer ward off the polar air.

The clanging pitch grew louder, but the landscape was unrecognizable due to the whiteout conditions. We couldn't see our hands in front of our faces.

I became disoriented.

Out of the white mist, someone grabbed my arm. "THEY'RE HERE!" screamed a Sherpa.

Burdened with severe exhaustion and hypothermia, we collapsed into their arms. Aloud, I thanked God and my parents. The Sherpas abruptly ceased banging their pots. We were home— we were at Camp 2.

Tashi gave me the biggest hug. He kept apologizing, saying that he had been looking for me. Reassuring him, I said, "It's okay, Tashi." You couldn't see us. It's not your fault."

Willard transmitted back to Base Camp with the walkie-talkie. He informed them that we were alive. We heard the screams of joy radiate from the portable two-way handheld radio.

Sitting in the community tent, I turned to Shelley and asked, "What's my name?"

"Same name that I told you ten minutes ago, Chanel."

"She's spunky! She's feeling better," I said, looking at Willard with a smile. He only cracked a slight grin.

After resting for thirty minutes, breathing supplemental oxygen, and submerging my hands and feet in warm water, I asked about the rest of our team. Disappointed that I hadn't seen Hans, I figured he was exhausted and resting. Removing the oxygen mask, I asked Willard, "Is everyone else back, okay?"

Solemnly, he said, "No."

"N-no? Who's missing?"

Looking me in the eyes, he hesitated, then said, "Hans."

"Oh sh-shit!" I cried out as I tried to stand. "Let's go find him. I can h-help. I'm gaining my strength b-back."

He touched my shoulders and softly said, "Chanel, he's gone."

With a raised voice, I challenged him. "H-how do you know this? He could be stranded like we were!"

Fighting back tears, he continued, "Hans' plight was unexpected. He was struck by an ice boulder that knocked him off the cliff to his death."

Feeling dazed, I fell back into the chair. The room was spinning. I was in disbelief as tears rolled down my cheeks. Hearing of his death, I had the illusion that my heart eviscerated, ripped right out of my chest. The sensation that the air was sucked out of the tent felt real. For a brief moment, I was catatonic, my eyes fixed in a stare and my breathing barely perceptible. The mental numbness gripped me hard, thrusting me into an out-of-body experience.

Then, I fainted.

Willard caught me before I hit the ground. Surrounded by Dr. Ziron, Shelley, and Tashi, I awakened in Willard's arms. Holding me tightly, we cried together.

As I was unfazed by the sounds of hunger, the borborygmi continued to wail excessively. Knowing that I hadn't eaten in hours, Willard was concerned.

"You need to eat something," he insisted.

With my head bowed, I avoided eye contact and muttered, "I'm not hungry."

"You must eat in order to trek back to Base Camp tomorrow, or you won't have the strength to do so."

Reluctantly, I solemnly said, "Sure, whatever." The last thing on my mind was food, but I knew that he was right. He gave me soup.

During the night, I was drowning in my sorrows. My thoughts were clouded. Why did the touch of death plague me again? First, the demise of my parents when I was an impressionable child. And now.

We stayed at Camp 2 for twenty-four hours, recuperating from the stress we had put our bodies through. By the following day, I had recovered fully in a physical sense, but I remained depressed. Hans' body would never be recovered for a proper burial. He would forever remain in the highest graveyard in the world.

Shelley was improving but was still a bit frail from high-altitude sickness. She received another injection of dexamethasone and continued on supplemental oxygen during the night.

At 6 a.m., we began the descent as a group. Our trek to Base Camp was uneventful. We briefly rested and had hot beverages at Camp 1. We could see for miles. The view was stunning, and finally, the unpredictable weather cooperated. It's mind-boggling how labile the conditions were on Everest—from treacherous to mild and vice versa, fluctuating without warning. Walking into Base Camp was bittersweet. Reminiscing about Hans and how our relationship had blossomed at this site was emotionally challenging. A large contingent of climbers converged at the entrance to the camp to greet us. Word had spread throughout the encampment regarding our horrid ordeal and the loss of Hans. They welcomed us with the most enormous group hug ever.

I had had enough of Mount Everest.

Desperate to leave and avoid the trek down to Lukla, I chartered a helicopter to pick Shelley and me up in the morning. I gladly paid for our extrication from this damn mountain. A helicopter can reach Base Camp at 17,700 feet, but any higher, the air is too thin. It would be risky to maneuver the aircraft. Such a challenge could result in a catastrophic event.

Gathering my belongings in the medical tent, I found Hans's favorite wool cap among my stuff. It was gray with the German flag embossed on the front. Holding it tightly across my chest, I walked quickly to my tent and began crying. Shelley heard me and entered.

"I miss him too. I wish I could take your pain away," she said, trying to console me.

She passed me tissues and continued, "I owe both of you my life."

I sobbed, "I, too, owe Hans my life. Now, he's dead. Our future is gone."

Finding solace in cradling the cap, I felt close to him. Assuming the fetal position, I cried myself to sleep. Shelley left when I dozed off.

Shelley and I bid our goodbyes to the team the following day. Looking up toward the summit, I thought about my journey. On one side of the spectrum, it was an epic adventure. On the other side, it was cruel and tragic. Everest was a fierce mountain to reckon with.

We boarded the chopper and departed Mount Everest forever. Conquering our goal was an accolade, but unlike the others, we had no desire ever to return.

I checked Shelley into the local hospital. They admitted her for three days. She responded beautifully to the treatments. Being only 4,600 feet above sea level enhanced her speedy recovery. I stayed in a motel but spent my days at her bedside. Even though I was eager to go home, I wouldn't leave her there alone. Once she was discharged, we spent an additional twenty-four hours in town to decompress. We knew that we would be lifelong friends; it was inevitable.

At the airport, we hugged, cried, and hugged some more before departing on our separate flights home. During my flight to New York, I recalled my extraordinary journey. Everest forced me to push my body to the limit—and beyond, stripping me raw and leaving me defenseless. I prayed for all the souls that unknowingly gave their last breath for the climb. The only person who would understand what a mountaineer does is another mountaineer. We were born to challenge Mother Nature.

After completing the expedition, I felt an internal shift, a calmness permeating my soul. Standing on top of the world does that to a person. I can imagine the jubilation astronauts feel.

Returning home, I knew I would hold my head a little higher. It's official: I'm part of an elite group that has seized the infamous mountain. Suddenly, I found myself grinning, displaying a newly arrogant persona that's duly deserved.

My footprints are up there!

I arrived at Kennedy Airport, and my family was anxiously waiting.

"Lawd my gosh, pickney, you look mawga (Lord my gosh, child, you look skinny)," said Aunt Birdie as she hugged me. "You're too likkle (You're too little)."

"Yes, Auntie. I lost weight. I'm counting on you to fatten me up with some home-cooked Jamaican food."

After enjoying a delicious meal at home, I shared the diluted version of my Mount Everest journey with my family, purposely omitting the gruesome sights and my close encounter with death. Eager to blame feeling jet-lagged, I retired to bed early. I showered and put on my nightgown. As soon as I lay in bed, there was a knock on my bedroom door.

"Come in."

Genesis and Jewel entered and immediately confronted me. "Why are you acting so weird?" snapped Jewel.

"I'm just tired, guys."

"Bullshit!" blurted out Jewel, crossing her arms in front of her chest. "Behind that cockiness that you've acquired, there's sadness. What happened up there?"

"Yup, what she said," remarked Genesis.

Teasing her, I said, "You're such a church mouse that you won't ever curse."

"Well, you're not a church mouse like I am. You're free-spirited, and I love that about you. Please, talk to us!"

After a long sigh, I decided to tell them everything. "For starters, I fell in love on Everest."

Perplexed, Jewel said, "Seriously? You were there for only eight weeks!"

"I fell in love with him on day eleven." Picking up my camera, I scanned through the pictures to show them Hans. "He was a caring, wonderful man. I believed that he loved me too."

"Why are you referring to him in the past tense?" asked Genesis.

"Because he died after saving my life." I grabbed a tissue to dry my eyes.

Jewel gave me a stunned look."Oh shit!" she murmured.

Momentarily speechless, Genesis stood with her mouth gaping open. "You almost died?"

"Twice," I responded with my head bowed.

"Oh, cousin," she cried out, hugging me tightly. Tears streaked her face, rolling onto mine.

Jewel gently rubbed my shoulder. "You have to tell us everything, girl."

Genesis released her tight grip on me, saying, "Yes, every detail."

"Okay, but you can't tell the family. Swear?"

"We swear," they echoed.

Sitting facing me, they were attentive and motionless, hanging onto every word. I talked until 2 a.m., sparing nothing. Shaking their heads, both women looked at me in disbelief. They were shocked and dismayed to hear of my turbulent experience on Everest.

The Army

A month later, I arrived at Fort Lincoln, Washington, for my elite commissioned officer's training with the aptly named ASTO, Aggressive Soldier Training for Officers. I attended the second group of this newly formed team. The first few weeks were grueling, but I welcomed the challenge. Aside from the leadership training, weaponry sessions, and lessons of military history, the agility training was intense, even for an athlete like me. Staying focused on the feat of climbing Mount Everest was my inspiration. I frequently referred to the picture of me standing on the summit. I kept the photograph in my pocket.

I conquered the infamous twelve-foot wall climb using a nontraditional technique. Bypassing the rope, I ran almost perpendicular to the wall, then did a 360-degree flip off the top ledge. The higher-ranked officers, along with my comrades, stood in disbelief. I used the unique training discipline of free running, or parkour as it's known, moving rapidly through an area by running, climbing, vaulting, or leaping over obstacles with stealth-like precision.

A few months later, I graduated in the top 5 percent of my class and received my orders to proceed to a modern-day MASH unit, a Mobile Army Surgical Hospital, in the combat zone. I was headed to the "ultimate sandbox," Taliban-infested Afghanistan! My first week at war was an eye-opening experience. The echoes of gunfire 24/7 from the not-too-distant battlefield were unnerving. Gone were the long, peaceful eight hours of sleep. Now, just infrequent naps of exhaustion sufficed.

The pace in the trauma unit was fast, the atmosphere noisy, and the floors bloody. Medical school didn't prepare me for anything like this. My adrenaline pumped constantly.

The majority of the traumas were sadly the same: young soldiers with catastrophic injuries. Most sustained severe burns, amputations, and traumatic deaths. Upon the arrival of wounded soldiers, the report of their condition consisted of swift medical jargon.

A combat medic accompanied a critically injured soldier and reported: "Twenty-four-year-old male US soldier sustained traumatic RLE amputation status post stepping on an IED. I applied the CAT above the stump, but he continued to bleed profusely. An IO was placed in his sternum, and we gave him two units of O-neg. blood. En route, he became apneic. He's intubated with a 7.5 ETT and bagged via Ambu. He remains tachy, with a rate of 150 BPM and BP holding at 80/52."

At a slower pace, my mind transcribed his report to be: A twenty-four-year-old male sustained a traumatic amputation of his right lower extremity after stepping on an Improvised Explosive Device, a simple bomb that's strategically placed under a layer of dirt, sand, or vegetation. It detonates on impact when pressure is applied. The explosion blew his right leg off. In other words, his right leg was severed—traumatically amputated as a result of the explosion. The medic placed a sophisticated Combat Application Tourniquet above the severed leg in an attempt to decrease the bleeding. As an emergency procedure, an intraosseous needle was drilled into the breastbone of his chest to allow the passage of fluids rapidly. He was given two pints of O-negative blood through this IO. Regardless of a soldier's actual blood type, each medical helicopter stocked two to four pints of O-negative blood in a cooler, ready to administer at a moment's notice.

While in flight to the MASH unit, the soldier developed difficulty breathing, so he was intubated. A 7.5 mm Endotracheal tube, a breathing tube, was placed in his mouth, progressing to the back of his throat and entering his trachea to supply oxygen to his lungs. The distal portion of the tube protruded from his mouth, and an Artificial Manual Breathing Unit was attached so that the medic could squeeze oxygen directly into the injured soldier's lungs from an oxygen tank. The medic is essentially breathing for him.

His heart was racing, tachycardia at 150 beats per minute. His blood pressure was severely low at 80/52. The condition of this patient was critical. A normal blood pressure is 120/80. His vital organs were compromised because he'd lost too much blood.

Unfortunately, this scenario was repeated way too often. Within a week, the rapid military jargon became second nature to me. We received patients, had them x-rayed, and then rushed them into the operating room within minutes. I also assisted with surgeries.

On rare occasions, I was assigned to the TMC—Troop Medical Clinic. That's an area designated for noncritical injuries and ailments, such as lumps, bumps, lacerations, abdominal pain, and asthma attacks.

With my eagerness to learn, I volunteered to join the helicopter medical evacuation team—MedEvac, as it's known. They retrieve injured soldiers from the battlefield behind enemy lines. It's hazardous, but I could finally put my elite training to the test.

On my first mission, I was sent out to perform a field amputation. An army tank ran over an IED, ejecting their sergeant. Then, the tank rolled over, pinning his left leg for seven hours. This was a serious rescue because of the extensive crush injury that he sustained to his leg.

Due to the remote location of this detail and their damaged communication equipment, no one knew of their precarious situation. A British military reconnaissance unit was tracking and observing the enemy when they stumbled upon the team of five. They rendered aid and bandaged the four ambulating soldiers but were unable to rescue the sergeant from the perilous grip of the overturned, mangled tank. They contacted the Army and provided a protection perimeter around the men as they waited for us to arrive.

A field amputation was imperative to save his life. I anxiously jumped into "the bird," a UH-60 Black Hawk helicopter, the Army's workhorse. Used to transport troops and provide armed escort, its primary purpose was to provide medical evacuations along with search and rescue missions. The giant medical decal, a red sign with a white cross, proudly displayed on the doors concerned me because they looked like the perfect targets to shoot us down.

With my oversized medic bag containing the amputation kit—an eight-fluid-ounce bottle of betadine (medical soap), sterile scrub brushes, an assortment of sutures to stitch his wounds, sterile bandages, medical tape, rolls of six-inch ace wrap, a battery-operated bone saw, extra batteries, surgical blades, sterile towels, a protective face shield, gown and hair bonnet, an assortment of IV or intravenous needles, bags of saline solution to run into his veins via IV tubing, medication for pain and sedation, an intubation tray, and packages of silver mylar metalized blankets—I was ready to prove myself worthy for this mission. The units of blood, a small oxygen tank, and an Ambu bag were already onboard the aircraft. My plan was to sedate, intubate, and extricate him.

The destination was definitely remote. Before descending, air command warned us that the area was hot-infested with Taliban insurgents. We'd infiltrated enemy lines. The men and I were on alert for an aggressive act of violence.

These guys took the title "hero" to a surreal level. The crew consisted of the pilot, Warrant Officer Mark Riddick, the support gunnery team, Staff Sergeant Rob Wilson and Sergeant Rafael Annucci, and the medic, Specialist Four Richard Axelrod, known as Axe. They rocked! I was proud to be a part of their team. As a twenty-two-year-old female Jamerican physician and an Army officer—I rocked, too!

The pilot sat the bird down on a cleared sandy field 180 feet from the soldiers. I grabbed my bag and weapon, an M4 assault rifle, capable of firing both semi-automatic and automatic modes. Keeping vigilant and rotating my head constantly as if it were mounted on a swivel board, I scanned the area.

Reaching the British soldiers, I introduced myself and thanked them, expressing America's appreciation of their unwavering support as our ally. Moving toward my patient, I said, "Hello, Sergeant! I'm 2nd Lieutenant Doctor Johnston, or you can call me Lt. Are you ready to get out of here?"

In between moans, he replied, "Hell, yes, ma'am, um, Lt."

"What's your name, soldier?"

"It's Timothy, Timothy Tuggle, Lt."

"Nice to meet you, Sergeant Tuggle."

I knelt beside him, held his hand, and explained the procedure that was necessary to free him and save his life. Losing a limb is a catastrophic event for anyone. While talking, I caught a glimpse of a sniper in my peripheral vision. With a swift move, I rotated my weapon to the shooting position as I draped my body over the sergeant and simultaneously fired a single round, striking the insurgent in his right shoulder. Immediately, his right arm became limp, and the weapon dropped. Shooting him in the brachial plexus, a group of nerves that originates from the spinal cord in the neck and travels down the arm, I had rendered his arm immobile. The bullet severed the nerves, causing immediate loss of movement. Within a blink, Staff Sergeant Wilson shot the same Taliban warrior between the eyes. Shocked and dismayed, I turned to him.

"I shot him in the brachial plexus, which incapacitated him. He wasn't able to shoot us."

He sarcastically replied, "He definitely isn't able to shoot us because I killed him, ma'am. This is war!"

Lifting myself off the sergeant, I asked, "Are you OKAY?" He nodded yes.

I injected pain medication into his left deltoid, his upper arm, to help ease his discomfort. I needed to redirect my mind to the task at hand. So much had happened within the ten minutes since we'd landed. The stress of this situation was intensified since we were sitting ducks waiting for additional snipers to pick us off. I knew I needed to stay focused.

Sergeant Tuggle was suffering from a prolonged crush syndrome. Aside from the obvious trauma to the compressed limb, with crush syndrome, the muscles are deprived of oxygen, resulting in muscle death, known as necrosis. Rhabdomyolysis also occurs: The skeletal muscle cells break down rapidly, leading to a potentially life-threatening situation. Due to the damaged muscle tissue, enzymes and toxins are released into the bloodstream, electrolyte integrity is severely compromised, and kidney failure occurs.

Even if we were able to lift the sixty-ton vehicle, his injury would quickly lead to his death.

Amputating his leg was the only option available. After Axe took our patient's blood pressure and pulse, I announced, "I'm ready for the IV, Axe."

"Copy that, Lt."

After cleansing the sergeant's arms with betadine, he inserted a large needle in each one. Then, he connected the tubing from the bags of normal saline and infused them to run wide open. I attached him to the portable battery-operated cardiac monitor. After cutting his left pant leg up to his thigh, I exposed the belt that his crew had applied as a tourniquet.

My next step was to sedate and then intubate. I injected a sedative into his IV, putting him to sleep and enabling me to intubate. After my successful intubation, Axe manually controlled the sergeant's breathing via the Ambu bag attached to the oxygen tank.

I vigorously scrubbed his left leg with betadine soap, maintaining a somewhat limited sterile field on the desert ground. I used a scalpel to make a deep circumferential incision, then severed his leg below the knee with a motorized bone saw. Now, he was extricated, no longer trapped beneath the tank. Well, the crushed portion of his leg was still under there.

I left a flap of skin at the end of his leg stump to pull up and over the exposed bone. After suturing the skin flap, I applied a bulky sterile bandage and a six-inch-wide ace wrap to the newly formed stump. With the saline fluid rapidly infusing into his veins, I administered sodium bicarbonate slowly into the IV tubing to counteract the elevated potassium ion that accumulated in his blood due to the trauma. I planned on giving him a blood transfusion when we returned to the helicopter.

Even though we were in the hot desert, my patient would lose body heat due to his severe injury. To prevent hypothermia, I wrapped him in a silver mylar blanket. My team carried the unconscious soldier, continuously bagged on oxygen, to the helicopter on a basic seven-foot-long army green canvas stretcher anchored by two rods. I lugged the cardiac monitor beside them.

The ambulatory wounded soldiers trailed behind me.

Pilot Riddick anxiously waited for us at the chopper. As the wounded soldiers entered the aircraft, he briefed me about our return flight. He planned to take an alternate route back to the base in an attempt to avoid insurgents. As Sergeant Tuggle was placed behind the pilot's seat, the cable to the cardiac monitor became dislodged and fell to the ground. Bending down to pick it up, I heard the distinct sound of a single gunshot. The bullet passed over my head, striking the pilot.

His body fell on me.

"Oh shit! No, no, no," I shrieked.

His final exhaled breath brought silent tears to my eyes. The high-powered bullet entered through the right side of his helmet, exiting through the left. Clumps of blood and brain matter dripped from the wounds. Performing CPR would have been futile. I pronounced him dead. Cradling his body, I said a prayer for his soul.

In my heart, I knew that the bullet was meant for me. My team returned fire, killing the sniper. A minute later, an insurgent was positioning a shoulder-propelled rocket launcher. Staff Sergeant Wilson took him out. We all took a moment to regain our thoughts. Our pilot, comrade, friend, and brother died on our watch. In silence, we placed his body in the helicopter. Removing a unit of uncrossmatched O-negative blood from the cooler, I initiated the blood transfusion to Sergeant Tuggle. Axe continued to squeeze oxygen into him through the Ambu bag, giving him a breath every six seconds. Wilson was the first to speak.

"We have to get the hell out of here, but how? We don't have a pilot! Who's going to fly the damn bird?" he said in disgust.

"I am," I said confidently, "unless one of you guys can fly?"

The men shook their heads no.

I reflected on my demo flight training on a small two-seater helicopter while vacationing in Hawaii years ago. Attempting to quell any fears and concerns, I announced, "I'm not a licensed pilot, but I acquired a helicopter flight certificate in Hawaii. I flew a two-seater under supervision. I acknowledge that this bird is much larger and possesses a hell of a lot more controls, but I'll figure it out."

Wilson sarcastically responded, "Well, this ain't Hawaii! This bird has live artillery attached to its frame, Lieutenant! It's not the toy helicopter that you flew, ma'am."

Hearing his comment made me see red! As my auntie would say, "I'm a drop of chocolate syrup in a tall glass of white milk." I was damn tired of having to prove myself.

Through clenched teeth, I angrily ranted, "I'm aware of that, Staff Sergeant! I realize that you're a lifer in this man's army. You've been a soldier for several years and probably plan on retiring from the military. I also realize you're not accustomed to having a female giving you orders, especially a young female. I know that this is a culture shock for you, but I am an educated woman, a wise woman, a Black woman, and your current superior officer! You need to cut the crap! We're at a fork in the road, Staff Sergeant. Either you're with me, or you're not! The decision is yours! I'm determined to get us out of this predicament, so either get in the chopper or take a damn hike!"

The silence was deafening as he stared me down. My return glare was unrelenting. In a less than apologetic tone, he said, "Let me know how I can help, ma'am." Disgruntledly, he climbed into the helicopter, occupying the co-pilot's seat.

Before climbing in, I inconspicuously said a prayer, then pulled my summit photo for a glance and whispered, "I got this."

I instructed the staff sergeant to wear the headset and place a mayday air control call. I needed assistance to fly out of there, and most importantly, I didn't know the coordinates to return to base. It was a sophisticated aircraft equipped with GPS. Air control was capable of guiding me. Unfortunately, we were out of range and unable to make contact. I would have to raise the aircraft to regain communication.

Prepared to start the engine, I found the key in the ignition. Turning it on, I did a safety check of the gauges. The fuel gauge indicated that the tank was empty.

"Oh, hell no," I muttered under my breath as I placed my headset on.

Before entering the cockpit, I performed an exterior check of the aircraft. No fluid leakage was present. The bullet that struck the pilot, penetrating his head, lodged in the side panel. Since I could visualize it, I felt confident that no damage occurred. Resorting to old-fashioned troubleshooting, I tapped the gas gauge's glass cover twice with my right index finger. The needle suddenly rose, pointing to a little more than half a tank. It would be enough to get back to the base. I minimized the possibility of it being inaccurate.

The rotors were oscillating at full power, and I was ready to lift off. With one hand on the cyclic and the other raising the collective level, I gained momentum, taking flight. Suddenly, at the height of 100 feet, alarms were blaring, and lights were flashing as we went into an uncontrolled tailspin. It initiated a sand and dust tornado, and my armed team couldn't visualize any insurgents that were surely on the ground. With sand in their faces, they couldn't see us either. The only thing in our favor was that the communication was restored. With the guidance of air support, I gained control of the aircraft.

The cacophony ceased.

As I maneuvered the helicopter out of the area, Sergeant Annucci, who was positioned at the open door, fired upon an insurgent who aimed a rocket launcher at us—just in time.

The remainder of the flight was uneventful, but the mood was somber. No one spoke except for me, who was transmitting communication. Using the MEDEVAC protocol, I radioed information regarding our casualties. Each section depicts specific information regarding the recovery of soldiers. Unable to recall the exact sequence due to my stress, I decided to wing it.

"Attention air control, Lieutenant Johnston here. I will proceed with my report. Transporting the wounded, US military times five. One intubated and requires immediate surgical intervention for a traumatic leg amputation. Four ambulatory with noncritical injuries. And one DOA. Two gurneys are needed."

"Ten-four Lieutenant. Continue your approach. We're waiting for you."

I remained unflappable despite the dire situation. As we neared the Army base, air support instructed me to change my communication frequency so the flight tower could guide me with the descent.

"Staff Sergeant, please switch the radio frequency to one, two, six point two."

"Roger that," stated a cooperative Wilson.

Unaware of aviation lingo, I said what came to mind.

"Hello!" No response. "I mean, um, Tower, this is an unlicensed pilot attempting to land on the base. I'm transporting injured US soldiers and a DOA. Please, assist me."

"We hear you loud and clear, aircraft Echo Niner-Niner-Two. As you enter our airspace, I want you to reduce your speed and pay attention to the illuminated markers indicating where you should land. I am halting all incoming and outgoing air traffic. We're waiting for you, Lieutenant."

"Ten, um, ten-four Tower," I nervously replied.

I felt better entering America's pseudo airspace. To my chagrin, rows of fire engines and ambulances, accompanied by at least 100 military personnel, lined the airstrip.

"Oh shit! No pressure here," I whispered, forgetting I was still on an open line.

"You're doing great, Lt. This is a cakewalk for you."

"Thanks for the confidence, Tower."

My mind was racing because I knew that if even the slightest spark was created when I landed, it could ignite, creating an inferno due to the artillery adhered to the sides of the aircraft. The fire department was on standby, ready to extinguish the flames.

I lowered the torque and collective lever to decrease my speed and altitude. Pushing the cyclic forward, I positioned the nose of the helicopter downward. Struggling to maintain the rpm— revolutions per minute or rotational speed—I hovered over the landing site. Continuing to lower the collective lever, I performed a less-than-smooth landing. Fortunately, we arrived safe and sound.

We were finally home.

The ER staff met us on the tarmac with gurneys for Sergeant Tuggle and the pilot's body to place them in the waiting ambulances for the brief five-minute ride to the MASH unit. The sergeant was swiftly taken to the trauma room and prepared for surgery to thoroughly clean his wound in a proper, sterile environment.

As the medics removed Warrant Officer Riddick's body from the rig, I had my team and the walking wounded soldiers assemble in alignment as a squad.

Facing them, I ordered, "Detail, Fall In! Attention!" They stood erect, at attention.

With a distinctive inflection and tone, I continued, "Present arms!" We saluted as the pilot's flag-draped body was carried past us.

Once he was taken into the MASH unit, I commanded that they terminate the salute, calling, "Order Arms!" Then, I released the soldiers: "Detail Dismissed."

When I returned to the chopper to retrieve my medical bag, I realized the staff sergeant had followed me. I didn't notice the team congregating near the unit's entrance.

Shyly, he said, "Ex—excuse me, ma'am." He hesitated. "My apologies for being such a jerk earlier. I would be honored to fly with you any day."

"Apology accepted, Staff Sergeant. It was an intense situation. There was a lot of anxiety. You make a hell of a co-pilot."

"Thank you, ma'am." He escorted me to the unit. As I approached the door, he announced, "Detail, Attention, Present Arms!"

My team surprised me by saluting me. Standing at attention, I returned their salute. This was their way of thanking me for safely returning them to base. After executing my salute, I entered the facility. While inside, I heard Wilson command Order Arms and Detail Dismissed. The men disbursed.

The next day, Warrant Officer Mark Riddick's body was sent home to Winston-Salem, North Carolina. It was a sad day for me. I was consumed with survivor's guilt.

My act of bravery during the helicopter incident hadn't gone unnoticed. Authorized by the President of the United States, I received the Distinguished Service Cross. With 200 soldiers in attendance, Brigadier General McKenzie flew in from Washington, D.C., to present the award. I was also promoted to 1st Lieutenant. This was a humbling experience, especially since I had been deployed for only four months. After the ceremony, the general invited me to lunch. I met him in the mess tent, and we had a light and enjoyable conversation over burgers and fries. He asked questions about my background, medical specialty, and military plans. I told him that I was born to be an emergency room physician. Acknowledging that he had read my personnel file, he expressed astonishment regarding my top scores and unique wall-climbing techniques.

After lunch, I returned to work in the MASH unit. That night, the celebratory event occurred in the commissioned officers' bar. Not being much of a drinker, I indulged in a couple of beers while playing darts. The more I drank, the more I lost to everyone.

Sergeant Tuggle's stump was healing well. He was waiting for orders to transfer to the Army hospital in Germany for rehabilitation, then would return home to the USA. His life as a soldier had ended, but at least he had a life. I recognized signs of depression in him: He had a flat affect and an unemotional demeanor, and his eyes were downcast, not making eye-to-eye contact. He was dispirited. I spent most of my free time with him. Timothy began to experience "phantom pain," discomfort in his missing left foot. This is a common occurrence with amputees.

As he used a wheelchair, I frequently took him outdoors for fresh air. We shared family history, played checkers, and ate dinner together most nights. He was no longer my patient; he had become my friend. I reminded him that he had his whole life ahead of him and that he wasn't any less of a man.

He was the eldest of four and the only son. Lonely and homesick, he yearned to see his family. I could help. It would be the least I could do as his friend. When Tuggle's orders arrived, and we learned he was scheduled to depart for Germany in five days, I knew what to do. I emailed Sue, my travel agent in New

York, and requested that she arrange travel plans for his parents and siblings to fly to Germany from Florida for a first-class round trip next week. She had my credit card on file. This was my farewell gift to him.

Due to the severity of his injury due to war, he received the Purple Heart Medal and was going to be retired from the Army. He was offered employment at the VA resource center in a civilian capacity when he fully recovered.

For the next eighteen months, I alternated between the MASH unit and MEDEVAC missions. One day, I was sent to retrieve injured Afghani soldiers, an ill-fated task.

As I boarded the chopper, my comrades were happy to see me. Staff Sergeant Wilson, Sergeant Annucci, and Specialist Axelrod all had big smiles.

"The band is back together again," I gloated.

We laughed and gave each other high-fives. There were two additional men on board.

Private Reynolds and the pilot, Warrant Officer Gallup, introduced themselves. En route, we encountered heavy gunfire. My men fought back.

As the aircraft jolted, the pilot announced, "We've been hit!"

Alarms blared, indicating that the rear rotors were inoperative, likely disabled by the artillery fire. We had to make an emergency landing. As a dire maneuver, the pilot turned the engine off, allowing the aircraft to glide through the air with some precision. Cutting the engine in flight doesn't immediately result in the helicopter falling from the sky. The disengaged motor initiates the autorotation. This causes the main rotor blades to rotate from the air below the aircraft as it descends. But you can only use the autorotation for a limited time. Gallup had to find a landing site quickly.

Descending and gliding us toward a sandy clearing, Gallup yelled, "Hang on! Prepare for a soft crash landing!"

We glided in the air until we hit the ground hard. Remaining in motion, the chopper slid across the terrain, jerking our bodies about the cabin. Finally, we skidded to a halt. We sustained only lumps and bumps, and no one was seriously hurt. Regaining our composure, we exited the now-defunct helicopter. Our mission transferred to foot patrol: boots on the ground, as they say. Refusing to stay in the rear, I stood among those in the front, destined to find our brothers. We trekked through the dry, dusty, heat-scorched terrain in a staggered formation. Sand entered my eyes, mouth, and throat.

Realizing that I was carrying too much gear, I downsized, abandoning equipment and supplies by burying them in the dirt. I kept the bare necessities needed to render aid. Forging ahead, I was a soldier first and a physician second. I had to be equally prepared to handle the task at hand, holding my own.

Penetrating the Taliban's invisible barrier, we found our guys. They were exhausted and bruised but able to walk. I was happy to see my pal Ashi. The hot desert made us parched. With water in my canteen, I took a swig and then passed it around. As I tended to their wounds, Ashi told me that they had been pinned down and ultimately ran out of ammunition, so we shared ours. This was a United Nations event. International soldiers were on the same mission for the same cause—peace!

Our path was eerily quiet. Making our way through this enormous sandbox was as dangerous as when we arrived. Staff Sergeant Wilson took the lead and suddenly raised his right-fisted hand, silently instructing us to halt.

We had stepped right into an ambush. Everything went to hell.

A volley of bullets momentarily pinned us down. We fought back aggressively, giving it all we had. No longer prudent to shoot the enemy in the brachial plexus, I fought for my life. I had to kill or be killed.

In the distance, I heard the rotors of a chopper coming to our rescue, or at least I thought I did. The mind can play tricks on people, especially under duress. I remembered I had a flare in my medic bag. Being the highest-ranking soldier on the team, I made an executive decision to use it. Hopefully, our troops would be alerted to our location. The drawback was that it could also attract more insurgents, making our situation dismal. With a cease in the gunfire, I gathered the men.

"Listen up, fellas. We're screwed if we settle down here. I've decided to set off a flare to signal aerial support. The best location for me to do that will be on top of that ridge." I discreetly pointed to the colossal mountain in front of us.

"You're going up there?" questioned Wilson. "Yes," I proclaimed.

"How in hell are you going to get up there, Lt.?"

"I'm going to free climb and scale the granite side of the mountain. I'm an elite mountaineer, and this is going to be much easier than climbing Everest."

"Seriously? You climbed Mount Everest, ma'am?" asked Private Reynolds as his eyes widened in amazement.

"Yes, I did!" I pulled my tattered summit picture from my front pocket to show him.

The normally loquacious private was stunned as he softly said a single word, "Whoa."

"Guys, the insurgents won't expect anyone to climb that steep slab of rock. They are most likely positioned on the other side, on the grassy, rugged terrain. Trust me, this will be much faster and, yes, much more dangerous because I will be free climbing—not using ropes or supports."

They were perplexed.

"Yes, ma'am," they replied.

I removed my camouflage fatigue shirt and tan T-shirt, glad I was wearing a plain black sports bra. My abs were taut, showcasing my six-pack. Yup, they were gawking. I snickered to myself. As I'd be unable to climb in my army boots, I removed them. I planned on climbing in my socks, but they needed more padding.

"Private, remove your socks and hand them to me, please," I ordered nicely. "Huh?" he responded.

"I'm not able to climb wearing my boots, just my socks. I need more padding, so I'll put your socks over mine. You have the smallest feet compared to the other guys. No offense."

All the men chuckled except the private.

After pulling his socks over mine, I dusted my hands with loose soil instead of traditional climbing chalk.

"Now, I'm ready," I said aloud. "Let's do this, guys. Cover me. Watch my six!" That's military lingo for "watch my back."

"Roger that, Lt.," said the staff sergeant.

My team got into position by surrounding me with their weapons locked and loaded. "Be careful, Lt.," Wilson remarked, shaking his head in disbelief.

"Ten-four," I responded with confidence.

Surreptitiously, I made my way to the base of the rock face. Looking upward, I scoped out my path, then smiled. I knew this was going to be fun. But then I realized that I could be the perfect target for the insurgents.

Facing the men, Wilson gave explicit orders. "I don't want anyone to ever mention that the Lt. removed her shirt and climbed in her bra and pants. This woman is risking her life to save ours. Got it?"

"Understood, Staff Sergeant."

Limited to carrying only my 9mm handgun, the flare, a monocular telescope, and a walkie-talkie, I ascended. Slowly and methodically, I moved vertically and horizontally. The rock face was steep but jagged, perfect for free climbing. It possessed many cracks where my fingers fit nicely. I mostly used my upper body strength, leaving my legs dangling or swinging in midair. Midway on the massive slab of granite, I leaped up to grab an overhang, a protruding portion of rock, by literally jumping airborne. Feeling feisty, I hung on to it with one hand, dangling for five seconds at approximately 100 feet above ground. Without much effort, I raised my right leg to my face and then placed it on the overhang. Swiftly, I elevated my body onto the ledge.

I was definitely in my element, absorbed in my chi. I continued to climb, reaching the summit within minutes. Momentarily rolling onto my back, I exhaled and relaxed. After unclipping the walkie-talkie, with the volume turned low, I said, "The falcon is ready."

"Copy that," responded Wilson.

My team was elated.

Private Reynolds blurted out, "I think I'm in love. Did you see her hang on that ledge with one hand at about 100 feet? My heart literally stopped when she did that!"

"Stay focused, soldier," snapped the staff sergeant. "I must agree, that was pretty badass." In disbelief, he shook his head again.

"Look, she set off the flare," exclaimed Reynolds.

Gingerly, I made my way back down the rock face. Descending was definitely trickier. I sustained quite a few nicks and scrapes to my fingertips, but I was otherwise all right when my feet touched the ground.

The men all smiled as they patted me on the back for an incredible job well done. Returning Reynolds's socks, I realized that they sustained collateral damage. The heels had noticeably large holes.

"Sorry, private."

"No problem, ma'am. What you did was beyond amazing."

"Rock climbing is a hell of a sport. I love it."

"Well, you're damn good at it."

"Thank you, Reynolds."

"Hurry up and put your socks and boots on, private," Staff Sergeant Wilson said curtly.

"Yes, Staff Sergeant."

Redressing, I said, "Now, we wait for the cavalry. Hopefully, our birds saw the flare."

"Bravo, Lt.," stated Wilson with a thumbs-up gesture. "I owe you a beer or two, ma'am. What you did was nothing short of heroic."

Smiling, I said, "I am a bit thirsty. Think I'll take you up on your offer." He smiled brightly.

We took cover as a series of gunshots erupted. Back to work!

After a brief battle, the eerie silence resonated throughout the land. We took a breather and a head count, ensuring everyone was with us. Now, my men and I were banged up as well, but we could all ambulate.

We hunkered down in a shelled-out, mortar-damaged brick structure. The sergeant and staff sergeant aimed their M4 rifles through bullet holes in the walls, on the lookout for enemies and our rescue chopper.

Suddenly, Wilson yelled, "Incoming!"

An insurgent prepared to fire a shoulder-propelled rocket at us. We scattered in all directions, running out in the nick of time. The building was reduced to a pile of rubble.

An insurgent grabbed my neck from behind, placing me in a chokehold and attempting to force me to the ground. Using the back of my head, I struck him with a powerful headbutt, surely breaking his nose. Finding him dazed, I yanked his arm, extended my buttock into his hip, bent over, squatted, then lifted him as I tugged his arm forward. Completing my resistance, I flipped his body over my back and slammed him onto the ground, knocking the breath out of him. Reynolds was the first one to reach my side. He shot and killed my assailant. Slightly winded, I uttered, "Thank you, Private."

"No problem. Are you okay?"

"I will be in about five seconds."

I heard the oscillating blades of a Chinook helicopter. I knew that I wasn't having an auditory hallucination this time. Help was on the horizon. Engaging in aerial artillery fire, our chopper flew into view and then landed. We were being extracted from the hot zone. We made a run for it. Assisting the wounded, we ran toward the chopper. Most of the insurgents were killed, and those that weren't retreated—except for one.

Shots rang out, causing us to hit the dirt. I fell to the ground hard as an intense piercing pain penetrated my right ankle from a bullet that ricocheted off a boulder. Fighting back tears, I tried to take rapid, short puffs of breath, such as the breathing techniques taught to women in labor. I was shot but refused to fall apart in front of my men. The lone gunman was fatally wounded by one of my military comrades.

Stoically, I stood up with assistance. The pain was excruciating! I was sweating profusely. I could not walk, so Ashi and Staff Sergeant Wilson took me to the helicopter in a two-person carry position. The pilot gave me kudos for taking the initiative to use the flare. It was a risky decision, but worth it. We all survived.

We landed on base, and I was transported from the helicopter to the trauma bay.

Entering the MASH unit, my medic yelled, "She's one of our own!" As they moved me onto the ER gurney, he continued his report: "A twenty-four-year-old female officer sustained a GSW to her right ankle. Gross deformity noted. It's our Lt., Dr. Johnston, guys!"

My notoriety resulted in unwanted attention. Still holding back tears, I managed to speak. "I'm—I'm OK, everyone. This—um— is extremely painful."

My right boot was cut off, exposing my disfigured ankle. My right foot was freakishly positioned on the outer side of my leg. I needed immediate surgery. The bullet had fractured multiple bones, requiring metal hardware to stabilize my ankle and foot.

The future of my military career was in jeopardy.

After surgery, I awakened groggily to see Staff Sergeant Wilson sitting at my bedside, staring at me.

"Hello, sunshine! Welcome back," he remarked with a grin.

Groaning, I raised my head to look at the bulky splint applied to my RLE. Plopping my head back on my pillow, I groaned in agony again.

Addressing Wilson sarcastically, I said, "It's Lieutenant Sunshine to you, Staff Sergeant."

"How do you feel?"

"Like I got shot in my ankle."

"Imagine, it took nine screws and a metal plate to put you back together again. I wonder how many millions of dollars this is costing the average Joe Blow taxpayer?"

"Oh my goodness! First of all, how do you know the details about my surgery? Did you read my chart?"

"I didn't have to. I know people in high places. What kind of person would I be if I didn't tell you stuff? By the way, I was surprised to see that you wear bright orange nail polish on your toenails. Who knew? I've been on the battlefield with you a few times and had no idea."

I laughed. "Oh, so you've got jokes. I'm in too much pain to keep laughing, Wilson."

Smiling, he stood up and said, "My friends call me Rob. Get some rest. I'll check on you tomorrow, Lt."

Smiling through the pain, I said, "OK, Rob! Thanks for the visit. I truly appreciate it."

At that moment, we became friends. The following afternoon, he brought me goodies. "Howdy, Lt. I come bearing gifts."

He placed a strawberry banana smoothie on my bedside table along with a couple of celebrity gossip magazines.

Beaming, I sat up in bed. "Well, hello to you, Rob. Thank you! You really are a cuddly teddy bear."

"You better not tell anyone, Lt."

We laughed.

I took a long sip. "Where did you get the smoothie? It's delicious!"

"Well, I know a guy with a blender and another guy with milk, strawberries, and bananas."

"And the rag mags?"

"I confiscated them from a couple of female privates."

After laughing loudly, I wolfed down the smoothie while rummaging through the magazines.

"Oh no, I didn't know that these actors broke up. They were such a cute couple," I blurted out.

Mocking me in a high-pitched voice, imitating a female, he placed his hands on his face and said, "Oh no!"

He erupted in a hearty laugh.

"Oh, be quiet, Rob," I said jokingly. "We've been friends for only twenty-four hours, and you're already annoying." Smiling, I winked at him.

Days later, sitting in a wheelchair, I was positioned in front of my platoon and received the Silver Star Medal, the third highest military combat decoration for gallantry, from the Battalion Commander, Lieutenant Colonel Ferrell. I was awarded the medal due to my heroic decision to scale the mountain, plant the flare, engage in enemy fire, and get shot while leading my squad. He also promoted me to captain.

The following week, I received my orders to go to the Army hospital in Germany. There, I would spend several months receiving physical therapy. I had a long road ahead.

Tearfully, I told my military family goodbye, leaving the sandbox forever.

Jane Doe

The 7 a.m. morning rounds at Shepherd Medical Center were filled with endless hustle and bustle from the staff. Young interns were preparing their morning reports for the senior residents. Senior residents were preparing their presentations for the attending physicians. Each patient's medical history is explored, along with current vital signs, lab reports, and plan of care.

Now, they were in the intensive care unit, inside room 16—my room.

With interns, residents, and attending physicians in attendance, a nervous intern started his insight about me. Fumbling with papers, he began.

"Here is an unidentified Black female that we call Jane Doe. She's approximately 20–25 years old. Two days ago, she walked into the ER and collapsed in the waiting room. Within minutes, she coded—she stopped breathing, and her heart stopped beating. CPR was initiated, resulting in a successful resuscitation. We intubated and put her on a ventilator to stabilize her respiratory status." Flipping through his notebook, he added, "Her cardiac, renal, and liver systems are severely impaired. She's even been placed on hemodialysis to lower her elevated potassium and assist in eradicating any possible toxins." Scratching his head, he uttered,

"This is puzzling. There's no rationale for such multiorgan failure. As you can see, her physique is toned, resembling an athlete's. She apparently took care of her body." He briefly paused.

"As for her neurological status, she remains in a coma, not waking up fully or following commands like squeezing our hand. She has bouts of agitation exhibited by an increase in her heart rate, and she fights against the restraints. Then, she requires sedation. Her arms are tied down to prevent her from pulling the tube out of her mouth or any of the other tubes that are attached to her body." Shrugging his shoulders, he said, "The urine drug test came back negative. She didn't overdose. White linear lines developed on her fingernails. These are known as Mees' lines, an indication of possible toxin ingestion. To explore the possibility of her being poisoned, her hair follicle was submitted for testing. The results are pending."

Donning latex gloves, he opened my eyes. "She doesn't voluntarily open her eyes, but I found them to be bloodshot, red. See?"

The team of spectators walked closer to me, the comatose woman.

"I ordered an ophthalmology consult. Perhaps the eye specialist can shed some light on this medical mystery. As we do not know what ailment we're dealing with, I propose that we continue to treat her symptoms as they occur. Her morning lab report shows a slight improvement in her cardiac markers and the liver and kidney functions."

Removing and discarding his gloves, he concluded, "She arrived without identification or a purse. The police have already taken her fingerprints in hopes of identifying her and locating her family."

With his head held high, he stood proudly as his senior resident discreetly nodded his approval. The medical team then moved on to the patient in the adjacent room.

My mind tracked his every word. Good job, young man! Finally, I had some details about my condition, although it was a mystery.

Locked into this bizarre level of unconsciousness, I could hear him speaking but wasn't able to communicate, not even gesture.

My circadian rhythm was altered, actually nonexistent. I had no idea what day it was or the time of day, for that matter. Mentally overloaded, I became frustrated and anxious. I was suffering from a gauntlet of challenges. My heart began to race as my respirations increased, causing me to resist the efforts of the ventilator, setting off the alarms.

Like clockwork, my nurse administered a sedative through my IV. Strangely, as a diversion from living in this nightmare, I found solace in being somnolent. Residing deep within my thoughts, I could retrace the steps of my extraordinary life.

Now, I sleep. Now, I dream.

Spy School

Upon my arrival at the Army hospital in Germany, the splint and surgical staples were removed, and a cast was applied. I had nothing but idle time over the next several weeks. Depression stared me in the face. I didn't want to socialize with anyone. I couldn't shake the fact that my military career was probably over.

Six weeks later, my cast was removed. The surgical incision healed well. Determined to push the depression aside, I gave my physical rehabilitation all I had. I attended physical therapy three times a week and continued my own therapy during the remainder of the week. A bucket of ice was my new best friend. I soaked my right lower leg three times a day. After a few months of rehabilitation, I finally felt like my old self.

I had Genesis retrieve Hans' cap from my drawer at home in New York. Then, I had a memorabilia display case created with the cap and a picture of Hans on the summit. Since I was in Germany, I planned on presenting it to his parents. I emailed Willard for their phone numbers. After visiting them, I was going to admire the Black Forest in his honor.

The general and I kept in contact every couple of weeks. I shared my plan to honor Hans. He expressed his condolences and said he loved the idea. He didn't know that I had climbed Everest. We laughed when he said I was full of surprises.

Genesis shipped the display case to me. I cried as I opened the box. It was such a beautiful tribute to him. I no longer used a walker and was walking with a cane. As a wonderful gesture, the general arranged for me to have a private military driver for the entire day. I dressed in my military Class A pantsuit uniform, adorned with all my medals. Meeting Hans' parents gave me closure, and receiving my gift gave them closure. I was unaware that twice from Everest, Hans had called his folks via satellite and jubilantly talked about me. We shared stories about him, became emotional, cried, and laughed. We missed him dearly.

He was my first true love.

Later that afternoon, my driver drove me to the Black Forest. I remember Hans raving about this place. It was everything he said it would be and more. As I could not hike the trails, we drove along the scenic route as the picturesque panoramic view unfolded, revealing breathtaking, dramatic landscapes and waterfalls.

I felt him; his spirit was there.

The general visited me. Once again, his visit was pleasant. He reassured me that I would be ready to resume my duties before long. I concurred. Unexpectedly, the conversation reverted to my skills of mountaineering and free running. He applauded me for my bravery in the war and my achievement of climbing Mount Everest.

"Have you ever heard of the Quantum Agency?"

I said, "No."

"Well, it's an elite undercover government division manned by the military. I recommended you to their superior officers."

I was stunned.

"Seriously? Is this because I have a degree in international relations along with my medical degree, or is it because I'm a linguist?"

I didn't know you were a linguist. What languages do you speak?"

"I'm fluent in Arabic, French, German, Italian, Russian, and Spanish, to name a few." We laughed.

"You're perfect for the job! It requires extensive international travel and expertise in blending in yet being invisible. You're an athlete, master of scaling walls and mountains, a linguist, and if you don't mind me saying so, beautiful."

Blushing, I replied, "Thank you, sir. What about my military career? I have a four-year contract with two years remaining."

"This would be a lateral move with an increase in your pay grade. Your salary will more than double, and you'll work for the Feds in the capacity of a CIA agent. Your true identity will be sealed, and you will be provided with a couple of aliases. You aren't allowed to reveal your employment with QA, as it's called. They will assign you to a bogus occupation with the government. Two of their agents will visit you tomorrow."

Smiling, I said, "I'm speechless, General. I appreciate the faith you have in me."

"Sleep on it."

We hugged, and he left.

Who could sleep? I would be going from the battlefield to the world of espionage. I chuckled as I wondered what my spy name would be. My ER career would have to be placed on hold. There's no way I could turn this down. The next day, I returned to my room after physical therapy and found two distinguished, stoic men in expensive designer suits at my door. They introduced themselves as Supervisory Special Agents Richard Nichols and Mike Lazo from the Quantum Agency. They acknowledged having an in-depth conversation with the general. I admitted that I hadn't slept since seeing him last evening. I received their recruitment speech. Unknown to them, I had already made up my mind. After handing me their generic white business cards, they left. The agency expected an answer from me when I was cleared for duty, which was in about two weeks.

As they walked out the door, I whispered, "Oh yeah, I'm in!"

Three weeks later, I flew to New York for a week to see family, then to Colorado for my spy training in the mountains. I was more than eager to get started. During the next four months, I would be training at high altitudes, which would be more challenging than training at the FBI's campus in Quantico, Virginia.

My first day of orientation left me stunned. Being the first to arrive, I entered the classroom for the didactic session and noticed twenty-one books on each desk. Within ten minutes, the remaining trainees arrived.

A six-foot-tall Caucasian man in his late twenties with rugged good looks walked in. His deep blue eyes, chiseled chin, loose, shoulder-length, dirty-blond hair, and toned stature caught my attention. As I glanced back over my shoulder, we made brief eye contact. He seduced me with his cheesy yet sexy smile. Exuding arrogance, he was unable to hide his natural swag. He resembled Brad Pitt.

Slowly, I turned my head back to the front as if I wasn't interested, but I was. Extending his hand, he approached me.

"Hello, I'm Johan Ramesh. I prefer to be called Ramesh," he said in a somewhat cocky manner.

Smiling radiantly, I shook his hand. "Hello, Ramesh. I'm Chanel, Chanel Johnston."

"Guess I'll have to hire someone to read these books for me," he boasted. "I don't think I'll have time, being a spy and all it entails."

"Wow, bending the rules already?"

Our banter was refreshing. He informed me that our group would have seven participants, all exhibiting particular traits. Ramesh was known for being a master of disguise, a chameleon, and an astute impersonator. He was orphaned as a toddler, and his adoptive parents worked in Hollywood as mask creators and costume makeup artists who had converted their garage into a studio. He bragged about having the best Halloween costumes from elementary through high school.

He didn't see action in war while serving in the Air Force, and I could tell that he yearned for it.

Staring at me, he said, "I'm going to call you C.J. from now on."

"Seriously? That's my cool spy name, my initials?"

Laughing, he remarked, "It fits!"

Oy vey, I've been here for five minutes, and this fool is already hitting on me.

"What are your secret powers?" he questioned.

"Well, I defy gravity, as in scaling walls and mastering the art of parkour. That's the art of movement creatively expressed in flips and acrobatics. I vault over obstacles from various heights, landing with grace. I'm also polylingual, fluent in six languages other than English. Oh, I'm also a medical doctor," I said proudly.

"Seriously? That's an impressive resume. I'm glad you're on my team."

The next trainee was Cody Never, an electronics expert with an unusual surname. Following Cody was Daniel Ludwig, an explosives expert. He was a demolition specialist in the Marines. The last male was Ramon Miranda, an elite hacker who hadn't met a computer that he couldn't crack. The women arrived at the same time. Bernice Ford was a firearms specialist and a sharpshooter from the Air Force police. Penny Remington completed our group. With a degree in mechanical engineering, she would be our logistics specialist.

Once again, I'm represented as the only Black person in the room. I was ready to leave my mark, make a difference, and, hopefully, pave a path.

Special Agent Holmes led the orientation. "Today is the day that your life and name change. You'll be provided with two aliases to use when you're on assignment. Your true identity will be sealed, including your fingerprints. They will be permanently blocked."

We were all on a contract. Extending the contract was by invitation only. Those who declined the invitation would be placed on inactive status and could convert back at any time or when needed. If we betrayed the agency or engaged in criminal activity, our employment would be terminated, and we'd be placed on the erstwhile list as a former agent, possibly facing federal charges. We would be considered "burned" in the world of espionage, perhaps labeled a traitor.

We stood and read the oath in unison. Everyone received a package containing our aliases, passports, and secure government-issued mobile phones and was assigned a code to use when calling the agency. My code was CJ2210: my initials and time of birth in military time, 10:10 p.m. civilian time. I was given the aliases Crystal Diamond and Chloé Thibodeaux. Ramesh was given Harrison Steele and Xander Cucuta, which were such cool spy names.

Our team was ordered to focus on domestic and foreign terrorist activities, relying solely on intel. Our first week was jam-packed with information. There was also new lingo to learn. A "Code Armageddon" meant an agent was in the worst situation possible. "Agent down" meant that an agent had been injured or incapacitated. We were assigned our handlers. Mine was the major general.

We learned how to apply "Invisible Fingers," a fingerprint cream that eradicates prints by filling in between the whorls of the pattern as it hardens. This transforms into a smooth, undetectable fingerprint. We were taught how to pick locks and perfect hand-to-hand and boxing techniques. I witnessed Ramesh's art of brutality. He would immediately go for the kill. He had enormous upper body strength. I preferred to disable or disarm my opponent. I would have to be in imminent danger to take someone's life, such as in war.

We had defensive-driving lessons in an area known as Stunt City. It was so sick; it was awesome! We learned how to elude being trailed, perform maneuvers during a pursuit, and even drive a tilted vehicle on two wheels. I felt like a stunt woman!

I suggested defensive motorcycle lessons, and QA complied. I was the only motorcyclist in the group. During the two-day session,

I learned outrageous street and freeway maneuvers. I rode my Kawasaki 650 CC motorcycle on the freeway concrete retaining wall. Lowering my head, which curved my back, decreased the centrifugal force. It was such a rush! I'm definitely an adrenaline junkie. Just another anomaly, I thought. My helmet was upgraded with a communication grid that connected to QA with the touch of a concealed sensor button.

The first six months consisted of nothing but paperwork, doing deep dives into the lives of potential domestic and international terrorists. Nothing really panned out. We were anxious to get into the field, ready to flex our new espionage knowledge. It was a full year before we were assigned a high-security-clearance mission. Finally, an epic assignment was handed to us. Ramesh, Ramon, and I were going to England to perform a cloak-and-dagger operation. The remainder of our team headed to Alaska to infiltrate an anti-government extremist group.

Ramesh and I were part of a diplomatic delegation accompanying the president of the United States on her trip to England in three weeks. We were assuming the role of newlyweds. Our mission was to retrieve data from a computer in the presidential suite at the Miltenburg Manor. QA's intel informed us that the grandson of one of the European dignitaries had been associating with terrorists. Supposedly, he had a red laptop that contained the locations of worldwide terrorist cells, including the names of their members. We were instructed to download, not delete, the list. Ramon would assist by hacking into the computer. Getting access to the secured suites was the ultimate challenge.

Ramesh and I had an appointment at the highly classified spy room. We were fitted with the gadgets required to accomplish our assignment. The spy room manager, Nancy Winslow, was a grumpy woman in her fifties. Rumor has it that no one had ever seen her smile. She had been with QA for about twenty-five years and apparently designed most of the espionage equipment.

We were fitted with communication earbuds color-coded to our pigmentation that positioned snugly into the ear canal. Since I'm

Black and Ramesh was white, we probably wouldn't screw this up. The buds were impeccably designed so that we could hear ambient sounds and simultaneously communicate with our team. Ramesh was fitted with a designer belt that had a 120-foot thin climbing rope embedded in it. That was my first clue that I would be scaling a building on this assignment. As my left ring finger was sized for the costume engagement ring and wedding band, I wondered if they had hidden spy powers. They did! The engagement ring was actually a sedation ring. A needle was ejected through the center of a cubic zirconia stone and injected a concentrated dose of the sedative ketamine upon contact. The opponent would fall asleep in mere seconds. Nancy saved the best item for last. I was fitted with a spy bra. There were carabiner clips designed into the underwire bra.

With excitement, I said, "I love how this bra makes my boobs look perfect! Can I have it?"

"No, agent," snapped Nancy.

"Well then, can I buy it?"

"You can't get this at the mall," she replied.

Even though I was disappointed, I laughed to myself.

Two weeks before our departure, we received an itinerary. We were going to attend two events at the Miltenburg Manor. The first night was the Unity Gala, and the following day was the Commonwealth Luncheon. The residential suites were on the second to fifth floors and heavily guarded with armed security.

I flew to Los Angeles for the weekend to shop for the perfect dresses. Concerned about what Ramesh would wear, I invited him to accompany me on my shopping spree. I found a cute boutique on Rodeo Drive in Beverly Hills that had the perfect outfits. Convinced that his old brown suit would suffice, Ramesh lost interest in shopping. I told him my dresses were extraordinarily gorgeous and his suits must complement them. I had prepared a plan to gain entry into the residential area, and it required everyone's eyes on me. On that day, I didn't want to be invisible; I needed to be seen.

My next mission was to dress Ramesh. As we explored different designers, he became a whiny child, complaining that he couldn't afford the clothes.

"This is too expensive for my budget. I can't afford this."

"Well, I can." I flashed my platinum credit card and winked at him.

By the end of the day, I had my elegant dresses, and he had two Armani suits. One was a Herringbone two-piece, and the other was a tuxedo with a classic black tailcoat, including a Victorian top hat. The tailored suits were sent to him the following week as a rush order.

We were ready for London!

Two nights before leaving for Washington, D.C., to board Air Force One, bound for London, I invited Ramesh over for dinner to discuss my plan. Since I don't cook, I had spaghetti delivered from my favorite Italian restaurant. We ate, then focused on work. Intel provided QA with the building blueprints and the possible location of the laptop—suite 402. I told Ramesh that we would ascend the upper floors in plain sight. He smirked.

It was time to move on to the next phase of the evening. Our undercover decoy was to portray a newly married couple. We would be dancing at the gala and needed to be comfortable with each other, so we practiced dancing.

Jokingly, I said, "For a white boy, you've got rhythm."

"I know," he said matter-of-factly.

The British band would be versatile, playing an array of music genres. From the tango to salsa and hip-hop, we danced the entire night. It felt more like a date instead of a rehearsal. There wasn't any doubt that we were attracted to each other, but he was my work partner.

Two days later, we boarded the infamous Air Force One presidential plane. It was an incredible aircraft. Because we had top-secret clearance, we could take a personal tour. President Williamson summoned me to her airborne Oval Office. She was the first female Black president of the United States. As a former prosecutor, she couldn't be intimidated. As a senator, she implemented an abundance of good changes. She was a positive role model, paving the way for women of color. I idolized her.

Entering the room, I gleefully addressed her with a salute. "Hello, Madam President." Surrounded by several assistants, she asked that the room be cleared of all personnel except me. She told me to close the door and take a seat.

"Hello, Agent Johnston, or should I call you Crystal Diamond? We have a mutual friend. Major General McKenzie told me so much about you."

"I admire the general. He's a mentor and a friend."

"Funny, you don't look like a spy," she chuckled.

I smiled, "Do I look like a physician? Well, I'm both, ma'am." We laughed.

"This is your first mission, and it's a dangerous one."

"Yes, ma'am, I agree."

"A lot of people have faith in you pulling this off. It will be a Herculean effort to gain access to the residential floors of Miltenburg Manor."

"I have a plan, ma'am."

"Godspeed, agent! As you know, if you're caught, I must disavow any knowledge of your assignment."

"Yes, ma'am, I know."

"You're dismissed, agent."

I stood up and saluted her. "Thank you, Madam President."

We arrived in London late in the evening. Ramesh and I settled into our room. Since we were supposed to be married, we shared a suite and actually shared the bedroom. We portrayed a loving couple. I thought about meeting Shelley for drinks, but Ramesh was against it. He stated that I should remain in character as Crystal Diamond.

Ramesh ordered room service. After we ate, we talked a bit and then retired to bed. In the bathroom, I changed into an oversized T-shirt and sweatpants.

Vigorously shaking his head, he said, "That's your sexy nightie?"

"Au contraire, agent Ramesh. We're a fake couple, remember? And by the way, you'll be sleeping on the sofa." Handing him a pillow, I added, "If you come near me, I will hurt you! And you know that I can fight since you attended the self-defense class with me."

Hearing him sigh, I grinned and turned the lights off.

The next day, we went over the plans for the evening. Getting ready for the affair, we got dressed in separate rooms and met in the sitting quarters when we were done.

Staring at me with the biggest smile, he said, "You look absolutely stunning. So beautiful!"

"Well, thank you, sir." I deliberately kept my dresses a secret from him. I wanted the "wow" factor. Ramesh looked so fine.

"You clean up well; so handsome. You resemble that debonair spy in the movies."

He blushed.

The gala began promptly at 7 p.m. in the luxurious ballroom. Upon arrival, all bags and purses were closely examined, and everyone was subjected to the manual metal detector.

Awaiting Queen Elizabeth II's entrance, the POTUS requested that I stand beside her. I was starstruck to be in the company of two of the most powerful women on the planet.

Adorned in their traditional red tailored attire, Britain's prestigious Fanfare Trumpeters of the Royal Air Force played a familiar ceremonial tune preceding the queen's arrival.

At the moment of her sophisticated entrance, the herald gallantly made the introduction, "Her Majesty, the Queen!"

The trumpeters rejoiced in their infamous rendition of "God Save The Queen."

The monarch extended her hand to the president. "I've longed to meet you, President Williamson."

"The pleasure is mine, Your Majesty," the president responded, smiling.

Merely a couple of feet from the queen, I was overcome with a frisson of excitement. As a wave of goosebumps swept over me, I began biting my lower lip. Noticing that I was fidgety, Ramesh discreetly nudged me to get it together.

Turning to me, the POTUS said, "Allow me to introduce Crystal Diamond. She's one of my delegates."

"Good evening, Ms. Diamond," she said stoically.

I executed a flawless curtsy as a respectful gesture. I had been practicing for three weeks. "It's an honor and privilege to meet you, Your Majesty."

Somehow, I managed not to faint.

President Williamson gave an articulate speech about unity and allies. The queen gave an exceptional speech as well. Her exquisite jewelry collection bedazzled me.

After an eloquent dining experience, the queen departed, and the evening event transformed into a night of dancing and socializing.

Ramesh and I mingled, then hit the dance floor to a contemporary R&B tune. About an hour and a half before the end of the event, the band performed a Latin tune. At the time, I was unaware that Ramesh had placed the request. Hand in hand, we walked to the center of the floor. Dancing, we stared into each other's eyes. He twirled me ever so gently. Moving to the music, our bodies were as one, oblivious that all eyes were on us. His transformation was spontaneous. He was no longer Ramesh; he was his alias—the exotic Xander Cucuta.

As the song ended, we passionately kissed. The guests clapped and cheered rambunctiously. The atmosphere shifted, and our attraction to each other entered another dimension.

Ten minutes later, Ramesh and I approached an armed guard at the foot of the grand staircase. He complimented us on our dance. I asked if there was a place where I could lie down because I was jet lagged and nauseous. Ramesh stated that I was six weeks pregnant. I thought, *Way to go, Ramesh! Why didn't I think of that?*

The guard congratulated us and then said, "Follow me."

President Williamson grinned as she witnessed Ramesh and me being escorted by the guard as we ascended the stairs to the residential suites.

We were led into suite 202. The target room was 402, so we were two floors below. The guard stated that the room was ours for an hour. He even brought me bottled water. I thanked him profusely. The guard exited the suite, closing the door behind him.

Ramesh turned to me, asking, "Are we going to talk about what happened on the dance floor?"

"Yes, but not now. We have work to do."

Turning my back to him, I asked him to unzip my dress. He complied. Removing my dress, I noticed Ramesh gawking at my body.

Tilting my neck and crossing my arms in disapproval, I said, "Stop staring! We have work to do!" I wore a skin-tight black dance leotard under my elegant dress.

"Your abdomen is so taut. You actually have a six-pack."

"I know! I'm an elite athlete, remember?" Gently slapping his left cheek twice, I added, "Snap out of it!"

I removed the carabiner clamps from my spy bra. My clutch had a pair of thin black ballet slippers embedded in the lining. I quickly put them on. Next, I removed the flash drive that was concealed in the seat of my stiletto's right heel. I detached the computer password extractor from the seat of the left heel. I needed both items to complete the task of retrieving the computer files. As I inserted my earbuds, Ramesh removed the climbing rope from the lining of his belt. After he had inserted his earbuds, I did a radio check.

"Ready for takeoff," I said softly.

Ramon was positioned in a surveillance van a block from the manor. "I read you loud and clear," he responded. Ramesh nodded and gave a thumbs-up gesture.

As a precautionary measure, I applied additional fingerprint cream. Hopefully, my dark attire would keep me undetected as I scaled two stories of a brick wall. Stepping onto the balcony, I swung the rope to the third-floor railing like a lasso and looped it to the carabiner clamp, then around my waist. Using leverage, I ascended carefully and methodically in the dark. I reached the third floor and unclamped my support rope. I swung the rope to the fourth floor and continued climbing. Unnoticed, I reached the balcony of suite 402. Climbing over the railing, I found the sliding door ajar. I donned night vision goggles and peered into the darkened room, confirming it was empty. Slowly, I slid the door wider and entered the suite.

After a deep breath, I whispered, "The bird has landed."

Ramon reassured me, "You've got this!"

Gingerly, I entered the first bedroom. No laptop. The second bedroom was a goldmine. The red laptop was on the desk. As I advanced toward it, I felt the cold tip of a gun barrel on the back of my neck.

Exhaling, I muttered, "Oh shit!" In a louder tone, I said, "Armageddon!"

"What?" said Ramesh in a panic.

"What's going on?" said Ramon.

I replied, "Please hold!"

The guys were perplexed. Mocking me in unison, they said, "Please hold?"

I startled the guard by raising my arms, then quickly spinning my body around while simultaneously rotating the spy ring. Facing him, I aggressively hit the right side of his neck with my open left palm, causing the needle in the stone to inject him with a concentrated dose of ketamine.

As his head slumped forward, he dropped the gun. I caught his body as his knees buckled and propped him on the floor against the wall in one corner of the room. He would wake up in about thirty minutes without recollection of what had happened.

Patting his head, I whispered, "Nite-nite!" Reassuring Ramesh and Ramon, I announced, "All clear. I'm OK."

The guys gave a loud sigh of relief. Ramesh responded, "That's my girl!"

There was a knock on the door of suite 202. Although alarmed, Ramesh reached for the doorknob. The guard who escorted us to the room had returned to check on me. He peeked into the unlit bedroom and saw the covered figure in bed. Part of my dress protruded from under the blanket, and my stilettos lay on the floor.

"She's sleeping soundly, but I'll wake her up in thirty minutes," whispered Ramesh. "Thank you for everything."

The guard nodded, then left.

Luckily, the bedroom light was off, and the hallway light slightly illuminated the room, or the security guard would have noticed that pillows were placed under the bedding with my dress spread over them as a decoy to resemble the contours of my body. Having my shoes under the bed was a nice touch by Ramesh.

Reliving what had just occurred upstairs in suite 402, I had to share it with the guys. I was rambling over the wireless mic. "Oy vey! I swept through the rooms and couldn't believe a guard was hiding inside in the dark. He had his gun to my head, but I managed to use the sedation ring. It worked like a charm. He's out for the count!"

Ramesh interrupted my shaky speech. "Take a break, C.J.! Stop yip-yapping and focus on the task. Hurry up and get the hell out of there!"

"Roger that! Sometimes, I'm loquacious when I'm nervous." I took a slow, deep breath, then inserted the flash drive and extractor into the laptop. "I'm ready to download."

Ramon replied, "I will be compiling a variation of letters and symbols to recreate the password from the extractor." He continued the computer jargon.

Perplexed, I remarked, "Dude, I'm a linguist, and I have no idea what you're saying."

We had the password within five minutes, and I opened the computer. Searching through the numerous icons, I selected the one titled "ghyr almwmnyn". In Arabic, it meant nonbelievers. Once I clicked it, a long list of names, addresses, and aerial photos of worldwide iconic images appeared on the screen. It gave me chills; then, it angered me. My better judgment was to delete the list, but my orders were restricted to download only. The list consisted of fifty terrorist cells that were strategically placed around the world.

Once my mission was completed, I removed the appliances and turned the computer off. Upon reaching the balcony, I climbed over the railing and began my skillful descent. All of a sudden, a guard who was smoking a cigarette came into view below. He was pacing in the yard.

I froze.

Beads of sweat accumulated on my forehead. I slowed my breathing down in an attempt to slow my heart rate. I waited impatiently, but time wasn't on my side. The worst-case scenario was that the smoker looked up and saw me clinging to the brick wall. Or, the sleeping beauty in suite 402 wakes up, peels himself off the floor, and steps onto the balcony for fresh air—or both. Unexpectedly, someone called the guard, telling him to hurry up.

He extinguished the cigarette and immediately ran toward the voice. Now, the coast was clear.

"C.J., what's your twenty?" said an anxious Ramesh, asking for my location.

"I'm descending, scaling the north wall. Meet me on the balcony."

"Ten-four."

Ramesh was waiting for me and assisted me over the second-floor railing. He embraced me. After redressing and concealing our spy gear, we exited the room and blended in with the guests downstairs. My peripheral vision captured the president looking at me. I turned my head toward her and gave her a discreet grin. She's proud of me, I thought. The evening ended on a high note. My mission was complete and successful.

And I'm attracted to my partner.

We held hands during the ride back to the hotel in the limo. Unbeknownst to me, Ramesh ordered champagne and a dozen long-stemmed roses for the room. I was pleasantly surprised when we entered our suite. We toasted the evening. I shared the story of the guard holding a gun to my head.

Ramesh was shaking his head in disbelief. "I can't believe you told us to hold on. I was ready to fight every guard as I made my way to suite 402 to save you."

"Awww, you do care about me. That's so sweet." He blew me a kiss.

"Listen to this," he said. "Our friendly armed guard came to the room to check on you. He glanced into the bedroom and saw your dress protruding under the blankets and your shoes aligned on the floor. I whispered to him that you were asleep and I would wake you up in thirty minutes."

We laughed hysterically. I believe the champagne had something to do with our giddiness. At times, we stared at each other silently and then kissed. We never spoke about the romantic dance. We no longer needed to. Fraternizing with a team member was forbidden at QA. We knew that we had crossed the line. Facing sanctions or disciplinary infractions was possible. But we didn't care.

It was late, and we needed to sleep after such a mentally exhausting evening. I changed into my pink negligee in the bathroom. I'm unsure why I packed it, but I'm glad I did.

Ramesh exited the bathroom and began settling under the sofa's covers. I lay in bed, then pulled back the sheets on the unoccupied side as an invitational gesture. Without saying a word, he got up and lay down next to me.

Within minutes, we were naked, then made love.

Late that night, the local British TV news aired a clip of the POTUS and her entourage meeting the queen at the Unity Gala. The video captured me curtsying to the queen.

In the morning, Ramesh and I ordered room service instead of going to the hotel restaurant. We wanted to be alone as much as possible. We showered together, then made passionate love again.

By the time breakfast arrived, we were famished. We ordered two bowls of oatmeal, a fruit plate, a glass of milk for him, and orange juice for me. Neither of us drank coffee.

We talked and rested until it was time to prepare for the Commonwealth Luncheon on the Miltenburg Manor lawn. Since this was a British Pomp and Circumstance affair, I expected nothing less than a spectacular event. All of the British Commonwealth blue-blooded aristocrats would be in attendance. I was proud to represent the United States alongside the president.

My navy blue dress was a head-turner. Ramesh loved it. He especially favored my fascinator. I had ordered it from London three weeks prior and had it shipped to Colorado. I wasn't sure how it would stay on my head, but it did.

Ramesh looked magnificent in his tuxedo, tails, and top hat. I had color-coordinated his tie and vest with my dress.

"You look quite dapper, Sir Xander Cucuta," I remarked.

"You taught me how to dress, my lady."

We kissed.

At the luncheon, Ramesh and I couldn't stop touching each other. We were either holding hands or hugging as we strolled across the lawn. I felt uneasy, as if everyone was staring at us. I even thought the president gave us an odd glance.

"It's all in your mind," said Ramesh. "By the way, we should be acting like newlyweds." I agreed, then resumed holding his hand.

The luncheon was lovely. The weather was perfect—not a rain cloud in sight—and the food was succulent.

The following morning, we boarded Air Force One, homeward bound. In flight, the president summoned Ramesh, Ramon, and me. Once she'd cleared the room and shut the door, we sat down.

The president spoke. "Agents, congratulations on a job well done! Your seminal work will provide a safer world tomorrow. Many lives will be saved due to our acquiring the terrorist list of targets and intercepting their planned carnage. It gave me great pride having you on my detail."

Ramesh interjected. "Excuse me, Madam President, but Agent Johnston is the real hero. She masterminded the entire plan and assumed all the risks, making this a successful mission." He added, "Her plan was a nail-biting experience, ma'am. On a danger scale from 1–10, it was a twenty. She made it look easy."

I spoke up. "Thank you, Madam President, and thank you, guys, but I couldn't have done it without you both. It was a team effort."

"Well, you've all made your country a safer place. Take the flash drive to the electronics rooms down the hall to your left. As soon as they download it, our government will initiate plans to eradicate the insurgent cells. You are dismissed."

We stood and saluted her. "Thank you, ma'am."

This was an extraordinary experience—such a rush. Ramesh, Ramon, and I were given a week off with pay as compensation for our mission. Ramesh and I spent quality time together, but I also hung out with my friends. While eating dinner with the girls from my health club, the sports bar's big screen TV interrupted the football game with breaking news. The commentator stated that several worldwide terrorist cells had been raided simultaneously, resulting in several arrests. I smiled to myself and ordered a round of drinks for the table.

Upon our return to QA, the guys and I were hailed as heroes since the cells had been destroyed and their mission was thwarted. We received accolades for perfecting the art of smoke and mirrors in the spy world.

The general flew up to congratulate me personally. We went out for a celebratory dinner with Ramesh and Ramon. He acknowledged that he knew I could pull it off. As the weeks flew by, it was challenging keeping my relationship with Ramesh a secret because he was so damn nice to me and a bit possessive. I was always concerned that someone would catch him winking at me. Our team noticed the banter between us. Penny and Bernice repeatedly asked me what really happened in England.

I would shrug my shoulders and say, "Nothing really."

The following week, we were told that intel was tracking a pyrotechnic company that had ties to a domestic terrorist group. They were suspected of making dirty bombs, explosive devices packed with screws, nails, bolts, and metal fragments. Once detonated, the force of the contents would cause irreparable harm to anyone nearby.

QA was assigned to provide the eyes and ears on the inside. That mission required my entire unit. All hands were on deck, as they say. Dan provided the smoke bombs with disintegrating outer shells. As the harmless bomb ejected massive smoke, the shell would shatter into unrecognizable fragments. Cody and Ramon collaborated to create the device to be inserted into the USB port of the company's video monitor. Penny and Bernice would keep the building under armed surveillance as I penetrated the perimeter.

Ramesh was my observer for this mission. Intel provided an aerial photograph of the layout. His eyes had to be on me at all times as I executed parkour techniques to jump from rooftop to rooftop on the compound. The plan was to create a diversion so the guards would leave the video room unattended. Everything was to commence in eighteen hours, at 1 a.m.

At midnight, I donned all-black attire: a leotard, yoga pants, tennis shoes, and a balaclava to conceal my face. With everyone in position, Ramesh gave me the order to scale the wall of Building A. Once on the roof, I began a rapid pace across the flat coal-tar surface in pitch darkness. The full moon assisted in illuminating the edge of the roof as I took flight, jumping over the fifteen-foot gap between the buildings. Landing lightly, I rolled my body into an acrobatic ground-level somersault, then stood up to run again. I repeated this maneuver across the roofs of Buildings B and C until I reached my targeted Building D.

Ramesh was ecstatic after I conquered the final jump. He proudly said, "Yes," to himself, but everyone heard it via the earbuds.

I quickly launched the smoke bombs, throwing them around the building. As the smoke billowed, it gave the pretense of an active fire. While the guards called 911, I rappelled down and hung above the video room's door. As the two guards ran outside with the fire extinguisher, I surreptitiously entered the building before the door closed. After inserting the electronic transmitter into the back of the primary video surveillance monitor, I slipped out of the room. The fire department hadn't arrived yet, and the guards were still fighting the replicated fires. I ascended the exterior wall, returning to the rooftop unnoticed. As I leaped from Building D, the firefighters arrived. All eyes were on them, not me, so my leaps across Buildings C, B, and A went undetected. I descended safely, then quickly edged off the premises in the shadows. Ramesh met me as I passed through the gate. Cody and Ramon remained in the van and acknowledged receiving a live feed from the monitors, including audio capability.

Ramesh and I high-fived. Now, Homeland Security had the capability of monitoring their malicious activities. We were too excited to sleep, so I suggested we meet at an all-night diner for a celebratory breakfast. Indulging in eggs and pancakes at 3 a.m. made us hyperactive and then plunged us into lethargy.

QA gave us two compensation days off. Ramesh came home with me, and we slept for ten hours. The assignments for the two of us grew exponentially. We became the poster couple in the world of espionage.

Morocco Mission

Special Agent Parker called me into his office.

"C.J., there's a mission that has your name written all over it. Since you're fluent in Arabic and a doctor, you're going to Morocco as a field physician in the Berber villages. The real mission is to extract a sleeper agent who's been missing for a week and presumed to be held captive somewhere in the rural community. Ramesh will be your medic. You both will leave in seventy-two hours. You'll fly to Madrid, Spain, then onward to Marrakech, Morocco. A driver from the US Embassy will pick you up at the Marrakech Menara Airport."

Our travel vouchers and passports reflected our aliases, Crystal Diamond and Harrison Steele. The tickets had us seated in coach. I upgraded our status to first class. The flight was long, a tiresome fourteen hours. Ramesh slept for the majority of the plane ride. He awakened only to eat. I updated myself with the latest medical journals: my pastime. Upon clearing customs in Morocco, a thirty-something-year-old male Moroccan held up a sign bearing the name C. Diamond and H. Steele. He greeted us with the broadest smile. His name was Habib, and he was our designated English-speaking driver.

When we arrived at the upscale Marrakech hotel, he said he'd pick us up after breakfast and escort us to the US Embassy. He also offered to take us to the Medina, a tourist mecca, this afternoon if we were interested. We nodded yes.

Habib picked us up three hours later. Marrakech personifies the hustling and bustling city life. Pedestrians, cars, motorcycles, trucks, and bicycles converge on the abundance of roundabouts, known as traffic circles in the US. Since driving is on the right side of the street, all traffic directions for roundabouts are counterclockwise. No one paid attention to the right of way. It was a hazardous free-for-all. After we had a few close calls, I discreetly held Ramesh's hand while we sat in the back seat.

The Medina was culturally diverse. A nation of Africans was present and embellished in brightly colored attire. Individual souks were scattered about, filled with a plethora of goods for sale. The array of multicolored mounds of spices was intriguing. Patrons were haggling over the price of handmade beaded jewelry and carved artifacts. The snake charmer amazed Ramesh, although he was unsuccessful in coaxing me to hold the creepy, scaled, elongated reptiles.

Habib wasn't just our driver but also our guide and my protector. A man selling his bracelets touched my shoulder to get my attention, and Habib aggressively pushed his hand off me and then told him never to touch me. Men frequently conversed with me, admiring my micro dreadlocks or locs, as they are also called. They all called me Reggae Girl. They had migrated from Senegal. I could tell that Ramesh was irritated with them, and though I was enjoying myself, I was also uneasy. I'd never been a paranoid person, but ever since we left the hotel, I felt like someone was following us. Perhaps I was just jet lagged.

Being an unmarried couple and maintaining Morocco's culture, Ramesh and I stayed in separate rooms. We met in the hotel restaurant for breakfast and then checked out. Habib arrived to transport us to the embassy.

The US Ambassador Jillian Bledsoe greeted us. "Hello, agents; please have a seat."

"Thank you, Ambassador," I responded.

"Nice to meet you, ma'am," said Ramesh.

We listened attentively as she briefed us on our mission to retrieve Tristan Richards.

"As you know, your mission is to locate a sleeper who has been missing, presumed to be held hostage or dead. He had been an invisible entity, infiltrating the desert communities until we decided to wake him up. He was ordered to take an active role and obtain intel regarding radicalized citizens from other countries that have permeated the borders of peacekeeping nations such as Morocco. Tristan was probing for leads and gathering information when he suddenly vanished a week ago while traveling through the Atlas Mountains. Finding him is vital to national security."

The ambassador gave us each a white medical bag with a caduceus medical symbol on both sides. It was packed with essential medical supplies and even had a hidden compartment that concealed a 9mm semiautomatic handgun and three full clips.

In a carry-on bag, I received hijabs, Muslim headdresses, and short-length kaftans that could be worn as a dress or an accessorized top worn with jeans. It was imperative that I dress appropriately, maintaining their clothing etiquette by covering my hair and most of my arms and legs. Ramesh received gandoras, a customary long, loose-fitting top that men wore.

"And agents, Habib isn't privy to the intricate details of your mission."

I responded, "Understood. And thank you for the clothes."

Ramesh added, "Yes, thanks."

Her parting words were a classic spy redundant rhetorical statement.

Leaning back in her chair, she said, "Remember, if you are caught, I will disavow any knowledge of your actions."

Such a repetitive statement in the world of espionage.

Ramesh and I stood. "Yes, ma'am."

It was a beautiful spring day for a road trip. I had brought a load of granola bars from the US, and Habib picked up a large box of dried, sweet, sticky dates. After packing the bags and a cooler filled with bottled water in the jeep, we were off.

Once we left the outskirts of town, somehow, we drew the attention of local police at the checkpoints. A young rookie stood next to a seasoned officer. He gestured for us to pull over to the right shoulder. Habib lowered the window as the officer approached the driver's door. His partner stood at the rear.

The nervous rookie said, "mrnbaan. 'ayn satakhudh alrukabi? (Hello. Where are you taking the passengers?)"

"Salaam alaikum (Hello)," responded Habib. "'inahum taqim tibiyun yadhhab fi muhimat limusaeadat sukaan alquraa albarbariati.(They're a medical crew going on a mission to help the Berber villages.)"

"'ahtaj 'iilaa jawazat safarihim. (I need their passports.)"

Habib turned to us in the back seat and asked for our passports.

Understanding the language, I already had my passport in my hand. Ramesh watched me and followed suit.

In a tremulous voice, the rookie said, "Al'amrikiuwna? (Americans?)" He scratched his chin, looked over at his partner, then back to Ramesh. "alfiraq altibiyat qadimat min 'uwruba. 'arni haqayibahum altibiyata. (The medical teams come from Europe. Show me their medical bags.)"

Habib nodded and exited the jeep. Ramesh grabbed the door handle, preparing to get out, too.

"Don't do it," I warned. "They could view your actions as being aggressive, so just sit still."

He released the handle.

Habib removed both medical bags from the rear storage area and handed them to the officers. With our passports and bags in tow, they entered their small checkpoint booth.

Twenty-five minutes elapsed, then they returned with our belongings. Obviously, they didn't find the weapons, or we would have been arrested. The rookie peeked at Ramesh and me in the back seat, then looked at Habib.

"yumkinuk aldhahabi. (You can go.)"

"shukran (Thank you)," said Habib pleasantly. We drove off.

"That was nerve-racking," said an annoyed Ramesh.

"Yes, it was. That's why we need to remain calm and cool," I responded as the voice of reason.

A mile down the road, we were stopped again. It was obvious that the authorities had been alerted about us. The unfriendly officer requested our passports. He stood stoically at Habib's door, flipping through the passport pages. When he finished, he, too, peeked back at us. The passports were returned to Habib. As he handed them to me, the silent officer gestured for Habib to move on. He started the car, and we left.

We had traveled ten miles since our last encounter with the police. Hopefully, that was behind us. I was relaxed and enjoying the scenery. With my window rolled down, the wind-blown air had me reminiscing about road trips through the countryside while vacationing with my parents in Jamaica when I was seven years old.

Passing a field of argan trees, I was amazed to see goats nonchalantly standing on tree branches, balancing effortlessly. The linear thorny branches curved slightly under their weight. My mouth gaped open, but no sound came out. Ramesh was asleep, so I shook him.

Drowsily, he said, "What's wrong?"

"Look at that," I pointed.

Rubbing his eyes, he muttered, "What the hell?"

Habib pulled over so that we could get a closer look. I jumped out of the car before it came to a complete stop. Ramesh followed. Standing among the trees, I gazed upward at the goats teetering above me. Some were eating the products of the nut-bearing tree. Others stood motionless, statuesque. Habib joined us.

"The argan tree is found only in Morocco," he said proudly. "It bears the argan nut from which the argan oil is extracted. The oil is used worldwide in the cosmetic and food industry. The goats first feed off the fallen nuts, but if they're still hungry, then they'll climb the tree and eat them from up there." He pointed.

Still in awe, I voiced my thoughts aloud. "This is incredible to see up close and personal. I probably wouldn't believe it otherwise."

After being mesmerized for about thirty minutes, we resumed our road trip. The ride was pleasant once again. We stopped at a roadside open-air café for a late lunch. Away from the city, the lifestyle was simpler and more primitive. Tagines, colorful glazed ceramic pots with lids, sat on hot charcoal and lined the top of cement walls at the entrance to the eatery. They were best used for cooking couscous, Morocco's staple dish of steamed wheat with vegetables and either fish, goat, or beef. We ordered the house specialty to share: couscous with beef. The waiter placed the massive plate of this hot, tantalizing dish before the three of us. Flatbread was provided as a tool to assist with picking up the food. Knowledgeable about Moroccan culinary customs, especially in the rural mountains, I informed Ramesh that we must eat with our fingers and use our right hands. The left hand is considered dirty and reserved for bathroom hygiene. Relinquishing customs, Ramesh asked for a fork. I watched the waiter scurry around, looking for one. He finally returned with a fork that had bent, multidirectional prongs.

Smiling, Ramesh said, "shukran. (Thank you.)"

The waiter responded, "shuhiat tayiba. (Bon appétit.)"

Knowing that he wouldn't be able to use the utensil effectively, he joined Habib and me in eating with his fingers. Limiting your food intake to the area of the plate presented in front of you is customary. Another waiter placed small, clear glasses in front of us. Then, he proceeded to pour sweet, honey-hued Moroccan mint tea from a metal teapot eighteen inches above each glass. With stellar precision, he didn't spill a drop. We quickly became satiated.

That night, we stayed at a hotel near the mountain's peak, again in separate rooms. We were equipped with walkie-talkies. Ramesh and I were in mid-conversation when the entire compound went dark, totally black. We continued to communicate, but after twenty minutes, we became curious. He suggested that we meet at the banister outside my room.

Opening my door, I was suddenly thrust backward, lost my balance, and fell on the floor. A large image forcefully pushed me down. As he came close to me, I heard Ramesh's voice.

"Hey! Stop!" yelled Ramesh

With his flashlight, Ramesh struck my assailant on the back of his head. I activated the stun gun switch on my flashlight and zapped him on his leg.

He collapsed.

We ripped a bath towel into strips and hog-tied him. I stayed with him, and Ramesh went to find the hotel manager. When he returned, he informed me that the police had been contacted via radio. He also stated that the electrical power was being restored.

Just as the police arrived an hour later, the lights came on. The intruder was placed in custody. He was a Libyan citizen and was wanted by Interpol, the International Criminal Police Organization, for human trafficking.

Ramesh watched over me for the rest of the night. I hardly slept. By the time we had breakfast, we were exhausted. Hot mint tea energized me.

The drive up the mountain continued. An elderly woman was ascending the road on foot. Habib asked us if it was OK to give her a ride. We relocated our additional bags to the rear storage area and made room for her. The woman was pleasant and grateful. She noticed our medical bags and mentioned to Habib that she had seen one just like it in the village. As I was fluent in Arabic, I understood what she told him. I didn't respond but took notice of this critical information. When we reached the Berber community, she got out of the jeep. Before walking away, she hugged me.

There was a plethora of dwellings, some even carved into the mountain. Even though we were in Morocco under false pretenses, I wanted to help the villagers. Their health complaints were minor ailments such as sore throat, cough, back pain, and wrist or ankle sprain. I treated them all. All of the families offered me hot mint tea, which I graciously accepted. The children playfully escorted me from home to home.

Riding further up the mountain, we noticed a tender-aged child walking alone. He was no more than four years old. Like most children, his clothes were soiled from playing in the dirt. Pulling his homemade car on a string, he expressed the biggest smile. We pulled off the road to interact with him. He gallantly waved at us, and I gave him two granola bars. Habib placed some dates in a bag for him. After that, he left. I voiced my concern regarding him being alone on the road. Habib tried to reassure me that he would find his way home safely by dinnertime.

Ramesh and I weren't really welcomed at the next small congregation of mountain dwellings. The villagers were suspicious of us. They watched every move we made. Putting them at ease, I entered their homes alone. The first home that I entered, I saw an identical white medical bag perched on a small table. As I was examining a young girl's throat, her mother stepped out of the abode. I quickly opened the bag and found it empty. Accessing the concealed false bottom compartment, I found the gun. After retrieving it, I saw a young teenage girl standing before me. Startled, I was unaware that she had even walked in. She turned and walked away, surely to alert the men outside. Instead, she picked up a scarf and covered the gun that was in my hand. Quickly camouflaging it, I placed the weapon under a pile of medical supplies in my bag.

"shukran (Thank you.), I mouthed.

She nodded.

She whispered, "tama 'akhdh alrajul allatif dhu alshier al'asfar 'iilaa almukhayam eind alkuthban alramliati. (The nice man with the yellow hair was taken to the campsite at the dunes.)"

With a smile, I whispered, "shukran limusaeadati. (Thank you for helping me.)"

She graciously smiled back.

That lead was crucial. I knew that it was the nomad campsite in the Sahara Desert. Due to their roaming lifestyle, it was going to be challenging to find him. I told Ramesh what had happened. The dunes were visible from our vantage point.

The word Sahara is Arabic and means desert. Located in northern Africa, its massive landscape spans 3,000 miles across and intercepts eleven countries: Morocco, Algeria, Chad, Egypt, Eritrea, Libya, Mali, Mauritania, Niger, Sudan, and Tunisia. In the desert regions, summers are extreme, with temperatures reaching 130 degrees Fahrenheit. During the winter, temperatures can plummet to below freezing. Rain is almost nonexistent—less than three inches a year. It's a harsh and desolate landscape.

Dunes vary in size. The largest dune in the Sahara is almost 600 feet tall. The most popular, larger dune belt is Erg Chebbi. Nomads, roaming tribes, are indigenous to this region and are accustomed to the austere living of simplicity.

Returning to the jeep, we descended the mountains. At the entrance to the Sahara, the jeep stalled and came to an abrupt stop. The guys inspected under the hood. Ramesh walked away to inspect the vehicle's exterior. A few fine white grains were visible near the fuel door. Taking his right pinky finger, he touched a couple of grains, then placed his finger on the tip of his tongue.

"Seriously?" I objected. "That could be poison."

"Relax, it's sugar." He opened the cover to the fuel tank filler neck. "See, there's more. The car was sabotaged while we were in the village. We were able to drive a few miles until enough sugar reached the engine, disabling it."

We were forced to abandon the jeep.

Changing my attire in frustration, I put on a T-shirt, jeans, and a baseball cap. Ramesh mimicked me. The medical bags were rearranged to carry only the necessities. The trekking commenced. The shortest route was to cut through the Sahara, omitting the road. The sun was brutal. It was hot as hell. After six hours, Ramesh exhibited symptoms of dehydration. He remained stoic, not wanting to consume what marginal water we had. Now, he was paying the price. He complained of having a headache and feeling nauseous. I checked his pulse and found that his heart rate was fast. His gait was becoming unsteady. We stopped beside a massive dune that produced some shade.

I started an IV on him and ran a bag of saline into his vein. For his nausea, I gave him an anti-nausea pill that dissolved in his mouth. Caring for him provided the time for us to rest. Within two hours, he was on the mend. We resumed the trek.

After traversing for a full day, we finally walked into a campsite. Once again, the community was skeptical about our presence. Many of the children had fresh abrasions on their arms and legs. I cleansed their wounds, then applied antibiotic ointment and a bandage. My caring treatments won over the mothers. As I assessed the residents of the peripatetic village, Ramesh and Habib remained outside the tents with the men. Entering the fifth tent, I immediately focused on a blond man—*a man with yellow hair*—in a fetal position on the floor, facing the canvas. I approached him. He appeared to be asleep. I tapped his shoulder, and he awakened. Perplexed, he stared at me.

"Hi, Tristan. The president of the United States said to tell you hello."

He managed to grin. While sitting up, he said, "I can't believe you found me. Thank you."

I lowered my voice and said, "Listen to me very carefully."

Ramesh stood with Habib as he was haggling for a couple of camels from the nomads. Unable to understand the prices offered, he could tell they were too high because of Habib's irritated demeanor. Distracted by my voice, he turned toward the fifth tent.

"Ram…er, Harrison, I need your help ASAP!"

Ramesh quickly ran toward the tent. Habib was right behind him. They entered the tent to find a blond man drooling and having a seizure. His medical condition scared the women, and they ran out screaming. Curious, the men ran into the tent.

Habib yelled at them, "man hu hadha alrajulu? (Who is this man?)" Before anyone could answer, he continued. "sataetaqiluk alshurtat walnisa' bituhmat aikhtitafih (The police will arrest you and the women for kidnapping him)," he seethed.

The women were afraid and began crying.

Habib made them an offer. "daeuni 'ashtari jamlin bisier al'asli wasakhidh alrajul maei. bihadhih altariqati, satatajanabun almashakila. (Let me buy two camels for my original price, and I will take the man with me. That way, you all will stay out of trouble.)"

The women pleaded with the men to take the deal. The offer was accepted. Ramesh and I paid them with a combination of Moroccan Dirhams and Euro currency.

The seizure stopped.

The camels were corralled behind the tents. After blankets were placed on their backs, we loaded up to go. At Habib's command, the camels knelt, allowing us to climb on. He led the first camel, and my new patient sat behind him. I sat behind Ramesh on the second one. Habib gave us a brief lesson on riding a camel. After we were out of earshot from the campsite and riding camels side by side, I made an announcement.

"Guys, I want you to meet Tristan Richards. I applaud him for being such a great fake patient."

"You're going home, Tristan," said Ramesh.

"Salaam alaikum (Hello)," said Habib. "I wasn't specifically told about you, but I heard rumors. When Crystal was so attentive to you, then it clicked. You must be the missing agent, the one kidnapped."

"Hello, guys! I can't thank you enough for finding me. Men from Libya drugged me and took me hostage."

Habib suggested that we travel to Erg Chebbi, a tourist attraction in the desert. From there, we could hitch a ride back to Marrakech. We traveled through most of the night. It was a clear, dark sky with an abundance of sparkling stars. After riding several miles, Habib kept moving his head back and forth.

Concerned, Ramesh asked, "Are we lost?"

Habib solemnly answered, "Yes." He loudly exhaled in frustration. "I can't recognize the markers at night. Everything looks the same. All I know is that we need to go north."

"Don't fret. I can help."

Ramesh was in his element. His knowledge of astronomy turned into a lecture.

"We need to find Polaris, the North Star. It will take us to Erg Chebbi," said a confident Ramesh. He scanned the ebony sky. "I'm looking for the seven stars that comprise the infamous constellation, the Big Dipper."

Briefly silent, he studied the astronomical map. With our heads flexed upward, we searched the sky too. Unfortunately, we had no idea what we were looking for. Suddenly, he pointed toward the heavens.

"There, there it is!" he jubilantly announced. "It's shaped like a pot with a long handle. The two bright stars that are a part of the pot are known as pointer stars. If I extend the length between these two stars five times, I should be near the North Star. Then, we'll be on the right track."

Ramesh held his right arm up to track the path of the stars. We were impressed. Well, I definitely was.

"I found it! Go left!"

By 4 a.m., we rested the camels and ourselves—mostly ourselves. Camels are adapted to this harsh, dry environment. We frequently passed around the water bottles to take sips and stay hydrated, which is not necessary for camels since they can retain water for almost two weeks. Lying against a dune, we decided to sleep for three to four hours. After a three-hour nap, I felt rejuvenated. The men were still asleep. I stood up and did a few modified yoga stretches. The sun slowly rose from behind the horizon, casting the dunes in a silhouette. It was an amazingly beautiful sight. The men awakened about thirty minutes later. We had consumed the remainder of the water before napping, but four granola bars were left. I passed them out. As we resumed our trek through the Sahara, the sky turned an eerie orange. The horizon was dark, unlike pending precipitation. This was different, ominous. A colossal sandstorm was approaching.

"It's a haboob!" shrieked Habib. "If we turn around, we won't be able to outrun it. We have no choice but to get through it."

The arid dust bowl quickly crept up on us. It was thousands of feet high and 100 miles wide. Habib gestured for the camels to kneel on all fours. They would provide us with a barrier, shielding us from the unimaginable terror that lurked ahead. We hunkered down next to them, covering our heads with the lap blankets, protecting our eyes. Camels possess thick, long eyelashes capable of preventing the sand from entering their organ of sight. The sandstorm was upon us and produced a high-pitched, raucous sound. Visibility was practically zero. The camels moved intensely. Agitated by the intimidating and deafening sounds, they stood up one by one and ran off, leaving us exposed.

The wind was fierce and almost blew me away. The men covered me with their bodies, weighing me down. Minutes felt like hours as the sand tornado pelted us and held us captive. I was mortified.

The dust devil passed.

Removing the blankets, the men rolled off me. We lay motionless, trying to relax our muscles from the tension initiated by the near-death experience. Since we were on top of the medical bags, they survived the ordeal, but my phone didn't. It was in pieces.

Without the camels, we resorted to traversing on foot. We reached Erg Chebbi, weather-beaten and battered. Habib found his friend, who was a tour guide. He treated us to a hot meal and cots to rest upon. The following day, we hitched a ride back to Marrakech in his mini tour bus.

We walked into the US Embassy sunburned, exhausted, and wearing tattered clothes. The ambassador gasped when she saw us. We returned the bags to her, and she removed the weapons.

We ate lunch together, and then I took an extended nap. I woke up to eat dinner with Ramesh, then took another nap. I overslept and was wide awake at 10 p.m. Becoming antsy, I decided to stretch my legs and take a stroll within the embassy. I found myself in front of the ambassador's outer office. The door was open. Peeking in, I noticed a jar filled with American milk chocolate candy bars. Unable to resist, I helped myself to a few. Unaware that the ambassador was inside the inner office, I suddenly heard her on the phone. Not wanting to pry, I had turned to leave when I heard something disturbing.

"I can't believe they found him. How was that possible? Now, I have to find a way to eliminate all three of them. Damn it! This was not the plan!" Bledsoe said on the phone.

I heard her heels clicking against the tile, indicating she was walking around the office. I quickly left.

I immediately went to Ramesh's room. My repeated banging on his door finally woke him up.

"Wha—what's wrong?"

"I can't sleep and wanted to visit you," I said, chuckling awkwardly.

I placed my right index finger to my lips as a gesture to keep him from speaking. A clock radio was on the nightstand, so I turned it on to blast music. Whispering directly into his left ear, I told him what I had overheard. Believing that our rooms were bugged with listening devices, I had to mask our conversation with the loud music.

"Shit," said Ramesh. "What are we going to do?"

"I need to contact QA. My phone is broken, but yours works, right?"

"Yes, but we can't call from this country."

"No, but I can get an encrypted message to them. I need paper and a pen."

He looked in the nightstand drawer. "Here," he said, handing me the items.

I started the message with the word "Armageddon," then gave explicit details of our plight.

"Are you having a stroke?"

Irritated, I said, "What? What are you talking about?"

"You aren't even writing words, just loops and lines. You're doodling."

"I'm writing in shorthand, sending a code to Ramon. He's the only one who's able to read it. I had a conversation with him about shorthand six months ago. OK, I'm finished. Take a picture of the note and email it to him."

"It's sent."

"Now, we wait for the cavalry."

After Ramesh sent the message, I turned off the music and went to my room. Unable to sleep, my mind ran through various scenarios for our escape. I decided to keep Tristan out of the loop and in the dark. Although he's an agent, I really didn't know him.

After breakfast, two men in suits approached Ramesh and me in the lounge. "Hello, I'm Agent Sullivan, and he's Agent Reynoso," spoke one of the men.

They flashed their badges.

He continued: "Ambassador Bledsoe requests your presence for a debriefing at a secure location. It isn't far from here."

"Good morning," said Ramesh.

"Morning," I replied.

"I hear that congratulations are in order. I also heard that you both had a couple of harrowing experiences here in Morocco. You're lucky to be alive. Oh, Agent Richards will also be joining us," said Reynoso.

I excused myself to go to the bathroom in my room. While I was there, Habib called the room phone.

"Hello," I answered.

"Morning, Crystal, it's Habib. I called Harrison's room, but he didn't answer."

"Harrison is waiting for me downstairs. A couple of suits are taking us to a secure location for a debriefing."

"A debriefing away from the embassy? That's weird."

"I know. It really is."

"Well, I was coming by to visit you guys before you leave tonight. Guess I'll see you later then."

"OK, Habib." The call ended.

Habib was parked on the street and watched our vehicle pull out of the embassy parking lot.

The drive took us through a multitude of complex labyrinth passages. We had no idea where we were headed. The car parked in front of a building encased in a facade.

"We're here," said Reynoso.

Entering the premises, we were greeted with an elaborately decorated open courtyard. Tall trees aligned the mosaic tile walkway that led to the residence. The high ceilings and bay windows accentuated the natural light. The main room was adorned with an array of Moroccan furniture with richly saturated colors. The subtle aroma of incense permeated the home.

We were escorted to a small, drab room in the rear. The decor was in contrast to the central portion of the house. It was bare-bones, containing only a few plastic chairs and nothing else. The walls appeared soundproof.

This was a torture chamber.

"What the hell is going on?" said Ramesh.

"Sit down and shut up," said Sullivan.

Looking at Ramesh, I discreetly shook my head no to any ideas of attacking these guys. Not yet, anyway. Someone was behind this attempt to kidnap us, and I had an idea of who it was. I needed to see this play out.

Holding a gun on us, Sullivan gave instructions to Reynoso. "Body search them."

"OK. You: Stand up. Keep your arms raised," Reynoso addressed Tristan.

After he frisked Tristan, Ramesh was next. Observing Reynoso's frisking technique, I saw it was marginal, amateur at best. When Ramesh sat back down, I stood up with my arms raised. He patted down my left leg, starting with my thigh and moving down to my ankle. As he prepared to pat my right leg, he clumsily touched my groin.

In a split-second reaction, I recoiled my right leg and violently thrust it into his stomach. He flew backward and fell.

"DO NOT TOUCH ME THERE!" I yelled.

Ramesh jumped to his feet. Sullivan pushed him back into the chair. Placing the gun to Ramesh's right temple, Sullivan said, "Stay down, tough guy." The ambassador entered the room just in time to view the disturbance.

"Stop," she ordered, raising her hands, palms facing forward. "There's no need to frisk them. I already took their weapons." She walked over to me. "Sit down. Please."

Angrily, I sat.

"Sorry, agents, this is nothing personal. I stand to make a lot of money, but you three have become an obstacle." She looked at Tristan. "Richards here was getting way too close to my operation. I decided to lose him in the desert. Unfortunately, you two super sleuths found him. Now, you all will have the same fate. Again, nothing personal."

Pissed off, I said, "You already betrayed your country. Now you want to add a triple homicide to the charges?"

"I know that your reputation is squeaky clean, agent, but sometimes things arise that lure a person to a different path."

With the door ajar, we could hear the sound of glass breaking.

She removed a 9mm gun from her purse and turned to Sullivan and Reynoso. "No one else is supposed to be here," she snapped. "You both check it out!"

Now, the gun was aimed at us. "Sorry, agents."

Reacting to this unplanned diversion, Ramesh nudged Tristan, then pointed toward the opened door behind the ambassador. Distracted, she turned to look.

A shot rang out.

Ramesh's deflection allowed me to remove the small .25-caliber gun from my back waistline. I had retrieved it from my room when I excused myself to go to the bathroom at the embassy.

Without hesitation, I fired a round into her right shoulder, decimating her brachial plexus. As her right arm went limp, the gun slid from her hand, dropping on the floor.

Glaring at her, I secured her weapon, then said, "Ambassador Jillian Bledsoe, I'm placing you under arrest. Nothing personal."

With the ambassador on the floor writhing in pain, she was no longer a threat.

Ramesh and Tristan went in search of Sullivan and Reynoso. Before they left the room, I gave Ramesh my gun.Tristan recognized this pearl-handled .25-caliber as his, the one that had been hidden in his medical bag in the mountains.

They scoured the main room but couldn't find the traitors. Moans were heard from the courtyard. They raced to one of the bay windows for an optimum view and saw the ambassador's henchmen unconscious, sprawled on the mosaic tile. Habib stood over them. Looking around, he caught a glimpse of Ramesh and Tristan peeking through the window, standing behind the drapes.

He yelled out to them. "Hurry, find something so that we can tie them up." The guys brought him a curtain cord from the window treatment.

"Yup, that will do."

After tying up the traitors, Ramesh was baffled about Habib's presence at the house of horrors.

"How did you know that we were here?"

"I was parked outside the embassy when I called Crystal in her room. She told me about the off-location debriefing. I was suspicious, and then I saw a car exit the parking lot with you all in the back seat. So, I followed it. This place is considered a safe house. Obviously, it's been used as an unsafe house, too. I had a difficult time picking the lock to the facade. It's been a while since I've done it. Guess I've gotten rusty. I hid when the ambassador arrived. Since the door to that little room didn't completely close, I heard and recorded everything on my phone. When she pulled out her gun, I decided to lure the guys out by breaking a vase. To incapacitate them, I used the stun gun option on the flashlight that Crystal gave me as a parting gift yesterday. I had no idea that I would be using it so soon."

He laughed. In a delayed response, Ramesh and Tristan laughed, too. "Come here, man." Ramesh gave Habib a male bear hug. "You're a hero!"

Habib called the embassy security to send backup and an ambulance. He was informed that the QA team from New York had arrived to extract Agents Diamond and Steele, responding to their encrypted distress message.

Our mission was over. Mentally drained, we were ready to leave. On the evening flight home, Ramesh said he needed a quiet vacation to recuperate.

"Where do you want to go?" I curiously asked.

"My patio."

The Bar

Boasting a disheveled man bun, Ramesh sat drinking beer in a darkened corner of a dilapidated shack converted into a bar on the outskirts of town. The walls were dingy and displayed multiple fading posters of old Western movies. The jukebox blared classic rock, and a pool table monopolized the center of the room. The players frequently made a ruckus, especially when losing or winning.

This was his second consecutive night there. The clientele left much to be desired. The cue ball popped off the pool table and rolled toward him.

"You don't know your own strength," he joked to the man approaching him to retrieve the ball.

"Sorry, bruh!" The man extended a hand. "I'm Brody." They shook. "Wanna play next round?"

"Sure, why not? By the way, I'm Ramesh."

Brody won the game by default. His opponent hit the 8-ball into a pocket other than the one designated.

"Yo, Ramesh," Brody summoned. "Rack 'em!"

Ramesh chugged the remainder of his beer. He racked the pool balls, arranging them in order within a wooden triangular border.

"We playing 8-ball?"

"Yup! Go ahead and break," suggested his new-found friend.

Ramesh removed the wooden rack and used the white cue ball to break the grouping of solid and striped balls. The game was lighthearted, and they laughed a lot as they indulged in another round of beer.

Ramesh let him win—twice.

On a sweltering Colorado summer night, the bar became hot and muggy. Brody and Ramesh convened outdoors for fresh air. Lighting a marijuana cigarette, Brody inhaled deeply, exhaling slowly. He offered the joint to Ramesh.

"Wanna hit?"

"Sure." He took a toke.

"You staying around here?"

"My girl and I are staying at the Shady Lane motel down the road. She's back east visiting her family for a week. She's returning the day after tomorrow."

"Mike, the bartender, is throwing a little cookout tomorrow around noon. Come on by and grab a burger."

"Hey, man, thanks for the invite. Well, I'm gonna get some shut-eye." Ramesh walked to his car.

"OK, bruh. Take it easy." Admiring the vehicle, he said, "This your car? A 1972 Chevy Chevelle SS 350? Nice."

"Yup, it's my baby. I rebuilt her myself. Clutch sticks a bit sometimes, though."

"She's a nice ride. I have a tricked-out Camaro myself. I'm waiting for my kid brother to bring it to me right now."

The engine roared to life.

"Guess I'll check it out tomorrow." Ramesh sped off.

When Ramesh walked in, the morning meeting at QA was about to begin. His appearance was evolving. With long sideburns and even longer, slicked-back hair, he looked thuggish.

He boasted arrogantly, "I'm in! Brody is practically in love with me!"

Everyone chuckled.

He continued, "I'm invited to a cookout today at noon. I have to meet the rest of his terrorist gang there. I'm introducing C.J. as my girlfriend tomorrow night."

"Oh, I can't wait to meet your new little friends," I sarcastically responded. "Check you out! You've really gotten into character, haven't you? How's life living in the hepatitis motel?"

"So, you got jokes! Don't forget that you're moving in there tomorrow," he snipped.

"Okay, you two, settle down," Special Agent Parker ordered. "I can't have you at each other's throats before the mission even begins. Ramesh, do you really think Brody will open up to you?"

"Definitely! He even mentioned his kid brother. I'm sure I'll meet him when I return for lunch."

Opening a file on the desk, Parker pulled out an 8 x 10-inch picture of a pimple-faced teenager and adhered it to the wall.

"This is Billy Menagerie, Brody Menagerie's seventeen-year-old juvenile delinquent brother," he said with disgust. "He's a menace to society. He's been a resident of juvie on multiple occasions. Now, he's a high school dropout, expelled because he brought a loaded weapon to school. He idolizes Brody. This kid is a wild card. I don't want either of you to underestimate him."

"Roger that, boss!"

At 1 p.m., Ramesh arrived at the cookout, toting a case of beer and a large bag of chips. Eight men and four women were gathered on the bar's rear patio. Brody broke away from the crowd when he noticed Ramesh.

"Hey, bruh, you didn't have to contribute, but thanks."

"It's the neighborly thing to do."

"Hey, everybody, this is Ramesh, our new bar patron. He brought more beer."

"Hell yeah, welcome, Ramesh," responded a man with extremely long mustache bars.

"Throw me one of those bad boys," commented a big-bellied man sporting a white wife-beater T-shirt.

"Come get a burger off the grill," said Mike.

Suddenly, Ramesh was quite popular. Everyone welcomed him except Billy.

"Damn, Brody, this is the best burger I've had in my life," marveled Ramesh.

"You can thank Mike. He has a secret grilling recipe." Acknowledging his brother's standoffish attitude, he called him over. "Billy, come the hell over here and meet Ramesh."

Reluctantly, Billy walked toward his brother. Ramesh addressed him: "What's up, Billy!"

"Hey."

After a single-word response, he walked away.

"Teenagers! They're so damn moody," remarked Brody. "I think I need to get him laid."

Ramesh let out a hearty laugh. "He'll be okay, man. He's just trying to find his way."

Opening another beer, Brody discreetly interrogated Ramesh. "So, what brings you out here to this deadbeat town?"

"I was stationed at Michaelson Air Force Base until I was released for being profiled as an unbecoming soldier. The shrinks said that I had anger management issues. They threw me out! I put my life on the line for my country. Screw them!"

"Damn, that's some crazy shit! I love my country, but that just ain't right." His face turned red. "Stories like that set me off!"

"Don't sweat it, man. I'll get my revenge one day."

"How would you like to have your revenge in about two weeks?"

"Oh, shit yeah! You possess some kind of magic powers?"

"Something like that! We'll talk about it later." He cheered up. "Let me show you my ride."

"I didn't see it when I pulled up."

"It's in the garage."

"Uw-wee! A 1968 Chevrolet Camaro RS." Ramesh walked around the flawless beauty with a custom maroon and black two-toned paint job. "Damn, those rims are lit! Where did you get them?"

"Special order from Canada."

"This Camaro is cool, man—a showpiece. You've put a lot into it. I could eat off the grill." Ramesh scratched his head. "Damn, it's sweet!"

"Yup, I modified the engine. It's barely street legal."

"My girl will flip when she sees it tomorrow." Laughing to himself, he said, "She's more of a car buff than I am."

The following evening, the bar was packed with revelers. Ramesh, Brody, Billy, Trevor, and Mike convened in the back room. The male bonding strengthened as they engaged in anti-government rhetoric and participated in a show and tell of their weapons.

Hours later, I entered the establishment. Perplexed, the patrons gawked at this young woman of color within their domain. The deluge of whispers circulated the room. Ramesh worked his way through the crowd to greet me.

"There's my chocolate chip! Hi, babe! I missed you!" He picked me up.

"I missed you too, babe!" We kissed. Expressing my love for him, I kept kissing his face. Approaching his left ear, I muttered, "Call me chocolate chip again, and you'll be sleeping on the sofa."

"Aww, I love when you say sweet things to me." He put me down. A nondescript man stood before me.

"This guy has been going crazy without you." He smiled widely. "Hi, I'm Brody."

Acknowledging him with a subtle wave, I responded, "Hi, I'm C.J. Wow! A pool table in the center of the room is a great idea."

"You play? " he asked.

"A little."

Ramesh handed me a beer. I took a sip as Brody challenged me to a game. "I'll rack it for you," he remarked.

"Don't embarrass me in front of my friends, dear," warned Ramesh. He's never known me to play pool.

"I'll break," I volunteered eagerly. Grabbing the pool stick, I applied blue chalk to the padded tip. Then, I placed the white cue ball in the optimum position to create the maximum impact. I took the shot, and my stick struck the cue ball, slamming it into the solid and striped balls, disassembling their formation. Two striped balls aggressively rolled into the side pockets. I was already in the lead.

"I call stripes," I exclaimed as I fed coins into the jukebox.

The music commenced, and I began dancing to the Rolling Stones classic "Brown Sugar." Brody acquired the solid balls.

"Number three in the far-left corner pocket," he predicted.

As his ball sank in, I was in full motion, moving to the rhythm around the pool table. I was the center of attention as I belted out the lyrics to the chorus. From my peripheral vision, I caught Ramesh biting his lower lip to refrain from laughing. I stopped dancing briefly to show off a little fancy work with my pool technique. Executing the most mundane shots, I added theatrics to challenge the tension in the room.

"Number nine in the pocket to my far right," I asserted.

I hit the cue ball with the required energy to make my nine ball roll down the entire length of the table, back-sinking it in the announced pocket.

A crowd formed around the pool table. The spectators tried to curtail their ill-concealed jubilation. Brody made a couple of interesting shots, but my extraordinary performance on the makeshift dance floor and the shots on the billiards table eclipsed his notoriety. My one-woman show ramped up as the song's extended version was winding down. The seductive gyration became another dimension as the pool stick became a prop. Gallantly twirling it to the beat transformed it into a baton, and I was a majorette. Still spinning, I threw it airborne, catching it behind my back. Everyone was in awe, especially Ramesh. He'd never seen this side of me. The song ended.

My final performance was to win the game.

The setup for my final shot was arduous. The targeted 8-ball sat at the edge of the pocket to my far right. The cue ball was near the pocket to my left. Four of Brody's balls were closely aligned, dividing the table in half. Shooting the cue ball in the direction of the 8-ball wasn't an option. Brody's balls were an obstacle, blocking the shot, and I would lose.

With an edge of cockiness, I called out my intention. "8-ball in the corner pocket to my right. Game over!"

"Not so fast, Lady C.J.," remarked Brody.

Ramesh walked around the table, examining my precarious situation. He approached me, shaking his head.

"You better make this shot," he said in an undertone.

Responding with confidence, I said, "Relax, bruh. I got this." I winked at him.

Removing a folded twenty-dollar bill from my back pocket, I tossed it on the padded table paneling.

Turning to Brody, I taunted him. "Wager?"

He was skeptical.

"Lady C.J., that shot is impossible."

"Well, I don't think so."

The wager grew. A pile of twenties accumulated; all were betting against me.

As I bent over the table, my left index finger curled around the distal end of the pool stick. I was ready to shoot. After intentionally stalling for ten long seconds, I stood erect and threw the stick high into the air. During the descent, I gripped it in the middle of the shaft. Holding it like a spear, I forcefully struck the side of the cue ball at a 75-degree acute angle, initiating it to spin on its axis and propelling it forward. As the ball advanced toward the far end of the table, its trajectory suddenly changed.

The audience gasped as they witnessed the cue ball curve to the right, avoiding a collision with Brody's solid balls. The white ball headed back toward my end of the table, toward the 8-ball. Making the connection, the cue ball tapped the black ball ever so slightly, rolling it into the intended pocket.

Game over!

Ramesh was uncontrollable.

"That's my girl," he announced as he picked me up. Our bodies twirled. We kissed. "You're amazing!" At the top of his lungs, he yelled, "SHE'S AMAZING!"

The patrons cheered. Brody stood speechless, shaking his head with the biggest smile. Clutching the $500 winnings, I was acknowledged for my pool shark antics. They all were flabbergasted.

"What the —"

"Oh shit!"

"Damn!"

"Way to go, C.J."

"You rock, girl!"

"We need to take you to Vegas!"

"Man, I lost $20. That was my gas money."

"Well, hot damn! I'm buying this gal a drink," said Mike. "C'mon up here!"

No longer ostracized, I was accepted by the tight-knit crew at the bar. Many patrons gave me high-fives or patted me on the back. Adroitly, I had won them over.

Mission accomplished.

Ramesh was animated during the ride back to the motel. His arms were flailing as he spoke.

"No one's going to believe me. There isn't even a video. Who taught you that trick? I didn't even know that you played pool."

I decided to put his curiosity to rest.

"When I was fifteen, a group of us hung out at one of my volleyball teammate's older brother's house. The only furniture he had in the living room was a pool table. He was a pool shark and taught us a lot about the game, including some tricks. It's been years since I've played. I actually doubted myself initially; then it came back to me."

"It sure the hell did, girl. It sure did."

Ramesh couldn't wait to share my escapades of the previous night with our QA team the following day. They were astonished.

I decided to skip the nightly bar festivities for a couple of nights. My body needed to detox, so I hydrated with bottled water. I researched anti-government groups on my encrypted laptop using my high-security clearance. I was capable of infiltrating their cyber chat rooms. Primarily, I was seeking correspondence with the names Brody, Billy, Trevor, and Mike, the men at the bar. The first night was unsuccessful. The second night, I hit pay dirt. The men in question were communicating with someone named Onyx.

It was 10 p.m., and Ramesh returned to the motel earlier than usual. Ecstatic, I said, "I found them!"

Clueless, he asked, "Who did you find?"

"Your bar buddies."

Smiling, he said, "Really?"

"They've been conversing with someone named Onyx in a chat room called The Back Room."

"That's clever."

"Have you heard that name before?"

"No, never."

"Well, he might be the lead perpetrator in their terrorist plan. Whatever the plan is, it will take place in about ten days."

Pacing the room while mumbling to myself, I blurted out, "There's going to be a Military Appreciation Day parade in Denver on the twenty-ninth, in ten days. That has to be the target."

"I have to get them to talk about Onyx."

"Yup, you do."

Even after his shower, Ramesh reeked of marijuana. He cuddled next to me in bed, and I gave him a concerned look.

"What? Why are you looking at me like that?"

"You need to stop smoking weed."

"I'm in character."

"OK, Mr. Character, don't come to me when you complain of abdominal pain and vomit profusely. I will diagnose you with Cannabinoid Hyperemesis Syndrome."

"What the hell is that? It sounds gnarly."

"It's an illness that's associated with chronic marijuana use; you know, potheads. Well, goodnight, ganja man!"

I turned the lights off.

Ramesh turned over onto his back, eyes wide open, staring into the darkness.

The following evening, I accompanied him to the bar. I was greeted with open arms and joined the women at the table. They were starting a game of poker and dealt me in.

Brody called out to Ramesh, "Hey, Ramesh, we're headed to the patio to smoke some weed. You coming?"

"Naw, man. I'm gonna sit this one out."

I discreetly smirked as I shuffled the cards. After the game, I got up to get a bottle of water. Billy stood beside me.

"How did you do that pool shot?" he asked without introducing himself.

"It's actually physics."

"Can you teach me?"

"Sure! When do you want—"

Brody interrupted our conversation. "Billy, we've got work to do in the back room!" The teenager walked away deflated, never speaking to me again.

That night in our motel room, Ramesh voiced his concern about Billy. "That kid is smitten with you. I don't trust him."

"Yeah, I see him eyeballing me like a pervert."

"Just be careful around him. He's a kid but built like a man."

"Don't worry. " I can beat him up, just like I can beat you up," I said, laughing as I flexed my muscles.

"You can beat me up?"

"Yup!"

Catching me off guard, he swiftly scooped me up in his arms and playfully threw me on the bed.

Startled, I confessed, "Maybe I'm more of a lover than a fighter." Ramesh removed his shirt, and then he removed mine.

At the end of the week, the bar boys held a clandestine meeting at Brody's apartment. I was the only female in attendance.

Singling me out, Brody stated, "I heard you can drive really fast."

"I hold my own."

"Good, I might need your skills."

Billy stared me down with his x-ray vision, incinerating every inch of my clothing. Pervert.

Brody pulled out a box that contained five two-inch metal toy cars. He aligned them on the kitchen table, resembling a caravan.

He announced with enthusiasm, "Lady C.J. and gentlemen, this is our target! We're going to intercept a military demolition convoy next week. Our mission is to confiscate the vehicle that will carry the C-4 explosives that we'll need for the main attraction."

"Well, all right," remarked Ramesh.

"How are we going to know which truck has the C-4?"

"Onyx is going to tell us," Billy blurted out.

"NO NAMES!" scolded Brody. He took a deep breath. In a softer tone, he added, "We'll have that covered. Don't worry."

"What's the main attraction?" asked Ramesh.

"Oh, you're gonna love this; it's the joint Military Day parade in Denver on the 29th. You're gonna pay them back for doing you so damn wrong."

"Oh, hell yeah!" exclaimed an exuberant Ramesh as he gave me a tight side hug.

The men smiled and nodded in agreement. Finally, we had concrete details of the proposed domestic terrorist plan. Too anxious to wait until the morning briefing, we called Special Agent Parker and woke him up. He was as excited as we were.

During the 8 a.m. meeting, Parker assigned our team the task of identifying Onyx. I believed he was an active-duty soldier.

Two nights later, at the bar, Brody introduced his friend to Ramesh. "Hey, Duncan, this is Ramesh. He was in the Air Force."

"What's up, Duncan!"

"Hey, nice to meet you."

Pulling his right hand out of his pocket to shake Ramesh's hand, a marble-sized rock fell out and landed on the floor. Picking it up, he gave a nervous laugh.

With an embarrassed facial expression, he said, "It's my good luck charm."

Ramesh shrugged his shoulders. "No biggie, I always carry a 1972 silver dollar coin my father gave me." Removing it from his pocket, he said, "See?" Replacing the coin, he patted Duncan on the back. "Let's get a beer."

A few hours later, I was tired and told Ramesh I wanted to sleep. He refuted my suggestion, saying that we'd go soon.

Another hour passed, and I became cranky. "Ramesh, let's go. I'm tired."

"Soon!" he said sternly.

His demeanor threw me off guard, but I remained complaisant. Thirty minutes passed, and Duncan said goodbye to the guys and headed toward the door. Ramesh followed him, and I followed Ramesh. Duncan entered a late-model Toyota pickup truck. For reasons unknown, we stood on the curb when he drove off. Once we entered our vehicle, Ramesh searched the glove box for a pen and paper. After writing something down, he handed the paper to me.

"Here, this is the license plate number for Onyx's truck."

"W-What?"

He explained the incident about Duncan dropping his good luck charm, the shiny black stone—an Onyx rock.

I was momentarily speechless.

QA did a deep dive on Duncan Link, a.k.a Onyx, and placed him under surveillance. He was an Air Force Airman First Class with a bad boy reputation, always in trouble. He worked in demolition and was an expert when it came to explosives. Link had been flashing cash lately. He uncharacteristically treated his squad to a few rounds of food and beer at the Non-Commissioned Officers' Club on base. The patron at the adjacent table despised him.

"What's he celebrating?" a senior airman asked.

"Who the hell knows? That guy is nothing but trouble," the technical sergeant remarked.

Initially, QA had overlooked Link due to his low ranking. He was not privy to any classified information.

Staff Sergeant Hugh McMillan, a team superior in the upcoming explosive ammunition convoy, was destined to be a military leader. He had many accolades, but he faltered when he drank too much, often revealing too much with his loose lips. Link was a member of his squad and homed in on the staff sergeant's proclivity.

Rumors circulated that Brody and Billy robbed a couple of check-cashing stores in downtown Boulder a few months ago, walking away with $20,000. They were paying their military contact $10,000 for information, and the informant had already been paid half.

The eve of the caravan heist was nerve-racking. Brody held another secret meeting but failed to disclose which military vehicle would have the C-4. To heighten my nerves, QA wanted those hoodlums to actually succeed in this caper. They wanted them to be caught red-handed before the bombs were detonated. I vehemently disagreed.

It was 1 a.m. on the night in question. With the help of Brody's buddies, detours and road closure signs were newly displayed on the side streets along the military caravan's route. To avoid drawing any attention, the convoy consisted of only three camouflaged jeeps, each carrying two soldiers.

Onyx, the driver of the first decoy vehicle, couldn't contain his contempt. "What the hell is this?"

"I dunno," said the staff sergeant in the front passenger's seat. "I guess the military didn't know about the street closures. We've done this convoy multiple times before, and no one bothers us. Just go with the flow."

Onyx expressed an unnoticed sinister grin, "Yeah, I guess."

Holding a sign displaying the word "Slow," I gestured for the first and second jeep to pass.

As the third jeep approached, I rotated my handheld sign to reveal the word "Stop."

Ramesh, wearing an orange high-visibility reflective construction vest and a yellow construction hat, was behind the wheel of a cement truck. With its flashing beacon of lights and audible backup alarm, he reversed into position to separate the first two jeeps from the third jeep, the one transporting the explosives. Unable to visualize the third jeep due to the truck's massive size, the other drivers waited patiently.

The plan was to abduct the soldiers in the third jeep, leaving them tied up on the side of the road unharmed, and then steal the jeep. At the last minute, Brody had a change of plans. A dark-colored utility truck pulled up behind the target jeep.

"Great. " Now a line is forming behind us," the driver of the third jeep complained.

Stealthily, Brody and Billy exited the unmarked vehicle, followed by an intense cloud of marijuana smoke. Even their pores exuded the uniquely popular musty stench. Approaching the jeep, one stood at the driver's door, the other at the passenger's side.

Tapping the driver's side window with the barrel of his.45-caliber handgun, Brody ordered, "Roll down the window, and you won't get hurt!"

Billy mimicked Brody's instructions to the passenger. The soldiers were compliant.

With the windows down, each of the brothers suddenly revealed a six-inch straw in his left hand. Each guy swiftly wrapped his lips around it, blowing a substance in the soldiers' faces. In mere seconds, they were overcome by the mysterious toxic agent.

I watched in amazement and disgust. What the hell was that? It wasn't the plan. The soldiers weren't supposed to be harmed in any way. I was torn between going into doctor mode and blowing this case or letting it play out. Reluctantly, I chose the latter.

The effects on the soldiers were instantaneous. Their pupils became pinpoints, their minds dazed, and they moved in slow motion.

"Get out of the damn truck and go to the rear," Brody addressed the men, who now possessed a submissive, somewhat obsequious behavior.

Speechless, the driver surrendered to the commands as his partner nodded off.

"Hey, wake your ass up!" demanded Billy as he shook the passenger. "Hurry up and get in the back!"

Under the influence, their gait was unsteady, but they complied without hesitation. Pointing his gun toward the driver's head, Brody stipulated, "Now unlock the case, or else!"

As a precautionary measure, the military had divided the code to the lock between them. No one person was capable of gaining access to the explosives.

The occupants in the first two jeeps became impatient, waiting for the colossal cement truck to leave, enabling them to continue their caravan to the civilian demolition company. They decided to walk over to jeep number three. Perplexed, they realized the driver had abandoned the cement truck that continued blocking the road. They found the soldiers asleep in the jeep and the case containing the explosives opened and empty.

Back at the bar, the Menagerie brothers celebrated their success in relieving the military of its cache of C-4.

I approached Brody.

"What drug did you use to subdue the soldiers?"

In a cocky tone, he responded, "It's called Devil's Breath! It was quite effective, don't you think?"

The following day, when Ramesh entered the back room, Brody was aligning a stack of C-4. Billy was sitting in the corner, nursing a soda.

"Hey man, what's the target?"

"Trash cans," answered Brody.

"A dumpster?"

"No, trash cans."

"Trash cans will be all over the place. People will be injured or killed."

Nonchalantly, he replied, "And?"

"Oh, hell naw! I'm not down with innocent people being killed."

"Brody, I told you that he would be an asshole," remarked Billy. "What are you, a cop?"

"Screw you, kid! I'll tell you what I'm not—a murderer!"

"All right, we can pick another target."

Pacing, Billy waved his arms around wildly. "No way! Why are we changing our plans because of him? You and I planned this for months!"

Enraged, he threw the bottle of soda against the wall, spraying the corner with carbonated lemon-lime fluid and glass fragments.

"Damn it, Billy! Settle down!" fumed Brody.

Billy headed toward the table with the C-4. "Fine, I'll place the bombs myself!"

Pointing to Billy, Ramesh ordered, "Sit your ass down!"

"Ramesh, we can find an alternative site," pleaded Brody. "It's not a big deal."

As Ramesh turned to answer Brody, he dropped to his knees. He was sucker punched by Billy in the region of his right kidney, sending shockwaves throughout his body.

Hastily entering the back room to complain about Billy, I began talking as soon as I reached the doorway.

"That stupid kid damn near knocked me over as I came into the building." Observing Ramesh struggling to stand, I ran to his side. "Are you OK? What happened?"

Using the table for support, he stood up. "I'm Ok. Go and get that crazy kid! He's planning to set off bombs to kill as many people as possible. He took some C-4 and timing pins."

Concerned, I asked, "Are you going to be alright?"

"Yes! I got this! Go and get that teenage son of a bitch!"

"He's got this," I said aloud as I left.

Brody stood in front of Ramesh. "You're a cop? Really, a cop?" he ranted.

Ramesh was still moving a bit slowly when Brody positioned himself behind him, placing a chokehold behind his neck, attempting to restrict his airway. Ramesh was unsuccessful in wiggling to get free; Brody's left arm was pressed against his neck while his right arm supported the left arm in applying pressure. Continuing to struggle, Ramesh managed to position himself in front of the wall. With determination and agility, he walked up the wall and flipped over backward, landing behind Brody. Gaining the upper hand, he knocked Brody out.

As I exited the bar's parking lot, Onyx pulled in. Although I was concerned about Ramesh, I was on a mission to capture a bomber.

Billy blew through a stop sign, and so did I, but I did it with caution. He was at least a block and a half ahead when he was forced to stop as a moving van pulled out of a driveway. I needed that edge.

Breaking multiple traffic laws, I caught up to him as he entered Burrow's Highway, a two-lane pathway with one lane in each direction. I was on his heels, then by his side, driving on the wrong side of the road and in the wrong direction.

With the passenger window down, I yelled, "BILLY, PULL OVER! PULL OVER RIGHT NOW!"

Briefly looking to his left, he glared at me, then flipped me off with his left middle finger. Flooring his accelerator, he drove over 100 miles per hour. I had to give him credit; he could really handle a car, but so could I.

The highway was practically deserted. I caught up and pulled alongside him once more. As we drove side by side, he looked at me with an obnoxious grin and pointed his right index finger toward the windshield. I turned my head forward and looked right into the beam of headlights from a big rig truck. In my determination to reach Billy, I had been oblivious to the ambient noise of the truck's thunderous horn.

Unable to position myself behind Billy because a car occupied the space, I quickly peeled off to the far left, driving eastbound on the westbound shoulder. Billy and I were driving parallel, with a caravan of semi-trucks between us. The shoulder was narrow, and periodically, I had to scrape the railing with my left front fender. Finally, the trucks passed, allowing me to regain my position in the eastbound lane.

Driving at an impressively high speed, I saw a sign indicating a sharp curve ahead. Although unfamiliar with the area, I'd heard rumors about Deadman's Curve. I downshifted on the entry to the hairpin turn by engaging the clutch, shifting to third gear, clutch, second gear, slowing down, and gripping the steering wheel to accommodate the hard right turn. Screeching as if in agony, the tires hugged the contour of the road. Each tread clung to the asphalt, maneuvering the sharp and treacherous arc. Exiting the acute bend, I gained momentum by up-shifting. I engaged the clutch—third gear, clutch, prolonged grind, fourth gear—and I was off.

Billy was within my sights once again, and I was in the sights of the local police. A lone cruiser with colorful oscillating flashing lights and a piercing high-decibel siren was tailing me. Deciding not to slow down, I sped up.

A high-speed pursuit evolved.

The cop car was in my rearview mirror and gaining on me. If I was stopped, a bomber would get away, and many lives would be at stake. I tapped the com in my right ear and updated QA with my precarious situation. Taking control of this predicament, I was inclined to utilize an unauthorized Precision Immobilization Technique, a PIT maneuver. The police frequently perform this driving procedure on a targeted perpetrator during a car chase to incapacitate their vehicle.

Pulling up beside me on my left, they announced, "PULL OVER!" via their external PA system.

Abruptly slowing down, I aligned my vehicle next to the police cruiser's right rear bumper. Without hesitation, I swiftly turned the wheel to the left, allowing my car to collide with the cruiser's right rear. Their vehicle catapulted into an uncontrolled 180-degree turn in front of me; they ended up disabled in the ditch. Driving off, I watched the officers self-extricate through my rearview mirror. They were waving their fists in the air in anger. I was glad that they were all right. QA would definitely have to bail me out of jail for that stunt.

Now, back to Billy.

Puffing on an illegal Cohiba Cuban cigar, Onyx entered the back room to find Ramesh standing over Brody, who was sprawled out on the floor. He drew his gun as he walked over to Ramesh. Brody moaned. Turning to look at him, Onyx became distracted. Ramesh took the opportunity to land a right hook to his face, knocking the lit cigar out of his mouth and sending it airborne; it landed in the trash bin adjacent to the table. The gun was kicked out of his hand, skidding across the floor to the rear of the room. A fight ensued between the men. They tossed each other around, unaware that smoke billowed from the receptacle. From throwing punches to wrestling on the floor, they were fiercely engaged in killing each other.

The dramatic high-speed chase between Billy and me continued. Due to the increasing number of cars on the highway, Billy exited onto an empty country road. Accelerating, I navigated the narrow, never-ending, winding road. Unable to pass him, I tailgated. We ended up at the entrance to the rock quarry. Driving into the mesh iron fence, he knocked it aside.

The rugged sand and gravel terrain didn't deter us as we hastily sped off, each vehicle leaving a residual cloud of dust. My car careened into the air when I hit a pothole due to limited visibility. In slow motion, I thrashed about in the seat with a death grip on the steering wheel. After the top of my head hit the headliner, the car succumbed to a hard landing. Gaining control, I downshifted to third gear, obtaining the thrust I needed to return to the race.

Clutch, shift, then back to fourth gear.

We drove around the enormous mounds of granite and soil. Suddenly, we found ourselves on a dead-end path that led to a stone cliff with a drop of over 100 feet. Turning around wasn't an option. Stopping his car, Billy panicked. He was near the edge. Aside from shooting this fool, I had just one trick up my sleeve. Revving the engine, I drove onto his rear bumper, pushing his vehicle toward the cliff edge.

Petrified, he screamed, "WHAT THE HELL ARE YOU DOING?"

With his wheels skidding on the gravel, his brakes could not stop the car. He swung the driver's door open and jumped out of the Camaro mere seconds before it plunged over the cliff. I abruptly braked my car, ran out, tackled him, and slapped handcuffs on his wrists.

Below us, a powerful explosion shot out of the quarry. Quickly, I covered his body with mine. He was a criminal, but he was a teenager, and my duty was to protect him from hot flying debris.

Back at the bar, flames rose up onto the table legs, encasing the tabletop and the bricks of the C-4. Ramesh noticed the imminent danger lurking. His aggression peaked as the situation neared total annihilation. With intense adrenaline, he picked up Onyx and threw him against the wall. Then, he ran out of the building to save himself.

The police sirens were audible and getting louder by the minute. Exiting their vehicles with guns drawn, Billy and I were in their line of fire.

Presenting my badge, I shouted, "It's OK, guys, I'm an undercover federal agent!"

"Get off me, bitch cop!"

"Shut up, Billy!" Assuming the standing position, I reported, "This is Billy Menagerie, my prisoner. He stole a brick of C-4, and it detonated on impact along with his brother's car."

Holstering his weapon, the senior officer approached me.

"I'm Sergeant Burns. An APB was dispatched for this kid. The Feds contacted the local police. We'll gladly transport him for you."

"Thanks, Sergeant. I appreciate that."

The officers yanked Billy up and escorted him to the back seat of their cruiser.

A second explosive shook the quarry. Spinning around, I witnessed the mushroom-shaped plume of smoke rapidly ascending the sky from the center of town.

"Oh no, Ramesh!" I shrieked. "Sergeant, I need an officer to drive me to the site of that bombing with lights and sirens. My partner is in trouble."

"No problem, agent."

As I ran past the cruiser detaining Billy, he was laughing hysterically. "The bar is gone! Ramesh is dead!" he chanted.

I ignored the little creep.

Pulling up to ground zero, we witnessed a large crater surrounded by a wall of fire at 5150 Holcomb Road, formerly known as The Bar. Ashes fell from burning trees.

Jumping out of the police vehicle before it came to a complete stop, I yelled, "Ramesh, where are you? Ramesh!"

The police sergeant and I searched the scorched terrain as the fire department arrived on scene. The fire captain ordered me to stand down and move away from the scene, but I was defiant.

Annoyed and flashing my federal badge, I ordered back, "You stand down! This is a crime scene, and I'm not going anywhere!"

The sergeant yelled, "Over here! I found someone!"

Ramesh was prone, flat on his stomach. Slightly lifting his head, he revealed a face blackened by smoke and ash. His eyebrows were scorched, and a thin stream of blood trickled from his ears. Glass and wood were embedded in his long, greasy mane.

"Are you OK, babe—um, Ramesh?" I gently touched his back.

"HUH?"

Compensating for his sudden hearing loss due to the impact of the explosion, he spoke extremely loudly. I had to speak louder so that he could hear me.

"ARE YOU OK?"

Attempting to sit up, he replied, "I THINK SO."

"NO, STAY STILL," I instructed. "THE PARAMEDICS HAVE TO PLACE YOU IN C-SPINE PRECAUTIONS UNTIL YOU'RE MEDICALLY CLEARED BY THE ER PHYSICIAN. BE PREPARED TO HAVE A SERIES OF X-RAYS PERFORMED."

Sighing in disapproval, he mouthed the word, "Great."

I accompanied him into the ambulance. After a battery of tests and close monitoring for twenty-four hours, he was discharged. Being stoic, he refused to ride in a wheelchair. Instead, he walked out of the hospital with a steady gait, practically unscathed—well, except for his perforated eardrums, which caused the loss of hearing, and his missing left eyebrow. The prognosis was good. As his eardrums healed, his hearing would return completely, and his eyebrow would hopefully grow back.

That afternoon, QA informed us that the remains of Brody and Onyx were recovered. A week later, Ramesh and I attended separate debriefing meetings.

Supervisory Agent Coleman scolded Ramesh. "Your actions were reckless and dangerous! You could have been killed!"

With his hearing returned to normal, he heard every word perfectly. Coleman's non-supportive rhetoric continued, but Ramesh summed it up as hearing just blah-blah-blah.

Special Agent Parker took a very different approach with me.

"Our unit commends you for your bravery and courageous tactics in apprehending Billy Menagerie. As for your unconventional PIT maneuver on the police vehicle, well, let's just say that the government extended its deepest apology to the local law enforcement agency. We also reminded them that this was a case of national security, and you thwarted the nefarious plans of a deranged domestic bomber. If he succeeded with his agenda due to your detainment or arrest, it would have been a black eye for the police. Good work, Agent Johnston."

After our briefings, Ramesh and I met in the hallway. "How did it go, C.J.?"

"Better than I thought it was going to be. What about you?"

"Well"—he ran his fingers through his clean, freshly cut hair—"it was better than I thought, too."

Armageddon

Over the following couple of months, my team and I progressively closed most of our cases. With our success rate unparalleled, all eyes were on us.

Intel informed QA that a local travel agency had engaged in suspicious activity by newly converted, radicalized men. It was under surveillance, but they were unable to obtain further information. With Ramesh's diligence, he discovered that one of the suspects, Atolli Saad, participated in a soccer game every Sunday afternoon at the local park. Befriending him, Ramesh joined a pickup game.

One fateful Tuesday morning, Ramesh went to Atolli's job at the travel agency and hadn't been seen since. Now, it was Wednesday afternoon. His actions might have cost him his life. Without backup, he had gone there on his own accord, running an unauthorized shadow investigation. Fortunately, he was wearing earbuds. That's how QA knew that he went there. The last word he said was muffled: "Armageddon." Then, the communication ceased.

Ramesh had been missing for forty-eight hours, and I wanted to panic at the thought of him being tortured. But, as a highly trained agent, I had to remain professional. Thoughts of him being killed consumed me. I couldn't eat. Drinking only orange juice sustained my existence.

The girls cornered me in the hallway.

"Okay, C.J., we're concerned about you. We're worried about Ramesh, too, but you're taking it to another level. You're not eating or sleeping. What's up?" Bernice asked.

Avoiding revealing our relationship, I had an outburst. Raising my voice, I said, "This isn't a routine K&R, people!"

In my heart, I knew that this wasn't a kidnapping and ransom situation. No one was going to call us with a ransom demand. We would have been notified by now. This was an old-fashioned abduction to obtain vital information. Unfortunately, there was a high probability of him being murdered.

QA initiated a task force to locate him. Accompanied by an FBI agent, I interviewed Atolli's wife, Nela, outside her job at the candy factory downtown. After I showed her a picture of Ramesh, she acknowledged meeting him at her husband's soccer game on Sunday. She stated that his name was Xander something. A couple of days later, Atolli had told her that this man unexpectedly visited him at his job, which upset him, but she didn't know why. She also mentioned that the man was very nice but had an odd compulsive behavior of rubbing his hands together excessively.

Six months prior, I had diagnosed Ramesh with Raynaud's disease. This condition results in periodic narrowing of the blood vessels in fingers or toes as a reaction to cold temperatures or stressful situations. When that occurs, blood flow is minimized and unable to reach the affected areas, causing the fingers or toes to become blue, white, or even produce a waxy appearance. Vigorously rubbing the appendages enhances circulation by warming them. QA wasn't aware of his medical condition.

We were responsible for finding him. Our team was paralyzed and unable to focus on our current missions, so we transferred our open cases to other units. I devised a plan.

"I want to do a sneak-and-peek at the travel agency. I can plant listening devices in plain sight," I said confidently to my unit.

"You're fearless," remarked Penny.

"No, I'm motivated!"

"You go, girl! Do you!"

My immediate supervisor rejected my proposal, calling it too risky. Unsatisfied with his decision, I ran my idea up the flagpole, consulting the regional supervisor. He gave me the thumbs-up to proceed. My plan was convoluted, requiring many moving parts to make it work.

The following afternoon, I wore a synthetic afro wig to hide my locs and dressed in what's commonly called "hoochie-mama" attire. After all, it was a sweltering day. Entering the establishment wearing a low-cut pink blouse, white short shorts, and stiletto heels, I appealed to the testosterone of the two male employees who were sizing me up. Besides the men falling over each other to assist me, the business was void of patrons. The air was stained with an overwhelming scent of cheap, noxious cologne. The extremely tall guy must have bathed in it.

Prepared to use my French alias, I stated, "Bonjour, er, hello."

"Please take a seat," the tall man said, gesturing to the chair.

"Je m'appelle Chloé Thibodeaux. (My name is Chloé Thibodeaux.)," After introducing myself, I slid my French passport across the table to him.

"How can we help you, Mrs. Thibodeaux?" the stout, shorter man asked.

"Oh no. Miss Thibodeaux," I replied with a smile.

I requested a flight to Los Angeles for the upcoming week. Although an antiquated computer was positioned on the desk, the plane ticket was handwritten. Scoping out the surroundings, I noticed faded, outdated travel brochures with curling page corners displayed on the shelves. They were at least five years old, considered obsolete by travel agency standards, and reflected inaccurate vacation prices. This was definitely a front for illegal activity.

The men gawked at my every move. After flirting and making small talk, I asked where the bathroom was. Luckily, it happened to be in the rear of the building. My gait was worthy of a model strutting down a runway as my hips swayed from side to side. Discreetly glancing into the adjacent room, I was ready to implement my plan of entering the bathroom briefly as a ruse. Exiting the restroom, I slowly walked to the doorway of the sole office in the back. The tall man approached me and kindly asked if I needed assistance. I giggled, then intentionally dropped my opened purse, spilling the contents. As intended, my things rolled everywhere.

Attempting to bend down and retrieve the scattered contents, I commented, "Pardon, so sorry."

"It's all right, miss," he remarked, then let out an odd high-pitched chuckle. "I'll gather everything for you."

"Oh, merci beaucoup!" (Oh, thank you!)

As he bent down and was occupied chasing my belongings, I entered the rear office and hastily placed transmitting listening devices on the curtain rod, under the desk, and under the phone. With the pretense of retrieving my lipstick that had rolled into the room, I met him at the door. As he handed me my purse contents, I gave him a kiss on the cheek and a big smile. I returned to the front office to obtain my plane ticket and placed a device under the desk.

Vigorously waving goodbye, I exited the travel agency. "Au revoir, messieurs! (Goodbye, gentlemen!)"

I couldn't wait to get away from Frit and Frat! I desperately needed a shower to wash away their sexist stench.

Sitting in my vehicle, I announced into my communication radio, "The seed has been planted. Mission accomplished."

Through my earpiece, Ramon informed me that the electronic listening devices were working loud and clear.

Laughing, he said, "They're drooling over you. I'll spare you their X-rated rhetoric. One guy has a peculiar piercing laugh."

"I know! They're both shady as hell, but the tall guy, Atolli, really creeped me out." Disengaging my earpiece as I drove off, I said aloud, "We're going to find you, babe!"

After going home to change, I went back to headquarters. Approaching my supervisor, I requested a lead role in this case. "I want to take a point position in this investigation, Special Agent Parker," I pleaded.

"You're too close to this, C.J."

"No disrespect, sir, but right now, I'm not close enough."

"OK, but if I feel that you're too personally involved, I will pull you off in a flash."

"Copy that."

I was determined to ensure every rock was overturned until we found him. That meant all hands on deck. We had to find Ramesh soon.

The audio guys picked up significant chatter between the two men at the travel agency. One guy was heard saying, "I don't want the cops poking around here."

Then, he mentioned something about the package being at the mountain. The other guy referred to the package being in the valley.

"They must be talking about Ramesh, but it doesn't make sense. They wouldn't have him at two locations," Ramon said.

Thinking aloud, I said, "Mountain. Valley. There's a seedy roadside motel on the south edge of town called the Mountain Valley Inn. It's a gamble, but I have a gut feeling that he's there. We've got to check it out, guys."

"Let's do a sneak-and-peek at the motel," suggested Penny.

"No, let's go one better. Let's get a search warrant, and we'll toss the place. We're going to break down doors and knock heads, people," I explained.

"Way to go, C.J.," remarked Birdie.

"It's premature for a victory lap. Let's get him back first. Suit up and grab your blackout clothes and bulletproof vests," I ordered. "If this doesn't work out, we'll go to plan B."

"What's plan B?" asked Daniel.

"I, um, have no idea."

The FBI joined our mission and steadily surrounded the residential suite of the rundown motel. With a no-knock warrant in hand, the plan was to aggressively gain entry with a battering ram, breaking down the door. Used for quick entry during tactical operations, this forty-pound compressed steel rod is thirty inches long and possesses two handles. When swung into an object with a single blow, it provides a high kinetic impact with 40,000 pounds of pressure. Taking the lead, I had everyone in position. A red sedan was parked outside the building. I had Daniel feel the hood of the vehicle for heat. If it was warm, then someone recently arrived at this site.

Daniel touched the hood. "It's warm."

I stood adjacent to the agent with the battering ram. Just as I was prepared to give the command to enter, a muffled rhythmic sound resonated from the small blacked-out basement window.

I whispered to the agent, "Do you hear that?"

"I do," he replied. "Someone's playing music."

"That's not music; it's Morse code."

Perplexed, he said, "Seriously?"

"Listen to it."

We heard three consecutive short pings, then three long pings, followed by another set of three short pings, and a brief pause. The grouping of sounds kept repeating. That was a repetitive SOS signal, a military distress call for help.

"That's Ramesh! He's in the basement!"

The agent remarked, "Oh shit!"

My strategy for this mission relied on the cooperation of the power company. "Go dark now!" I ordered into my walkie-talkie.

Within sixty seconds, the electrical power to the neighborhood grid was turned off, thrusting the homes into complete darkness.

"Hit the door," I commanded the muscular agent standing next to me. He swung a single forceful blow with the thick, heavy metal rod into the door, knocking it down.

Swiftly, I entered the suite, wielding a flashlight with my gun drawn, yelling, "Federal agents! We have a warrant! Come out with your hands up!"

The team was right on my heels; then they dispersed in search of the kidnappers. I was in search of Ramesh. Entering the kitchen, I saw there wasn't an obvious entrance to the floor below. I began tapping on the retro-patterned yellow and blue wallpaper covering the stucco, seeking the concealed basement. Within minutes, I found a hollow-sounding wall. I pushed on the panel, and a door opened, revealing a set of stairs leading downward. The pinging sound was definitely generated from there. I briefly thought about the cacophony the Sherpas on Everest provided when I was lost. Cautiously descending the stairs, I entered the pitch-black room. It was damp and musty. A stale, coppery scent lingered in the air, a familiar stench.

I smelled blood.

Gunshots rang out, and people were running on the floor above; then, the sound of someone being tackled echoed overhead. The perpetrator's gun was retrieved, actually knocked out of his hand.

An FBI agent yelled out, "I got him!"

Another announced on his walkie-talkie, "Attention, Denver Police Department. Be advised: shots fired at my location, 105 Lake Street, the Mountain Valley Inn. Plainclothes federal agents on scene."

"Roger that, agent. Backup needed?" replied the crackling voice of the police dispatcher.

"Negative. Code Four, suspect apprehended."

"Understood. Ten-four, agent."

Due to their curiosity, the local police arrived after overhearing the conversation transmitted. Since they showed up, the FBI had them cordon off the driveway to the inn. An officer retrieved a roll of yellow, 1,000-foot-by-three-inch barricade tape with the recurring message "POLICE LINE DO NOT CROSS" written in black capital lettering from the trunk of his police cruiser. Denver's finest tied one end to a light pole, then stretched the tape across the roadway entrance and secured the end to an electrical pole. This provided a crime scene perimeter.

Tracking the origin of the sounds, I found myself drawn to the corner of the subterranean dungeon. Clenching my small but powerful flashlight between my teeth, I aimed it at the mound of woolen blankets before me. With my free left hand, I removed each blanket and aimed my weapon with my right. Removing the last blanket exposed a slumped-over man. He had been tortured, sustaining severe facial and head trauma, even a gunshot wound to his abdomen. Extensive swelling, bruises, and lacerations with encrusted blood covered his face and head. His T-shirt was wet and drenched in blood, indicating that he had been shot recently. Although he was battered and nearly unrecognizable—it was Ramesh! Handcuffed to an old rusty cast iron radiator, he struck the restrictive metal bracelets against the accordion-style frame, reverberating the Morse code message through the chipped painted pipes.

I holstered my weapon.

Even as I knelt next to him, he continued to percuss. Cloaked in darkness and isolation, he was determined to send the distress message as he barely clung on to life.

I held his head to my chest, reassuring him, and whispered, "You're safe now, baby."

He relaxed his arms and stopped the cadence.

Holding back a flood of tears, I remained stoic. I was a federal agent, and it wasn't the time to be his girlfriend.

Clutching the walkie-talkie, I made a brief statement. "Agent down! I found him! Use the hidden entrance to the basement from the kitchen. I left the door ajar."

"Roger, C.J.! " We're on our way," Cody replied.

"Am I dreaming?" Ramesh asked in a weakened voice.

Stroking his face, I brushed his matted, blood-streaked blond hair out of his eyes. "No, babe, you're saved."

"I knew you would find me. I kept sending out messages—um, you, you know, Morse code."

Unlocking and removing the handcuffs, I acknowledged his creativity. "Yes, I heard it. That was brilliant! That's how I found you."

"Am I dreaming?"

"No, babe, you're safe now."

The team hastily ran down the stairs.

"Am I dreaming?"

Cody was the first to reach Ramesh.

"Oh, damn!" exclaimed Cody as he took his initial glance at him. "Er, I mean, we're all here for you, man."

"An ambulance is en route, C.J.," said Penny.

"Good, he keeps repeating himself. He has a brain injury and is in critical condition," I said in a hushed tone.

The paramedics arrived and placed him on a gurney, then gave him supplemental oxygen, attached him to a cardiac monitor, started an IV to infuse fluids, and bandaged his head and abdomen.

I introduced myself as a physician and informed them I wanted him transported to a large trauma center, bypassing the many small community hospitals. I also stated that I would be accompanying him.

"Wow, a doctor with a gun," stated the cocky medic.

Flashing my badge at him, I curtly asked, "Is that a problem?"

"N-no, ma'am," he cowardly responded.

As Ramesh was placed on the stretcher and carried up the stairs and into the kitchen, I remembered seeing a cell phone on the counter when I had previously scoured the room. Assuming it belonged to the kidnapper, I placed it in my pocket. Removing it from my jacket, I gave it to Ramon.

"Toss this phone. I want to know about every call made over the past seventy-two hours."

"Ten-four, boss."

"Guys, go through this place with a fine-tooth comb. I'm going to the ER with Ramesh."

Bernice responded, "OK, C.J."

Journalists are known to listen to police scanners. Suddenly, news vans encroached on our area. They had apparently overheard the communication between the FBI and the local police.

"And guys," I continued, "don't say anything to the press. We need to control the narrative."

My team nodded in unison.

The trauma physician ordered blood work, x-rays, and an array of Computerized Tomography scans, also known as CT or CAT scans. These radiographic imaging techniques can provide detailed internal images of the body. Ramesh's head, chest, abdomen, and pelvis were scanned, offering a detailed trauma scan.

During the extensive workup, I left the hospital for a little over two hours so that I could interrogate the subject who had kidnapped, restrained, beaten, and shot my boyfriend nearly to death. I needed to grill this villain before the FBI did.

Watching the perpetrator through the two-way mirror from the viewing room, I had an edge by observing his body language without his knowledge. I could see him, but he could only see his reflection, not me. The rhythmic tremors of his left leg were a tell-tale sign that he was nervous. I used that to my advantage. Entering the adjacent interrogation room, I read from the passport found in the motel.

In an authoritative tone, I said aloud, "Akbar Alam Abar from Lebanon. You're twenty-two years old. According to our files, you attended junior and senior high school here in the USA, then got in with the wrong crowd, a wanna-be insurgent gang. I need to tell you that lying to the police isn't a crime, but lying to a federal agent is. And guess what? I'm a federal agent," I cautioned.

"Well, hello, pretty chocolate lady," said Mr. Abar as his left leg shook faster.

"That's Agent pretty chocolate lady to you," I retorted while slamming his passport and a manila folder on the table.

He sat back in his chair and seductively licked his lips.

Ignoring his grotesque sexual advances, I continued: "Your DNA was found on the federal agent confined to your basement."

"Where? Where did you find my DNA?" he interjected.

"The way this works is that I ask the questions, not you!"

"Well, maybe the blankets in the basement came from my bed. They would have my DNA. I mean—well, I dunno."

"Who said anything about blankets? I'm referring to your DNA and fingerprints on the handcuffs that you placed on him."

There was an awkward moment of silence. Deciding to appeal to his attraction for me, I acted interested. Smiling, I moved close to him and sat on the table. Tilting my head while crossing my legs, I admired his ring.

"Wow! I've only known macho men to wear big, gaudy rings on their pinky fingers. It looks good on you. There's a distinctive design. What does it mean?"

"It was my father's military ring," he replied proudly. "It's the Lebanese Armed Forces logo."

"Hmmm, can you take it off so that I could get a better look, please?"

"Anything for you, chocolate agent. I never remove this ring. Papa gave it to me when I graduated from high school."

After placing a latex glove on my right hand, I held out my palm, and he placed the ring in it. "So, you never had anyone wear it?" I inquired.

"No way!"

"It's quite impressive."

He smiled with pride. His leg tremors ceased. I continued: "What's especially impressive is the speck of dried blood that I noticed in the crevice of the insignia. I'm sure it belongs to the agent."

I avoided mentioning Ramesh's name since they knew him by his alias, Xander Cucuta. I placed the ring in a plastic evidence bag. After removing the glove, I slid a picture to him.

"This is an enlarged photo of the left side of the agent's face. You can clearly see the crest of your ring imprinted on his skin," I seethed. "Your repetitive punches caused him to have facial and skull fractures, possibly. I bet you felt like a big man as you beat up a handcuffed federal agent. Well, macho man, there's an old saying: Don't do the crime if you're not ready to do the time!

"You're charged with kidnapping and attempted murder of a federal agent.Based on your criminal resume, that's at least twenty-five years of hard labor." Sliding off the table, I momentarily paused my ranting. "If you cooperate and tell me the names of your crew, I could persuade the district attorney to shave a few years off your sentence."

His smile faded into a grimace etched with worry. The leg tremors returned. "I want a lawyer," he demanded, pounding the table.

"You're going to need one!" I fumed. Gathering the passport, file, picture, and ring, I walked away, then turned back around to face him. "Oh, have you heard of a slide bite? Perhaps you shouldn't answer that since you lawyered up. I can no longer ask you questions, so listen. When you grip a weapon too high and fire the gun, the slide pulls back and clamps down on the web of skin between your thumb and index finger, leaving two wounds that resemble a snake bite."

He glanced at his left hand.

I continued to lecture, "Yup, it looks just like those wounds." He hastily moved his left hand from the table onto his lap.

My ranting raged on. "Unfortunately, you're an amateur at holding a gun. I'm sure that you're the one who shot the agent. Along with the bullet ballistics, we're going to match the blood and skin under the slide of the gun to you."

I exited the room. Giving my team an update, I recounted Mr. Abar's inquisition.

"He's preparing to be a lone wolf, possibly hoping for notoriety among his insurgent buddies."

"Such an idiot," remarked Daniel.

"His choice. I'm heading back to the hospital."

Ramesh was in and out of consciousness. He was diagnosed with facial fractures, rib fractures, and a skull fracture from the massive beatings. He sustained a liver laceration from being shot in the abdomen. All of his injuries concerned me, but the diagnosis of a subdural hematoma petrified me. He was bleeding in his brain.

I left his bedside for fifteen minutes so that I could cry outside. QA contacted his parents and arranged their flight to Colorado.

The abdominal surgery lasted two hours, and the neurosurgery took four. After his operations, I was permitted in the recovery room. He lay helpless and unconscious with his head bandaged and on a ventilator. It was a surreal image. I wasn't his physician and didn't know how to be on this side of the fence. I didn't know how to help him except to pray.

The following twenty-four hours were a whiplash of emotions. His condition could swing in any direction. I would be devastated if he died. He spent the next three days in an induced coma. On the fourth morning, he was extubated and removed from the ventilator. He was awake but lethargic and looked at me with a weak smile.

In a somewhat slow speech, he muttered, "Hi, baby! My head hurts."

Even though our team members were in the room, I no longer cared if our relationship was revealed. He had almost died.

I lightly kissed his lips and whispered, "Hello, my love."

Cody turned to Daniel and announced, "You owe me fifty bucks! I told you that they were a couple."

Everyone laughed. Ramesh even chuckled. Sarcastically, I responded, "Whatever!"

After spending three weeks in the hospital, he was still experiencing headaches and retrograde amnesia, unable to recall the events leading up to and including the kidnapping. But he was discharged home in fair condition. He remained on medical leave for two additional months, so I took a month off to care for him. By the time I returned to work, his headaches had subsided.

At the end of the second month, he returned to duty. I noticed a change in him, and so did everyone else. His moods were labile and erratic at times. Unfortunately, that wasn't an uncommon occurrence after experiencing a TBI, traumatic brain injury. But for Ramesh, his behavior was compounded by his tenacity to find the kidnappers who tortured him. At times, he accused our team of being lackadaisical and nonproductive.

Demanding answers, he shouted, "What the hell have you guys done during the ten weeks I was recovering?"

"Dial it down, Ramesh," I stated with authority. Trying to reason with him, I continued: "Don't let revenge consume you. We'll get them, and the law will prosecute them, but it'll take some time. You know that!"

Glaring at me, he remained silent. It was challenging for me to adjust to his erratic personality. Reluctantly, I told him that Akbar Abar was released on half a million dollars' bail. The trial was scheduled to begin in two months. The FBI surrendered his passport to the court. Abar's uncle owned the travel agency and motel. A warrant for his arrest was issued. Intel stated that he had sought sanctuary on his multimillion-dollar yacht, sailing out to sea. He was in a gilded cage, his own luxurious floating prison. If he docked anywhere on America's coast, he would be apprehended. Atolli was hiding, too. In disgust, Ramesh stormed out of the room.

Twenty-four hours after returning to work, he contacted Lalo, one of the teenagers who frequently played in the Sunday soccer games. Intending to make him his confidential informant, Ramesh offered money if he could locate Abar since he no longer lived at the motel.

Three days later, Lalo texted Ramesh's burner phone, an untraceable prepaid cell phone. The message bore three simple words: "I found him."

Meeting at the park that evening, Lalo told Ramesh, "He's staying with his girlfriend."

Wringing his hands and massaging his fingers, Ramesh responded, "Great job! You just made yourself 500 bucks. Spend it wisely!" Ramesh handed him five $100 bills rolled together, then left.

The following day, QA was notified of a dead body at an apartment on Tenth Street. He was identified as Akbar Alam Abar. The Denver police were aware of his pending federal trial, so as a courtesy, they called us. When my team and I arrived on the scene, a woman was pacing in the yard. She was pale and shaking uncontrollably and dissolved into tears. A female officer was attempting to console her. She must have been the girlfriend who found his body, I thought. Entering the residence, the coroner was in the process of her preliminary assessment. Prior to our arrival, the girlfriend briefly pulled it together long enough to give a riveting timeline to the police. She informed them that when she left for work in the morning at around seven, Akbar was in the shower. She returned home four hours later to retrieve paperwork that she had forgotten to take with her. Arriving home, she found him lying in a pool of blood on the kitchen floor.

She immediately called 911.

Ramesh spent the night at my house but left early in the morning to pick up something from his apartment. He kissed me goodbye and said that he'd see me at the office. By the time my team and I left headquarters, he hadn't arrived yet. I texted him to meet us at 2222 Tenth Street, apartment B.

The coroner was a middle-aged Black woman named Laquita Jones.

Usually, she wouldn't be at the site, but this was a high-profile death. I introduced myself to her and then asked her for details. She stated that she would update me in a few minutes. I acknowledged and remained patient.

Akbar's new cell phone was protruding from the back pocket of his jeans. Dr. Jones retrieved it and passed it to me. I passed it to Ramon.

Ramesh walked into the apartment, eating a breakfast burrito.

Approaching him, I asked sternly, "Ramesh, why are you eating at the crime scene?"

Nonchalantly, he replied, "Um, because I'm hungry?"

"I made you breakfast," I whispered.

"You made me toast. I'm a growing spy, and I need more sustenance."

"Oy vey!" I was livid. Shaking my head, I walked away from him. That white boy was working my last nerve.

Waving her hand, the coroner beckoned me over to the body. As I stood beside her, she began delivering her report.

"Here is Akbar Alam Abar, a twenty-two-year-old male with a defined muscular physique. He was a health nut—well, until this morning when he added a bullet to his diet. There's—"

Interrupting her, I questioned, "Excuse me, but are you saying that this is a suicide, not murder?"

"Yes, that's exactly what I'm saying," she confidently replied. Pointing to Mr. Akbar's head, she continued her medical findings. "There's stippling, burned skin around the gunshot wound to his right temple, suggesting that the weapon was fired at close range. Blowback of his brain tissue and blood are noted on his right hand and the.45-caliber weapon at his side. By the way, the gun's serial number had been filed off. There's no way to trace it back to its legal owner.

"He's entering the first stages of rigor mortis. After making a small incision in his right upper abdomen, I passed a thermometer into the opening and then penetrated his liver to obtain an accurate body temperature. His current liver temperature is 94.1 degrees Fahrenheit. A body loses 1.5 degrees Fahrenheit every hour after death. So, I estimate the time of death is roughly three hours ago, around 8 a.m."

After a long sigh, I blurted out, "It's JDLR! It just doesn't look right! My gut feeling says that it was staged to look like a suicide. His girlfriend denied that he suffered from depression, even though he was facing criminal charges. He was optimistic that he would be acquitted, having faith in the high-profile attorney that his uncle retained to defend him."

"My hands are tied, Agent Johnston. The death certificate will indicate suicide unless you provide evidence to prove otherwise or if I find additional information during the autopsy."

"Give me time, and I will. Thank you, Dr. Jones."

"Ok, agent."

I noticed that Ramesh was uncharacteristically quiet, standing next to the body of the man who had shackled and beaten him to a pulp.

Concerned, I asked, "Are you OK?"

He simply said, "Yes."

I left the apartment determined to find the truth about Akbar's death. I was a dog with a bone, a saying that Ramesh frequently said about me. Instructing my team to return to QA, I decided to canvass the apartment complex. I needed to speak to the residents and find out if they heard or saw anything between the hours of seven and eight, the time of the murder.

The neighbor to the right, apartment A, didn't answer the door. The neighbor to the left, apartment C, was quite informative. She stated that she was walking her dog around seven-ish and greeted Akbar's girlfriend as she entered her vehicle and left for work. After walking around the neighborhood for thirty minutes, she returned as her neighbor in apartment A was picked up by an airport shuttle around 7:45 or so. She's on vacation in Florida for a week.

So far, nothing led to murder. Damn!

That night in bed, Ramesh was scratching his chin and neck intensely.

Grimacing, he asked, "Do you have something to put on my neck? It itches, and it's driving me up the wall. I think I was bitten by a swarm of mosquitoes. Shit!"

"Stop scratching before you make yourself bleed. Let me take a look, babe."

Examining his chin, I noted, "There's a sticky residue on your neck." Washing the sediment off with a wet washcloth, I asked, "What have you been up to?"

He continued to whine. "I don't know! Could you please help me?"

"Yes, I'm going to help you. I see a fine red rash. This is contact dermatitis from something that came in contact with your skin, irritating it. I'm going to apply a cream that will soothe and eradicate the itching. Did you apply aftershave to your neck this morning?"

"I don't remember. Ahhhh, that feels so much better. Thanks, honey!"

"Good." I kissed him. "That will make you feel better, too."

He smiled. "Yes, it does. Come here, girl!" I giggled. One thing led to another.

The next evening, I came home from work and found a bouquet of flowers at my door. There wasn't a note.

"Pretty flowers," remarked Ramesh.

"You didn't send them?"

"Is it your birthday?"

"You know that my birthday is on November 11, Veterans Day."

Smiling, he said, "Well, they're beautiful. I say keep them, especially since I signed a contract to have fresh flowers delivered to you weekly."

"That's so sweet, babe!"

"You know that I will always, always love you, right?"

"Yes, I do! And I love you! They're so beautiful. Thanks again, babe!"

We kissed. Even though he was a narcissistic pain in the ass at work, he was also a gentle and romantic boyfriend.

Unfortunately, our colleagues never saw that side of him.

A week later, detectives paid a visit to Rhonda Smith, the resident of apartment A at 2222 Tenth Street. Holding their badges in view, they introduced themselves.

"Hello, Ms. Smith. I'm Denver Homicide Detective Teylor Rainey, and he's Detective James Pelham. We want to talk to you about the incident that occurred next door a little over a week ago when a man was found deceased. It was the same morning that you flew to Florida."

Opening the door wider, she gestured them to enter. "Come in, gentlemen. I heard that he shot himself. How awful."

"Do you recall seeing anyone arrive or leave apartment B between seven and eight that morning?" inquired Detective Rainey.

"Yes, I saw Analyn Harper leave for work around seven. That's when she normally leaves. I was waiting for the airport van to pick me up. I remember being anxious and looking out the window every five minutes. I hadn't taken a vacation in four years and couldn't wait to get out of town."

"Did you see anyone else?"

"Actually, I did. Around 7:40, I saw a man, a delivery man, approaching her apartment. I thought it was kind of early for a delivery."

"How did you know he was a delivery man?" interjected Detective Pelham. "Can you describe him?"

"Well, it was a shadowy male figure. The bright sun glared into my window, partially blinding me. He was wearing a jumpsuit and carrying a small parcel and a clipboard."

"Any distinctive facial features?"

"He had a full beard." Snapping her fingers, she recalled details about the man. "Oh, yeah, he did something rather strange before ringing the doorbell. Even though he was a silhouette, I noticed that he placed the box and clipboard under his arm and then vigorously rubbed his hands together as if he were cold. It's August! How could he be cold? Weird, huh?"

"Definitely strange. " Did you hear any gunshots?" Rainey asked as he diligently took notes.

"Sorry, but I don't know what a gunshot sounds like. I did hear a car backfire, though. I ran to the window, thinking it was my airport transportation van, but it wasn't. My brother had a muscle car that always backfired. My van arrived about five minutes later, and then I left home. That was around 7:50."

"Did you see the delivery man leave? Did you see what kind of vehicle he drove?"

"No to both," she replied. "Sorry."

Closing his pocket-size notebook, Rainey extended his right hand to the sole witness in this case. After a gentle handshake, he expressed his gratitude.

"Thank you, Ms. Smith. You've been quite helpful." Both men left.

Waving at the door, she commented, "Glad I could help. Goodbye!"

Sitting in their unmarked vehicle, Pelham pondered aloud. "So far, everything is circumstantial. On the other hand, this might have been a hit on Akbar. More than likely, the car backfiring that she heard was probably the fatal shot."

"I agree! The package delivery was probably a smokescreen to gain entry into the apartment. There wasn't a parcel left at the scene. I'll call the coroner when we return to the office."

As soon as Rainey sat at his desk, the phone rang. He answered it on the first ring. "Homicide, Detective Rainey here."

"Hello, Teylor! It's Laquita!"

"Hey, doc, I was just about to call you regarding the death of Akbar Abar."

"Well, I have interesting information to share with you. At the morgue, when we removed his remains from the body bag, strands of his scalp hair fell loose. Most of them had roots attached."

"His hair was pulled out?"

"Yes! There's also a hematoma and skin irritation at the occipital area."

"English, please, doc."

"His hair was forcibly pulled out from the back of his head. He was also hit in the same area, causing the hematoma, a collection of blood under the skin."

"He was assaulted, too?"

"Yes! I also found evidence of synthetic hair from a wig."

"Probably from a fake beard?"

"Sure, that's possible."

He brought her up to date with his findings. "I just interviewed a neighbor who saw a delivery guy with a beard ringing the victim's doorbell around 7:40. He was carrying a package and clipboard, but there wasn't a package found on scene. The girlfriend denied ordering anything."

"That's pretty early for a delivery."

"I thought the same thing."

"Gaining access to his arrest record, I read that Abar was left-handed. The gun was fired from his right hand. Most lefties don't shoot with their right hand. Oh, I almost forgot. When the deceased fell to the floor, his watch broke. The glass crystal cracked, and the hands of the timepiece stopped at 7:46. That's the precise time of death."

"So, in summary, he was hit in the back of the head to incapacitate him, probably with the gun. Then, he was held up by his hair as the gun was placed in his nondominant right hand. The perpetrator must have placed his hand over the victim's hand as he raised the gun to his right temple and pulled the trigger. The assailant really has a lot of upper body strength."

"Sounds plausible, Teylor. Agent Johnston was right. This was staged to look like a suicide. I'm revising the manner of death. This is now a homicide."

"Okie-dokie, doc! Now I have to find the infamous delivery man." Shaking his head, he said, "Good grief."

"Good luck, detective." She hung up. Detective Rainey called me with the update.

"So, the delivery man was a ruse to have Abar open the door. I knew that it was staged. I just knew it!" I said jubilantly.

"Unfortunately, there aren't any videos or other witnesses. Right now, that delivery guy is a ghost."

"I pity you, detective. Thanks for the information. Goodbye."

Pelham walked up to Rainey's desk, handing him the file on Akbar. "Did you tell Agent Johnston that the perpetrator was noticed rubbing his hands together repeatedly?"

"Hell no! I would sound stupid telling her that the guy was cold during a heatwave."

I stood up to make an announcement to my team. "Well, what do you know, the vic didn't commit suicide. The crime scene was staged, just as I thought."

Ramesh chimed in. "So, Abar was murdered. I'm not going to work on the case of that prick!"

"You don't have to. It's Denver PD's case now," I replied.

Ramesh denied having headaches even though he experienced them daily. He knew QA would sideline him from duty if he still had pain, which undoubtedly exacerbated his mood swings.

Early on a cool Saturday morning, I was snuggled warm in bed, determined to sleep in. Ramesh was up and dressed in a thin hoodie and jeans.

Still drowsy, I yawned, then asked, "Where are you going?"

"I'm going to get a couple of breakfast bagel sandwiches for us."

"Mmm, that sounds wonderful. Don't forget to order a large OJ for me, please, babe. Thank you."

"OK. Go back to sleep. I'll wake you when I return."

I fluffed my pillow. "Ok."

He kissed me on the forehead, then left.

After parking and exiting his vehicle, Ramesh chuckled to himself at the thought of a bagel bakery adjacent to a health club. Surely, this must be a cruel joke. Walking through the parking lot, he noticed four men leaving the club. One of them was quite tall, at least six-foot-six or even six-foot-seven. They looked familiar to him, but he couldn't recall where. Indecisive about whether they were friend or foe, he chose the latter. In a last-ditch effort to obscure his identity, he pulled the hood of his top over his head, past his eyebrows.

As they approached him, he realized that the tall guy was telling a story. The men were attentive to every word as they laughed, oblivious to the fact that Ramesh was staring them down. As their paths crossed, he avoided eye contact, preferring to be inconspicuous. The men engaged in hearty laughter at the conclusion of the story.

The towering, lanky man belted out a uniquely high-pitched, snort-like laugh. The piercing din made Ramesh shudder. A sudden barrage of symptoms cascaded over him. First, his chest tightened, then he had difficulty catching his breath, followed by vertigo. Beads of sweat accumulated on his forehead. His heart was beating so fast that he felt it was going to explode. His body trembled, and his knees became weak, on the verge of buckling.

Leaning against a lamppost was the anchor he needed to steady himself to regain his balance. PTSD gripped him swiftly and hard as his mind recalled events—as he recognized his kidnappers.

Still laughing, they drove by him, unaware that their lives were now in jeopardy. On his way back to my apartment with bagels in tow, Ramesh called a friend at QA.

"What's up, man? How's my favorite secret agent?"

"I'm holding my own, buddy. Look, I need you to access a license plate for me. Keep this on the DL, okay?"

"Definitely. I'll keep it on the down-low, just you and me. What's the plate number and make of the vehicle?"

"It's a late-model white Range Rover. Plate number is 8 FIGHTR."

"A fighter. That's cute. I'll get back to you."

"Thanks, man."

"Hey, Ramesh, when I grow up, I wanna be just like you."

"Be careful what you wish for. Later!" He ended the call.

Ramesh woke me up when he arrived with breakfast. We stayed in for the remainder of the day. He was distant and distracted. I figured he was in one of his moods. I kept myself occupied by catching up with reading my medical journals. My contract with QA was approaching the time for renewal. I was seriously considering declining. Ramesh's term would be ending as well, but he would definitely extend his contract and sign a new one.

The next day, I questioned Ramesh.

"Are you OK? You were distant yesterday and seem a bit bummed today."

"I'm all right. Just having flashbacks."

Hugging him, I noted, "Your muscles are so tense, babe. Why don't we get a massage for couples today?"

"I'm down with that."

"You know that you can talk to me."

"I know, honey, but I don't want to talk."

"How about talking to someone else, say a therapist, perhaps?"

Emphatically, he said, "No!"

I never knew what mood he was in. I wish he would consent to psychotherapy.

Ramesh micromanaged our assignments. The team was irritated with him. His decisions were sparking outrage. In his mind, everyone was incompetent—except him. His narcissistic personality had reached an all-time high. Everyone put up with his ego because he had almost died. A traumatic brain injury can cause a radical change in behavior, but in Ramesh's case, it caused rage. After being rescued from his captors, he was embarrassed and seemed to be taking it out on the world. Considering himself to be a top-notch spy, he felt incapable of being kidnapped and tortured. As a result of his captivity, he became mean and ornery. Morale in our unit was at an all-time low.

He and I argued frequently. I no longer saw him as my compassionate lover, and our relationship grew tepid. I tried to keep him calm and focused but failed. Suffering from severe insomnia, he often paced during the night.

Today, he was exceptionally irritating and verbally attacking everyone without provocation. Due to a lack of current leads on the kidnappers, Ramesh expressed his disappointment with a bitter, acrid speech toward our team.

Outside the lunchroom, I overheard Penny and Bernice talking.

"Ramesh is such a pompous ass! I don't know how C.J. can stand to be around him. She's so sweet and kind," seethed Penny. "She probably thinks she can fix him."

"He's broken goods, irreparable."

It saddened me, but they were right. During dinner at his apartment a week later, I pleaded with him.

"We're a team, Ramesh. I realize that you're angry, but this isn't the way to handle it. At this rate, you're going to tiptoe right to the edge. This rage is consuming you, babe. You should seriously consent to therapy. No one needs to know. It will help you defuse the urge for revenge."

He unleashed his rage. "SHUT UP! I don't want to hear your psychobabble!"

Grabbing my shirt, he catapulted me out of the chair, slamming me against the wall. His face was flushed, beet red. His eyes were bloodshot, demonic. Curling his right hand into a fist, he thrust it near my head and into the wall, punching a crater in the stucco.

I didn't know this man. I was afraid of him. Aware I couldn't outfight him, I yelled at him, "LET ME GO, RAMESH!"

Releasing his clutch on me, he took a step back. Now, *I* was enraged! "Damn you! Don't you ever touch me like that again! This is your first and final warning. WE'RE THROUGH! IT'S OVER!"

Without uttering another word, I gathered what belongings I had and left.

Ramesh had transformed into a violent, malignant narcissist, and his aggressive tendency toward me had changed the calculus of our relationship. We were no longer a couple; he was now a mere colleague. Working with him was awkward, but we remained professional. On many occasions, he attempted to speak to me about us. Since we were no longer an "us," I refused to listen. Our affair had fractured, and an apology couldn't fix that break.

"C.J., you know that I've been under extreme stress lately," he professed.

"Thanks for the non-apology apology," I replied curtly as I walked away. Witnessing our tiff, Bernice and Penny looked at each other.

Penny said, "She finally left him."

Bernice acknowledged by shaking her head.

My contract with QA was ending in less than a month, and although I received an extension invitation, I decided to submit my letter of resignation. After working for my country for five years, two in the war and three as a spy, I was ready to work for the people. I was also ready to get far away from Ramesh. My three-year stint as a spy had been an extraordinary experience. Even though I was returning to the world of medicine, QA placed me on the inactive list, enabling me to return anytime.

Anxious about getting hired in an emergency room due to my three-year hiatus, I consulted the general about my future. I was elated to hear that he had been promoted to major general. Returning my email, he stated that he would be in Colorado in two days and preferred to meet with me to discuss my options. I anxiously awaited his arrival.

We met at a restaurant for dinner. It was the first time that I had seen him out of uniform, in a civilian suit—such a handsome older Black man. He was truly my mentor, more like a father figure.

"Hello, General," I said, embracing him.

"Hello, my dear! You look beautiful as always."

Awkwardly gazing away, I muttered, "Thank you."

He continued: "I have a proposition for you. I spoke to the emergency department medical director of the Army hospital at Fort Lincoln in Washington State, and he's eager to have you reinstated to active-duty status as a senior resident in the ER, maintaining your captain status. This is a two-year commitment. What do you think, Captain?"

Without hesitation, I blurted out, "Hell yeah, sir!"

"I'm not much of a gambling man, but I pretty much bet that you would love that offer." After a brief snicker, he went on to say, "You received exceptional training on the battlefield, and a position less than senior resident would be substandard. Once you complete the commitment, you will be eligible to take the national exam and become certified by the American Board of Emergency

Medicine. You will receive an acceptance email from the Army within the next forty-eight hours."

Jubilant, I thanked him profusely.

"I may not say much, Chanel, but I see everything, and I definitely see you. You're an exemplary person, a trailblazer, a rising star, and definitely a role model for women and men of color. You've made us proud."

"Thank you, sir! I've made the Army proud?"

"Yes: the Army, America, and Jamaica. I'm a Jamerican, too!"

My eyes welled up.

I received the Army's acceptance letter the next day. I didn't hesitate to sign it.

After a week of procrastinating, I finally found the courage to tell my team I had resigned. Their reaction was worse than I had imagined. They wept, then became angry. The girls blamed my breakup with Ramesh as the reason for my departure. Somehow, they didn't believe me when I told them that I missed practicing medicine, even though they admitted forgetting that I was a physician because I was such a natural spy.

A couple of days later, Special Agent Parker held a brief meeting in the conference room.

Several other units were in attendance as well. I happened to be in the personnel office finalizing my discharge paperwork.

After clearing his throat, Parker began. "I take it that you've all heard about C.J.—er, Agent Chanel Johnston's resignation." Placing his hands in his pockets, he paced. "As a highly decorated and respected member of our espionage family, she has exemplified professionalism, leadership, and a strong sense of duty. Her exceptional character flourished in the war and infiltrated our world of fighting terrorists. Refusing to take sole credit for a job well done, she always illuminated her entire team. She's an asset to this agency and will be truly missed." His voice began to crack. "P-please take a moment to bid her farewell prior to her departure in two days."

A few colleagues noticeably wiped their tears.

The night prior to my flight to Washington State, the team organized a going-away party at Swanson's Bar and Grill, a local watering hole. That afternoon, Ramesh called me and said that he would miss the festivities because he didn't feel well. I believed he was ostracizing me.

Instead of resting at home, Ramesh initiated his cunning, diabolical scheme. Donned in black attire, he borrowed a friend's truck on the pretense of moving furniture from his storage unit. He drove to an alley and removed the license plates, hiding them under the driver's seat. Then, he went onward to the house in question.

Three cars were in the driveway, and a pizza delivery vehicle was on the street outside the residence. Aware that an international soccer game was televised and in progress, he patiently waited until the pizza guy left before exiting his truck.

With a shifty gait, he made his way to the rear of the house. Assessing the back door, he quickly picked the archaic lock, gaining entry to the house in under thirty seconds. No one was in sight as he slid a black balaclava over his head and face.

The game was blaring from the basement. Suddenly, he heard the sports announcer yell, "G-O-A-L!" Ramesh distinctively heard the familiar voices of four men. They were whooping and hollering with great enthusiasm for the winning team.

Standing on the top stair landing, he overheard one of the men say that he was going upstairs to get a bottle of water. Choosing to hide in a closet, Ramesh kept the door ajar. He heard the man singing in the kitchen. As the house phone rang, he abruptly stopped singing to answer it. The man was conversing with the caller as the super sleuth walked out of the closet and discreetly approached the stairs. Removing a weapon from his waistband and attaching a silencer, a metal cylinder-shaped rod that muffles the sound of a gunshot, he quietly descended. With his face concealed, he entered the downstairs family room, catching the men off guard.

With precision aim and rapid succession, he fired three muted rounds. Each man was struck between the eyes, mortally wounded before they even fell.

Three minutes later, the remaining house occupant went downstairs. He walked into the room and was horrified to see the massacre. Dropping the bottled water, he quickly pulled out his weapon, only to realize that he was alone with his deceased friends. He lowered it to his side. Ramesh was on the floor, camouflaged under the bodies. Quickly and aggressively, he pushed them off, then stood up, aiming his gun at the six-foot-seven-inch man.

Pulling off the balaclava, he cocked his head slightly to the right and said, "Hello, Atolli."

Atolli's face drained of color as he acknowledged the intruder. With a tremulous voice, he uttered a single word: "Xa-Xander."

Sniffing the air by deeply inhaling twice, the agent grimaced.

"Some things never change. You're still wearing that cheap cologne. Now, drop your weapon! I won't tell you again," ordered an intimidating Ramesh.

Compliant, Atolli released the gun, letting it fall to the floor.

Swallowing hard, he managed to speak. "Hey, man, I, um, I didn't agree to have you kidnapped. I'm so sorry about what we did to you."

His plea of innocence angered Ramesh. "Bullshit! Where's your stupid-ass laugh now?"

Fueled by rage and breathing heavily, Ramesh's squinted eyes glared at Atolli. After creating a brief sinister silence, he fired a single shot. The remaining kidnapper fell forward onto the floor. As an act of self-gratification, he fired a final execution shot, a coup de gras, into the back of Atolli's head.

Inadvertently, the man cave had been converted into a killing field. In his dark and twisted mind, Ramesh avenged his near-death experience by killing all of his abductors. Surreptitiously, he went rogue. His vigilante tactics quenched his thirst for revenge, turning him into a mass murderer.

After picking up the spent bullet casings, he left the house undetected. Retracing his steps, he drove to the alley and replaced the license plates before returning the vehicle to his friend.

Two hours after the festivities began, Swanson's Bar and Grill was packed and noisy. Everyone was enjoying themselves when Ramesh walked in. Snaking his way through the crowd, he found me.

"You came," I said with jubilation.

"I had to eradicate a headache. I feel so much better now. You have quite a turnout."

Smiling broadly, I remarked, "I'm popular."

My mood was likely wine-induced; I hugged him, then initiated a long, passionate kiss. The patrons erupted in thunderous applause.

Tearfully, I spoke softly into his ear: "I will miss you."

Looking at me with warm, loving eyes, he replied, "I will always, always, always love you, C.J."

The jukebox played one of my favorite reggae songs. "Let's dance," he suggested.

"No one else is dancing."

"When has that ever stopped you?" he teased.

We laughed as we walked hand in hand to the small dance floor. Our dance was fun and lively. The next song was a popular Latin tune. Our sexy, seductive salsa gained everyone's attention. Their mouths gaped open in disbelief as we swayed and twirled to the music as one. No one at the party had ever seen us dance like this. It brought back beautiful memories of our mission in England. I must admit, I was glad he came.

The following morning, the bodies were discovered when Atolli's wife arrived home from working the night shift at the candy factory. Neighbors heard her blood-curdling screams.

The Denver police informed QA.

I was on a plane heading to Seattle when Bernice left me a voice message on my cell phone.

"Hi, C.J.! Good news: We found Atolli. Bad news: He was murdered along with his three cronies. Call me when you land. Have a safe flight!"

Back at the office, the team was discussing the murders. "Obviously, there was a hit placed on those guys," said Daniel.

"Obviously," remarked Ramesh nonchalantly.

"They could have been your kidnappers."

"That's possible, but I can't remember anything," responded Ramesh as he walked away.

When I landed, I listened to Bernice's message. I was dumbfounded to hear of the atrocious crime that was committed. Perplexed, I wondered if their gang had them eliminated. The only other person who would have a vendetta against them was Ramesh, but he wasn't a murderer. Plus, he couldn't recall who kidnapped him.

Standing at the luggage carousel, I shook my head as I pondered about the kind of evil that ran through someone's veins, enabling them to commit such a heinous act as killing people in cold blood.

The Denver police were baffled about the murders. The calculated plan was well choreographed and scrupulously performed. There wasn't a trace of evidence, no one to convict, yet a gunman was at large—in the wind.

Army Emergency Room

A week prior to starting my ER assignment, I moved into the officer's quarters, a tract of bungalows on the military base. I had a one-bedroom with one bathroom, a kitchen, a living room, and a carport. My motorcycle had been shipped via a cargo van and was scheduled to arrive in a couple of days. Since I sold my Mustang to Daniel prior to leaving Colorado, I bought a brand new five-speed cherry red Mustang 5.0 on my second day in Washington. I yearned for speed. My neighbor was outside washing his compact four-door sedan when I arrived home from the dealership. Admiring my car, he walked over and introduced himself.

"Welcome, I'm Captain Emory Banks, but my neighbors call me Emory."

"Hello, I'm Captain Chanel Johnston, but my neighbors call me C.J."

We chuckled.

"Nice ride. No offense, but can you handle it?"

"Most definitely."

He walked around the car. "Huh, Ok. Do you race?"

Perplexed, I responded, "You want me to race your sedan?"

He laughed. "No, I mean, there's a public racing track nearby. It's called The Racing Strip. You can race another amateur driver and gain notoriety, you know, bragging rights, if you win. They even have semiannual competition events that attract the media, and the winner receives a trophy."

"That sounds very tempting. Thanks for the info. What about motorcycle racing? My Kawasaki arrives in a couple of days. I live on the edge of an adventure," I smirked.

"Whoa! I don't have an answer for you, but I can find out."

"Great."

"If you don't have plans, would you like to join my wife and I for dinner tonight? I believe she's making spaghetti."

"I'd be honored. What time?"

"1800 hours."

I arrived for the six o'clock dinner with a bottle of wine and a bouquet of mixed flowers. Emory's wife answered the door.

"Hello, I'm Madison. Come on in."

"Nice to meet you, Madison. I'm Chanel, but you can call me C.J. These are for you and Emory."

"That's so nice of you. Thank you!"

I heard a baby cooing followed by a bark-like cough. As I entered their living room, Emory was holding their six-month-old son.

"Hi, C.J.! This is our son, Wade."

"Well, look at this adorable little guy."

"Sorry, but he has a cold."

"How long has his cough sounded like a bark?"

"It started this afternoon," stated Emory.

"May I hold him?"

"Sure."

Holding Wade, I unzipped his onesie down to his stomach. Watching his chest concave with his breathing, I alerted Madison and Emory.

"Guys, we have to postpone dinner. Wade is sick and needs medical treatment in the ER."

"What, why?" questioned Madison as she set the plates on the table. "I'm taking him to the clinic in the morning."

"C.J., are you a nurse?" asked Emory.

"No, I'm a physician."

"A doctor? You're so young," he exclaimed.

"I completed medical school five years ago when I was twenty-two. I've spent a couple years in the sandbox."

"Afghanistan?"

"Yes. Next week, I'll start training interns in the ER. Now, back to Wade. He has a condition known as croup, a respiratory infection that causes his airway to become narrow. That's why he has that distinctive cough and chest retractions." I exposed Wade's chest. "See how his chest caves in when he takes a breath? He needs a breathing treatment and steroids to open his airway. He needs treatment now."

Madison quickly packed the baby bag while Emory looked for the car keys. They immediately left for the hospital.

The next time I saw my neighbors was two days later. My motorcycle was delivered that morning, and I yearned to take a long ride. Donned in my rider's attire—a T-shirt, black jeans, black leather jacket, short black leather boots, and a black helmet with a tinted shield, I was ready. I traded my Kawasaki Ninja for the newest model the previous year. QA granted me the same espionage upgrades as my old bike. Anxious to get it on the open road, I revved the engine multiple times just to feel the thrill.

I headed toward a street that exited the rear of the base. My route transformed onto a deserted country back road. Capable of going from 0–60 in 3.5 seconds, I engaged in pushing it full throttle. Ignoring the 40-mph speed limit, I periodically capped off at 100 mph. The two-hour ride was a rush, exhilarating. Pulling into my carport, Madison greeted me outside. I removed my helmet.

"Hi, C.J.! Emory and I can't thank you enough for diagnosing Wade. He was admitted for two days, arriving home an hour ago."

Turning the engine off, I responded. "I'm glad I could help. How's the little guy doing?"

"He's well now, thanks to you."

I signed up for the night shift at the Army hospital. The advantage is that fewer administrative staff hang around, and the camaraderie with the night shift staff is usually extraordinary. On my first shift, I was required to work during the day so that I could become familiar with the facility. I arrived an hour early. Even though I missed my spy buddies, I belonged in the ER. These newly appointed Army second lieutenants, my first-year medical interns, arrived early, too, thirty minutes before the shift. They looked hungry, eager to learn, ready to absorb everything that I was about to dish out. Boy, I thought *I* was young. They looked like teenagers. My group were Efren Panganiban, Diego Embolo, Lola Gilman, Allison Rollo, and Caleb Mitchel. I addressed them.

"Hello, and welcome, everyone! I'm Captain Johnston, a.k.a. Dr. Johnston, your senior resident for this advanced pilot program. I've been on the frontline in a MASH unit in Afghanistan for two years and on a special government assignment for three years.

"You are my newbies, specially chosen for this three-month ER rotation. I expect you to learn, ask questions, and learn some more."

I asked them to introduce themselves.

"I'm horrible with names, so I will call you by the initial letter of your surname." They all laughed.

"I will initiate a weekly didactic session with numerous mock situations."

I was granted a small conference room and the freedom to train them my way. As I was considered a war hero, I received pretty much anything I requested.

I continued, "I will review ailments and injuries from A to Z. OK, let's get started."

We convened in the emergency room. Lieutenant Autumn Becker, the charge nurse, approached me.

"Hello, Dr. Johnston, we're expecting a critically burned patient. I don't know any other details. He'll be placed in trauma room one. I have a respiratory therapist on standby in the room."

The patient arrived seven minutes later. The smell of burned hair and skin heavily permeated the room. The putrid odor lingered in my nose as it traveled through the entire ER. The paramedics stated that the patient created a homemade liquid explosive device that had ignited in an abandoned bunker. He was visiting relatives stationed on the base. This twenty-six-year-old male sustained burns to 80 percent of his body. Although his condition was grave, he was alive, barely.

Soot adhered to his face, discoloring it. The toxic particles had been released into the air during the explosion and consequent fire, and he unknowingly inhaled them. The soot had lodged in his lungs, and when he exhaled, the dark powdery dust coated his nares and philtrum black.

Burns are categorized as first, second, third, and fourth degree, depending on the depth of the damage. A first-degree burn is when the epidermis—the outer skin layer—becomes red and painful, such as sunburn. A second-degree burn affects the epidermis and the dermis, the layer below the outer skin. Besides the intense pain, blisters are formed. A third-degree burn extends beyond the epidermis and dermis, damaging multiple layers of skin. A fourth-degree burn is life-threatening. Besides destroying all layers of skin, muscles and bones are charred. Although this injury is extremely serious, pain is minimal due to the destruction of nerve endings.

Maintaining his airway was my priority. With the first- and second-degree burns to his face, the possibility of oral burns was high. The extensive burns to his chest were third-degree. In a matter of time, his respiratory status would be compromised.

I announced to the staff, "I'm going to intubate him." Turning to the patient, I said, "Manuel, I'm going to give you medication for your discomfort and place you on a ventilator to help you breathe easier."

His response was a moan.

He had arrived with an IV infusing a liter of normal saline in each hand. After sedating him, he was easy to intubate. The respiratory therapist placed him on the ventilator.

"Please remove his burned clothing and wrap his body in sterile bandages," I ordered.

As I observed his cardiac rhythm on the monitor, I noticed a steady, thin stream of water flowing upward from below the gurney on the opposite side.

"Oh no," yelled Brandi, his primary nurse. "A section of his skin sloughed off his left hand and fell to the floor with the IV fluid still running into the vein!"

On the floor laid a segment of burned flesh with an IV anchored in the dislodged vein. Angulated upward, the trajectory of the free-flowing fluid rose toward the ceiling.

Brandi turned the IV off.

"His skin is still burning under the surface," I affirmed. It caused his hand to deglove. His skin slid off as if he was wearing a glove and then removed it.

She started another IV in his left upper arm.

"Dr. G, I need you to observe the rise and fall of his chest continuously. Let me know immediately if there isn't any movement."

"On it, Dr. Johnston."

Within ten minutes, Dr. G. anxiously blurted out, "His chest stopped moving!" The ventilator alarms wailed.

"Brent, go to the operating room and get their cautery machine STAT," I instructed the EMT.

Looking at my interns, I emphasized, "I need to perform an escharotomy: cutting through his thick, leathery, burned skin to enhance his respirations. The excessive burns to his chest have fused and penetrated all layers of his skin, creating a third-degree burn. This is restricting his chest from naturally rising and falling, hindering his lungs from expanding. Everyone don latex gloves. I want you to feel how hard and rigid his chest is."

Diego was the first to touch the patient's torso.

Bewildered, he said, "Oh my God!" Turning to me, he asked, "Can he survive this?"

"Avoid the rhetoric, Dr. E. The patient may be able to hear you. We'll discuss his prognosis away from the bedside," I cautioned.

"Sorry, Dr. Johnston."

Touching his bared, crisp chest, Lola faced me with wide eyes and mouthed the word, "Wow."

Efren, Allison, and Caleb acquired the same perplexed expression after their tactile encounter.

Addressing my team, I explained the procedure as Brent arrived with the machine. "By using this electrocautery probe"—I revealed the pointed tip of the handheld wand—"I'm able to apply precise thermal current, intense heat, to cut through the burned tissue and muscle in his chest while simultaneously sealing the blood vessels to minimize bleeding. The short version is that I'm going to carve out a large rectangular track in his chest, allowing his lungs to expand. He's in an induced coma and won't feel this."

Everyone was speechless.

I applied a face shield, hair bonnet, surgical cover gown, and sterile gloves. I was ready, and so was the audience that gathered around his bed.

Slowly and methodically, I cut through the damaged muscle with the heated tip, revealing undamaged pink skin within the creases. Mentally, I deflected the odor of burned flesh.

Some of the onlookers became nauseous due to the smell, or perhaps it was the fact that they were watching such a barbaric procedure. My peripheral vision homed in on a few nurses and a couple of my interns, who decided to excuse themselves from the room. They found refuge at the nurses' station as they consumed saltine crackers to assuage the urge to vomit.

As I concluded creating a large rectangular-shaped groove from nipple to nipple, an audible "pop" was heard as the entire carved portion protruded from his torso. Then, it began to rise and fall, aligning with his inhalation and exhalation.

The procedure was a success. His breathing was effective, and his chest wall was able to move again, allowing his lungs to expand. Fortunately for me and my patient, I'd done this procedure multiple times in Afghanistan. Manuel was transferred to the burn unit on the fifth floor. Everyone bombarded me with questions. Once again, I began talking about the war.

Just as the interns were going to take a brief break, a pickup truck sped up to the ambulance bay entrance with its horn blaring. This is an ominous auditory sign for any emergency room, immediately triggering anxiety in the staff, who fear that a patient in one of the worst situations has arrived. As I stepped outside to investigate, EMTs Brent and Dillon accompanied me. The interns trailed behind.

Hysterically pointing to his fellow soldier in the bed of the truck, the driver stated that they were off duty and horseback riding on a farm outside the base when his friend's horse became spooked, and he was thrown off. The twenty-five-year-old male soldier was awake but exhibited loss of normal function in his arms and legs. Suffering from paralysis, he couldn't move; his condition was extremely critical.

I instructed the EMTs to get a neck brace, a backboard, and a gurney. After placing the neck brace on to protect his cervical spine, preventing further injuries to his neck, a rigid backboard was placed behind him, and then they gingerly moved him onto the gurney. His breathing wasn't compromised, even though he had suffered this catastrophic event. As he was brought into the

ER, I had him registered and ordered a CT scan of his head, neck, chest, and back to be done immediately.

The radiologist reviewed the images and called me with the report. Prior to answering the phone, I knew that the news would be bad, but I wasn't prepared for it to be that bad. The findings indicated a condition known as Atlanto-Occipital Dislocation, an internal decapitation. This rare and often fatal injury occurs when the ligaments in the neck have been severed. This patient's skull was literally detached internally, precariously teetering on the first vertebrae in his neck.

The patient was still on the backboard and wearing a neck brace, and I needed to restrict all movement to his head and neck. The slightest movement could prove fatal. To further secure his neck's immobility, I placed large rolled towels on both sides of his head and neck, anchoring them with six-inch-wide cloth medical tape across his forehead and to the edges of the backboard. As a precautionary measure, I sedated and intubated him. To limit manipulating his head, I decided not to insert the tube through his mouth but instead through his nose. Due to the extreme urgency of his condition, I arranged to have him airlifted to a specialized neurological center in Seattle. The medical helicopter arrived in less than an hour.

What a shift! I was definitely in my element. *Their exposure to such dramatic injuries will become priceless within their careers*, I thought. Due to my exceptional experience, not only was I capable of treating the patients, but I brought these new lieutenants under my wings. After having a debriefing session with them based on the back-to-back trauma patients, I ended the shift a couple of hours early, sending them home.

Settled into my bungalow that evening while sipping a glass of white zinfandel, I processed the day's events. My mind carried me back to Afghanistan, back to treating severely injured soldiers. This time, I wasn't dodging bullets; my life wasn't in peril. Being a spy was an attractive, intense career, but it derailed my first love— being an ER physician. The transition of trading global espionage with nail-biting adventures for high-intensity medical drama was easier than I imagined. In reality, I exchanged one form of adrenaline rush for another.

Jewel called to find out how my first shift went.

My initial response was, "Oy vey, girl! You're not going to believe this."

The following night, my interns were still riding a natural high from their experience the previous day. Our first patient was a thirty-year-old female with flu-like symptoms. She looked feverish and miserable. Her voice was hoarse; she complained of a sore throat, painful swallowing, and occasional shortness of breath with exertion. Her lungs were clear, and her oxygen saturation was 98 percent. I didn't notice any shortness of breath when I examined her. Reluctant to believe she had a viral syndrome, I ordered an x-ray of her neck.

Perplexed, Dr. M. questioned my decision to have her neck x-rayed.

"She only has a fever and sore throat, so why are you ordering a lateral soft tissue neck x-ray?"

"Excellent question! She has a fever, sore throat, painful swallowing, and a hoarse voice, but my preliminary findings are otherwise normal. I suspect she has a bona fide infection, and the neck x-ray will confirm or exclude my hunch. Meanwhile, I'm ordering labs, an antipyretic for her fever, and a liter of normal saline fluid into her vein to hydrate her. Now, let's see another patient."

A fifteen-year-old male was brought to the ER by his mother with complaints of right side and right back pain after he collided with a tree while on a homemade zip line a couple of hours before his arrival.

He was pale. The examination of his body revealed a large purple bruise that extended from his right side to his back. His mother gasped in horror as she saw the extensive discoloration for the first time. His vital signs were surprisingly stable, for now.

I confined him to bed rest, so he was not allowed to walk around. I ordered a liter of fluids to rapidly run into his vein, an abdominal and pelvic CT scan, bloodwork, and a urine specimen. Overriding his rebuttal, he was required to use a urinal, a plastic jug to pee in. He was not permitted to get up and go to the bathroom. Able to urinate with ease, my interns were aghast when he handed the half-full jug to the nurse.

His urine specimen was bright red, mostly blood.

The x-ray of the thirty-year-old female with a sore throat was available for viewing. My hunch was correct.

"Gather around everyone," I instructed. "Do you see anything peculiar in this x-ray?"

"Not really," commented Dr. R.

"Nope, nothing," chimed in Dr. P.

Pointing to an area above the trachea on the x-ray, I began to lecture. Some of the ER staff gathered around as well.

"This area is known as the 'thumb sign' because that's what it looks like, a thumb. Medically speaking, it's epiglottitis, swelling of the epiglottis, a highly emergent condition. As you know, the epiglottis is a thin cartilage at the base of the tongue. Its sole function is to cover the trachea when eating occurs, preventing choking. Epiglottitis is an infection of the epiglottis. The swelling could potentially occlude the airway, causing a life-threatening situation. She will be admitted to the intensive care unit, where her respiratory status will be monitored closely. I ordered a cool mist oxygen mask placed on her and IV antibiotics. Even though this is serious, I expect her prognosis to improve in a few days."

"I really didn't expect this diagnosis," uttered Dr. M. as he shook his head.

"I did," I said, expressing a suspicious grin.

I received the CT scan report on the male teenager. He sustained significant injury to his right kidney from the blunt force trauma. His right kidney had ruptured—torn—requiring immediate surgery. A nephrectomy, the removal of his right kidney, was urgently needed. We immediately prepared him for surgery.

I intentionally chose the unique cases to explore with my team. What better way for them to learn than by gaining exposure to the more challenging patients? There will always be noncritical patients for them to treat in the future. I preferred that they dive right into the deep end.

After much encouragement from Emory, I spent most of my days off practicing racing at the male-dominated establishment, The Racing Strip. He introduced me to a few of the guys. They were mostly servicemen, but I didn't divulge being a soldier, much less an officer. Amateur drivers and the average wannabes flocked to the Strip on the weekends. I avoided attending the mayhem, preferring to go midweek. For $30, anyone could participate in test runs, with restrictions. Vehicles had to comply with safety regulations: no engine modifications or use of N_2O, nitrous oxide, a gas that's used in racing vehicles to increase the horsepower exponentially with a 10–15 second boost.

I diligently practiced on the 1/8th mile linear track to enhance my speed and limit the lag in gear shifting. Feeling confident, I raced a few novice drivers, losing every time. Not giving up, I focused on my acceleration, maximizing the peak of speed versus shifting gears. Driven and determined, I yearned to compete in the upcoming amateur championship race. Obsessed with the auditory and tactile experience of racing, it filled the void that was created when I left QA. After challenging the sixth novice driver, I finally won, and I have been winning ever since. Now, I was ready to submit my application to compete in the main competition. My eagerness to enter the event was fueled by a group of fans that I acquired. They all backed me up except their previous champion, a guy named Oz.

During the next couple of months, Madison, Emory, and I became close friends. We engaged in bowling, shooting pool, and playing golf. They always tried to set me up with their male friends.

I casually dated, preferring not to get too involved. To some degree, I was still in love with Ramesh.

The championship weekend finally arrived. I changed my work schedule around to accommodate partaking in this exceptional event, although I was the underdog. Considered the newbie, I was placed at the bottom of the racing hierarchy. Everyone else had competed in this race last year. Sixteen drivers were selected and divided into two groups to compete. The losers were eliminated as the winners advanced up the standings.

I kept advancing.

The climax of the final race had me against Oz, their resident pro.

"You got this," said Emory.

"Go get 'em," remarked Madison.

I was glad that she came. She'd never seen me race. Her babysitter was able to watch Wade for the entire day.

With my racing helmet on and strapped into the harness, I retrieved my summit photo for a quick glance of spiritual encouragement. Purposely avoiding looking at Oz, who was to my right, I revved my engine and anxiously stared at the red racing light. The split second that it turned green, I peeled off the asphalt. With a quick sprint reaching 60 mph in 4.9 seconds, my clutch-to-gear ratio surpassed my wildest expectations. I crossed the finish line, 660 feet, in 8.55 seconds. Oz crossed the line in his Camaro in 9.23 seconds.

I became the new champion!

The crowd's jubilation was deafening. Holding my helmet in my right hand and pumping it into the air, my male racing buddies lifted me over their heads. It was a blissful moment.

The females chanted, "Queen Champion."

Oz was highly perturbed that I beat him. His friends mocked him for losing to a female. Aggressively removing his helmet, he threw it in my direction. It came close to me, but I didn't even flinch. Lucky for him, it didn't hit me.

Emory was pissed and yelled at him. "Knock it off, Oz! Don't be a sore loser!"

Walking over to pick up his helmet, he said, "You and that Black bitch can go to hell!" Then, he walked away.

"Ignore him. He's an immature hothead!"

"I already have."

The majority of the racers rallied around me. The women said that I was their hero. About fifty of us converged at a local bar down the street. I walked in carrying my enormous trophy and placed it on the bar's counter. Everyone applauded. Grabbing a chair, Emory and Madison joined me. She was in awe that I could drive like that.

Calling the bartender over, I said, "I'm buying a round for everyone in here. Here's my credit card."

"Well, okay, little lady." Turning down the music, he picked up the microphone. "May I have your attention? Our honorary top racer is treating everyone to a round of drinks."

The patrons cheered wildly.

On a pretty mellow night the following week, an Army sergeant presented to the ER with foot pain. During a practice session at a kickboxing studio, he was barefoot and sustained an injury to his right big toe. It was pointing toward his head, out of place and dislocated. This injury was severe and was affecting his nerves. I had to reduce it urgently: manually return the toe to its natural position. First, I had to numb the toe by performing a digital block, an injection into his toe. I injected the medication into several sites at the base of the toe. It was initially painful, but then his toe became numb. Manipulating the numb toe manually, I successfully moved it back into place. I had my EMT tape his big toe to the second toe with cotton placed in between, known as a buddy tape procedure, and then he applied a splint to his right foot, keeping the toe in place.

The sergeant received training on the usage of crutches and was discharged home. As he left, two Military Police officers escorted a soldier in custody for medical attention after a brawl at the NCO Club, the military Non-Commissioned Officers' Club. This was a popular military bar for the ranks of privates to sergeants. This wasn't an establishment for officers. After tossing back a few bottles of beer, the young soldier tossed a few blows at patrons playing pool. In retaliation, he sustained oral trauma, including a loose upper tooth, when he was punched in the face.

As the custody patient sat handcuffed to the chair with his head bowed down, I spoke to the MPs.

"What's his name?"

The senior officer responded. "It's Oscar McNichols. He definitely has anger issues, always instigating a fight. He even took a swing at me. This latest act of aggression is going to lead him to an Article 15, a military infraction that could progress to a demotion in his rank from private first class (E3) to private (E2), resulting in loss of pay. Any more complaints about him will surely end his military career, causing him to face a court-martial and leading to a dishonorable discharge."

I stood in front of my patient, and he raised his head. Staring intently at him, I finally spoke. "Hello, Oz. Remember me?"

"Oh shit, you're a captain?"

"Yes, private. It's amazing, since I'm a Black bitch and all."

The MPs were perplexed.

"You know him, ma'am?" asked the senior officer.

"Uh-huh." I nodded yes.

Oz shook his head in disbelief.

"Unlike you, Oz, I know how to be professional. This is definitely karma because now, I'm your doctor. Open your mouth, soldier."

Hesitating briefly, he complied. As I prepared to examine him, his loose tooth suddenly fell onto his tongue. Lucky for him, the now avulsed left lateral incisor tooth was otherwise pristine. All of his teeth were. His condition was upgraded to a dental emergency. With the tooth lacking chips, cracks, or dental caries (cavities) and the gum tissue surrounding the empty tooth socket also healthy, I quickly replaced the tooth into the gaping hole. Rolling a wad of gauze, I told the private to bite down, enabling him to hold the tooth in place. I instructed him that under no circumstances should he open his mouth unless I told him to.

The on-call dentist was notified and arrived in an hour. After a two-hour procedure, Oz was discharged from the ER. He left in handcuffs with the MPs, heading to a military jail cell. Now, he was wearing temporary braces that reinforced his once dislodged incisor.

The days turned into weeks, months, and then years. Before I knew it, I was instructing my eighth and final group of interns. After winning the racing trophy, I spent the majority of my free time diligently studying for the Emergency Physician Certification exam. I focused solely on enhancing my career, challenging myself with every extraordinary case. Being in Washington for the past two years had been therapeutic after my break up with Ramesh. We spoke occasionally, but I had no intention of rekindling our relationship.

The general called me upon hearing that I passed the certification.

"Hello, C.J.! Congratulations on your achievement."

"Thank you, General."

"Rumor has it that you're on the shortlist for promotion to major. You would be one of the Army's youngest."

"Seriously? Hmmm. That's tempting, but I'm considering leaving the military at the end of my term in a few months."

"That's a pity. Retiring from the Army would be lucrative for you. Since you entered as an officer so young, you'll be eligible for retirement at forty-two. And the way that you excel in rank, you could be a general by then."

We laughed.

"General C.J. does have a nice ring to it."

We laughed again.

"Give it some thought, my dear."

"Sorry, but I'll have to pass, General. I don't want to end up back on the battlefield. Getting shot once is enough for me. I want a more mundane, mellow life, a civilian life."

"Sad to say, but I understand."

It was time to leave the Army and Washington State, with its gloomy clouds and excessive precipitation. Deciding to stay on the West Coast, I applied to hospitals in Southern California. I yearned to experience the never-ending sunshine that flourished in that part of the country.

I accepted a night shift position in Los Angeles.

Los Angeles Emergency Room

Speaking to Jewel on the phone, I jubilantly said, "Guess who's going to Cali? I accepted an ER position at Wiltern Medical Center in downtown LA."

"Oy vey, girl! You didn't get enough blood and guts in the Army?"

"It's what I do."

She sighed, "Yup, I know."

Scheduled to start in thirty days, I spent two weeks in New York before my move. I welcomed the brief sabbatical. It allowed me to spend time with family and friends while also caring for my banking business.

After settling in LA, I headed to Irvine in Orange County to meet Jewel for an early dinner. Driving on the I-5 freeway was usually a permanent parking lot, regardless of the time of day. The five o'clock gridlock actually started at noon. Snaking my way through traffic, I noticed everyone driving around a disabled vehicle in lane #3, the middle of the freeway. Driving in lane #2, the plethora of luxury vehicles in front of me just slowed and stared, causing more congestion. Approaching the car from the left, I saw the bloody face of a middle-aged woman whose head hung out of the opened driver's window. Blood actually dripped onto the driver's outer door panel. Her car had front-end damage, yet there wasn't a disabled vehicle or any other vehicle with damage in sight.

Stunned that no one had rendered aid, I pulled over to the far-left shoulder. Clicking on my hazard lights, I grabbed a towel from the trunk and carefully ran across two lanes of traffic to reach her. I peeked into the opened window and asked the fifty-ish-year-old female driver her name.

She responded, "I-I don't know."

It was apparent that she was altered and disoriented. Leaning in further, I placed the towel against her bleeding facial wounds. It was then that I realized that her engine was still running. It was difficult for her to follow simple commands such as turning off the ignition.

Alerting her, I stated, "I'm going to enter the passenger's side and turn your engine off."

"OK," she responded calmly.

I entered her vehicle, turned off the ignition, initiated the hazard lights, then called 911.

As other drivers witnessed me interacting with her, they pulled off the freeway onto the right shoulder to observe the drama. I stayed seated next to her until the paramedics arrived. Even though I had limited information to share with them, the first responders thanked me just the same. Shockingly, they revealed that only one 911 call had been submitted—mine!

As I prepared to leave the scene, the medics closed down the freeway, enabling me to return to my car and drive off safely. This experience was disheartening. Were Californians so carefree, callous, or self-absorbed that they didn't give a damn about mankind? With her obvious blood-streaked face and possible brain injury, no one was concerned except me and the paramedics. I wondered if I had chosen the wrong state to formulate my civilian life.

Being in SoCal enabled me to rekindle my friendship with Timothy Tuggle. He had transferred to the VA resource center in

LA six months prior. He looked great! He was fitted with a dark brown skin-toned prosthetic and ambulated without a cane. He eagerly told me he was dating a registered nurse. I truly missed him; he was like a brother to me.

I met Monica, his girlfriend, a week later when we all went out to dinner.

In the restaurant foyer, he jokingly said, "Honey, this is the Army doctor who chopped my leg off."

Smiling and extending my hand to her, I said, "Au contraire, I'm the Army doctor who saved his life."

Instead of shaking my hand, she hugged me and graciously said, "Thank you!"

My first week on the job was an eye-opening experience. The onslaught of inner-city emergencies at night included a multitude of overdoses, victims of violence, and aiding a high homeless population. As a military physician, I was shielded from the raw essence of homelessness, drastic inner-city violence, and illicit drug abuse. No matter what, I treated all my patients with respect.

Being such a young physician, the night crew gravitated toward me, and I adored them. They called me Dr. C.J. Ketra, one of the charge nurses, was a Jamerican, too. We bonded immediately. In playful banter, we would attempt to speak Patois to each other and then laugh at how horrible we sounded.

Most of my shifts were busy with little to no downtime. Every night resulted in the kinds of scenes I would tell stories to Jewel about. For example, one night, a nineteen-year-old college student was brought to the ER by his fraternity brothers. Arriving in his pajamas and looking flushed, he told the triage nurse that he had a fever, body aches, malaise, and loss of appetite. His temperature was 103.1 degrees F. Reading the triage note, I suspected that he had the flu. I donned a basic surgical mask and gloves to protect myself.

During the examination, he complained of intense muscle aches and pain throughout his body. Then, he matter-of-factly mentioned a rash on his legs and feet. Rolling up his pajama pants to expose his legs and removing his socks, I noticed a scattered, non-blanching, purplish rash. The discoloration of the rash didn't fade when I depressed his skin with my finger. With the high fever, nuchal rigidity, and the non-blanching rash, the tell-tale signs were apparent. He was immediately placed in a negative airflow isolation room, a sealed and contained area where his contaminated exhaled breath was transported via an external exhaust system, not circulating in the room.

I instructed all personnel who entered his room to avoid exposure by wearing a hospital face mask, not a basic surgical mask, but an N95 respirator. The difference is that a surgical mask is a loose-fitting face covering that creates a physical barrier to block large droplets or sprays. An N95 respirator mask has a form-fitting seal around the nose and mouth, capable of filtering airborne particles like the germs from meningitis.

A lumbar puncture was necessary to complete and confirm the diagnosis, so I placed a needle in his back to withdraw samples of his spinal fluid. The samples were sent to the lab and confirmed my diagnosis of the highly contagious and often deadly bacterial meningitis.

The college sophomore was admitted to the intensive care unit and placed in their negative airflow room. The Los Angeles Health Department was contacted and alerted the university of a possible meningitis outbreak. Known as Frontline Workers, emergency room staff, paramedics, firefighters, and police officers respond to the aid of others while unknowingly subjecting ourselves to potentially deadly diseases. As a precautionary measure, my staff and I were placed on prophylactic antibiotics to hopefully prevent contracting meningitis.

Some nights, I barely had a chance to recover from one dramatic incident before the next would happen. As I stood in the hallway speaking to a nurse who handed me my dose of antibiotics, the next interesting case arrived. I had barely swallowed the pills when a twenty-eight-year-old male was brought in by his wife. I witnessed him having difficulty walking, but he refused to sit in the wheelchair that my EMT provided for him. As he shuffled into an examination room, I instructed the EMT to have him undress entirely and put on a gown.

I introduced myself to him and his wife and then asked him what was wrong. Noticeably embarrassed, he looked at his wife.

She responded, "We were having aggressive sex and heard a 'pop'; then he yelled out in pain, and his penis became soft."

"OK, I understand. May I take a look, Mr. Bernard?" Without looking at me, he nodded his head yes.

Lifting his gown, I examined his penis. Aside from the swelling and discoloration, it was bent in the middle of the shaft at a 90-degree angle.

Attempting to maintain eye contact with him, I gave my diagnosis. "You have what's known as a penile fracture. An erection occurs by blood filling the erectile cylinders. The forceful impact of your penis striking below the vagina and making contact with her perineum caused a buckling of the penile shaft. During this traumatic incident, the cylinder tore open, and blood escaped into the surrounding tissues, resulting in the immediate loss of your erection. You will need immediate surgery to repair and restore your penis to its full functioning ability."

"Surgery? Oh, hell naw! I will go home and think about it," he anxiously said.

"Are you nuts?" interjected his wife.

Lifting his gown, she pointed to his exposed genitals. "Look at it! Your thing is broken! The doctor said that you need immediate surgery. What do you mean you're going home to think about it? Think about what?"

Modestly pulling his gown back down, he meekly asked, "Will you do the surgery?"

"No, I will contact a specialist: a urologist. This is his field of expertise. Would it be all right if I called him and arranged the operating room, Mr. Bernard?"

He looked at his wife as she vigorously nodded yes, then looked at me. Barely audible, he said, "Sure—whatever."

"In the meantime, I will order blood work, an IV, and pain medication for you."

Casting his eyes downward and biting his lower lip, he maintained his introverted demeanor. Since he remained silent, his wife spoke up and thanked me. Ironically, he had nothing to say to me.

During my time in the LA emergency room, I saw many unique cases. One night, there was an unusually high influx of patients, many waiting for hours to be placed in an exam room. As I scanned the charts, I noticed that a patient who had been waiting for four hours was of great concern. This forty-three-year-old male construction worker complained of numbness in both legs, impairing his ability to walk steadily. He stated that he initially had numbness in both feet, but it had now progressed toward his knees.

This was alarming to me. Only one medical condition came to mind: Guillain Barré Syndrome. This is a rare occurrence in which the immune system attacks the nerves, causing numbness and then paralysis in an ascending order. The symptoms start with the feet and then move upward to the rest of the body. If the paralysis progressed to his chest, his breathing would be compromised, impairing his chest muscles from expanding. If that occurred, he wouldn't be able to breathe effectively, and I would have to place him on a ventilator. After ordering a battery of tests, I admitted him to intensive care for close observation.

A twenty-three-year-old female presented with generalized weakness after an intense eight-hour workout in preparation for a bodybuilder exhibition in two days. I ordered lab work, an EKG, and an IV of normal saline to run with the liter bag wide open. She suffered from Rhabdomyolysis. High levels of enzymes released into her bloodstream due to the overexertion of her muscles from her intense workout.

After she received three liters of IV fluids, she felt better and decided to leave the ER. Despite my determination to admit her to combat this potentially fatal condition, she decided to leave AMA—against medical advice. My explanation of the risks, including recurrent weakness and possible death, failed to dissuade her. She signed out of the ER, determined to compete in less than forty hours. A number of serious patients continued to pour in during my entire shift.

My least injured patient wasn't critical but was a bit odd. A twenty-one-year-old female was pushed into the ER in a wheelchair by a male friend. She held a blood-soaked wad of paper towels over a laceration to her forehead that she sustained from a fall. She was placed in an exam room, and I assessed her wound. After having a CAT scan performed on her head, it was revealed that no brain trauma occurred. As I prepared to suture, her male companion sat in the corner, unfazed and uninterested. I was perplexed by his annoyed and distant behavior. With the scent of alcohol on her breath, she exhibited a childlike giddiness. The laceration had occurred when she fell off a barstool on a date—her first date with this male companion. Considering his lack of concern for her injury, I presumed this would be their first and last date.

Jewel and I met for dinner at least every other weekend. She was amazed by the extraordinary work stories that I shared with her. She stated that she was friends with a couple of ER physicians, and they never experienced intense shifts like mine. She referred to me as a "shit magnet."

During a mediocre shift, I was called to the nursery to evaluate a newborn with shortness of breath. He had been born three hours earlier without complications. A chest x-ray revealed a rare anomaly, a diaphragmatic hernia. He was born with an undetected hole in his diaphragm, the band of muscle that separates the chest and abdominal cavity. It contracts and flattens as you breathe, creating a vacuum effect that pulls air into the lungs. His breathing was normal at birth until it wasn't. With each breath, the newborn's intestines penetrated the hole, entering the chest cavity. The x-ray showed coiled intestines smothering his lungs, preventing them from expanding and causing shortness of breath.

After intubating him, he was transferred to a children's hospital for emergency surgery.

A forty-six-year-old woman was brought in by ambulance with pain in her left forearm after a fall. She tripped over her small dog. Due to the pain, swelling, and deformity, the medics applied an air splint to support her arm. She required surgery for rod placements to realign her bones.

She was very emotional.

"Is there any possible way to avoid the surgery? Perhaps I can wear a cast?" she pleaded.

Being supportive, I said, "Unfortunately, your broken bones are displaced, out of alignment, and placing the rods is crucial."

Crying, she said, "But I'm scheduled for a procedure tomorrow. I told you that I have C-diff, but I didn't mention that I have prolonged C-diff."

"How long have you suffered from Clostridium difficile?"

"Fourteen months."

"You poor girl. Are you scheduled for a fecal transplant?"

Wiping her tears, she said, "Yes, in the morning. My sister is the donor. She was just discharged from the Air Force three weeks ago, returning from a three-year stint in Europe. She's my light at the end of this horribly long tunnel."

"Oh my goodness! I'm so sorry, but you really need this orthopedic surgery in the morning. You will have to defer the procedure until next week."

I wanted to give her a supportive hug, but I didn't. She was infected with a contagious intestinal infection. Returning to the office, I was swarmed with questions from the staff.

"Hey doc, what the heck is a fecal transplant," asked an inquisitive Derrick, EMT.

Robbin, the charge nurse, chimed in. "I never heard of that either."

Before I knew it, I was holding an in-service about C-diff.

"This patient has Clostridium difficile, a highly contagious intestinal infection that manifests frequent bouts of diarrhea and abdominal pain. Due to a disruption of healthy bacteria in the colon from previous antibiotic therapy, inflammation and possible colon damage occurs from the bacteria, also known as C-diff. The patient miserably experiences constant abdominal pain, fever, and diarrhea. This bacteria can easily spread from contaminated surfaces like clothing, doorknobs, and toilet seats. In rare cases, like with this patient, the infection is recurrent, lasting several months or even years. As a last-ditch effort for treatment, a fecal treatment, also known as a donor stool transplantation, is required. The transplanted donor stool eliminates the bad bacteria, replacing it with good healthy bacteria, promoting healing."

"What's the actual transplant process?" asked Robbin. Another six staff members curiously joined the group.

Leaning back in my chair, I explained. "Well, the donor supplies her stool. Once it's screened for harmful bacteria, infections, and drugs, it's sterilized, strained, and processed. It's administered to the recipient through a tube in the nose that enters the stomach or rectally through a tube into the rectum.

"Even though most donors are family members or close friends, they don't have to be. Some donors sell their stool in the name of science for a price."

"Seriously?" remarked Robbin.

"Whoa, sell your poop? Now, I've heard everything," exclaimed Derrick.

On another night, an ambulance brought in a thirty-six-year-old female in moderate distress. With her eyes closed shut, she arrived whimpering and intermittently moaning. The medics told me that she was having a panic attack. Glancing at her as the gurney rolled past me and entered the examination room, I noticed that her fists were clenched and her toes were curled. With that brief encounter, I surmised that she wasn't experiencing a panic attack but was having spontaneous sexual arousal.

After completing my full assessment of her, I ordered an antianxiety injection to calm her unwanted sensations. She suffered from PGAD, Persistent Genital Arousal Disorder.

"What? Is that a thing?" questioned Derrick.

"Most definitely. I heard about it in medical school."

"So, she suffers from pleasure?" he commented sarcastically.

Ketra walked over to us. "Get back to work, Derrick."

It's sobering sometimes to see how often life-threatening medical issues can happen to young people. A few months into my time in LA, a twenty-eight-year-old male with the complaint of a rapid heart rate and anxiety was transported to the ER. His heart was beating in an abnormal rhythm at 188 beats per minute and didn't respond to the multiple doses of fast-acting IV medication that the paramedics injected into him while en route.

Upon his arrival, I ordered a STAT EKG and prepared to perform electrical cardioversion to treat his rhythm, known as Supraventricular Tachycardia or SVT.

I needed to shock his heart back to a normal rhythm. The procedure is parallel to defibrillating or shocking someone who exhibits a fatal rhythm during a Code Blue when they're pulseless, dead. The difference is that a smaller dosage of electrical current is used, and the patient would be alive and awake, capable of feeling everything.

Besides placing the electrical gel pads on his chest and attaching them to the monitor, I ordered mild sedation for him, which is necessary medication to minimize the pain that would be inflicted by the electricity penetrating his heart. After the sedative was administered through the IV, he became drowsy. I gave the order to proceed.

"Charge the defibrillator to give fifty joules of synchronized current." This would give him a fourth of the electrical energy needed to restore the heart of a dead patient.

The defibrillator buzzed, indicating it was charged.

"Clear away from the patient," I announced as everyone stepped away from the bed to avoid being electrocuted.

Depressing the button, I initiated the charge.

"SHIT!" yelled the patient as his body performed a single involuntary jerky motion, arching his back when the current ricocheted through his chest.

Keeping my eyes on the cardiac monitor, I watched his rapid rhythm briefly transform into a linear flat line, then convert into normal rhythm at eighty-two beats per minute. The patient gave a long sigh, aware that his heart was beating normally again, no longer feeling like it was going to jump out of his chest. But he was unaware that his heart actually stopped beating for a tender moment. Thanks to our expertise and medical technology, we were able to restore his normal heart rhythm.

A few minutes later, paramedics alerted Ketra that they were coming in Code 3, lights and sirens, with a fifty-five-year-old male patient in cardiopulmonary arrest. CPR was in progress. The paramedics had intubated him and attached an Ambu bag, manually pushing oxygen into his lungs. As the patient arrived, he was swiftly moved onto the ER gurney and placed on our cardiac monitor. We continued cardiac compressions and manually squeezed air into him. We resumed giving advanced cardiac life support drugs. After a total of four rounds of epinephrine, administered in his IV every three to five minutes, along with a dose of sodium bicarbonate and calcium chloride, we felt a pulse.

He was in critical condition but alive!

Arriving at work one night, I was greeted with unpleasant yet familiar sounds. As I passed through the halls, the raucous sounds were deafening—noise that was generated only in an emergency room.

A toddler was exhibiting a piercing cry as a nurse was inserting an IV into her foot; a middle-aged woman was yelling that she had abdominal pain; a drunken middle-aged man was incontinent of urine and screaming at the top of his lungs as a nurse inserted a

Foley catheter, a urinary tube, into his penis; a woman in her early forties was hysterical, having a panic attack because she found her husband in bed with another woman; and a female gangbanger was cursing and threatening everyone that walked by. She was dissatisfied with her care and was requesting more pain medication. A victim of a drive-by shooting, she was shot in the right butt cheek and awaiting surgery. The last rambunctious patient was an agitated twenty-something-year-old male under the influence of crystal methamphetamine, PCP, and Lord knows what else. He was restrained on a gurney as he, too, yelled profanity at the staff. He was huge, possessed enormous strength, and kept rocking the gurney from side to side, almost flipping it over several times.

Damn full moon!

Many myths exist about working in a hospital at night during a full moon phase. Supposedly, there's an exponential increase in the number of women in labor and in the number of patients that arrive at the ER. Most of my staff, including myself, believed in these superstitions at work. We didn't care to work during a full moon, and we didn't say things like "quiet" or "slow." That's just asking for mayhem. As I walked past the nurses' station, Robbin, the charge nurse, shook her head.

"Make a break for it, Dr. C.J. Run back to your car. It's a real shit show tonight," she said in disgust.

I sighed as I thought about my strategic plan to bring peace and tranquility to the ER. Well, at least, to change the atmosphere from this dysfunctional chaos to a controlled, functional chaos, restoring the staff's sanity.

After receiving reports on all the patients, I made my rounds. The nurse successfully inserted the IV into the baby's foot, and she was comforted by her mother. I ordered pain medication for the female patient with abdominal pain. Antianxiety medication was given to the patient experiencing a panic attack as a nurse gave her supportive care. The Foley catheter was in place and draining urine from the drunken male patient. No longer in discomfort, he fell asleep. The gunshot wound victim received additional pain medication and then was taken to surgery.

The agitated male patient remained unfazed even though he was given sedation. Although restrained, he continued to wreak havoc in his corner of the ER. With his aggression escalating, he thrashed from side to side, raising the legs of the gurney off the floor. Nurses had to actually hold the bed down with their body weight. Determined to end this madness, I temporarily paralyzed him with medication and intubated him. He was placed in an induced coma, and now he slept.

An hour had passed, and a new ER had emerged. The fracas abruptly ceased. The next four hours were pleasant. Some of the nurses assembled in my office and asked me to share stories of my life in the war. I shared my profound experiences and tales of the camaraderie and the friends I missed. With just three hours left in the shift, I briefly left the ER to get a cup of hot mint tea from the physicians' lounge.

Suddenly, the chaos resumed!

It all began when five sixteen-year-old girls who were on a sleepover walked into the ER and vomited all over the lobby floor as a result of ingesting edible marijuana. They had scarfed down large amounts of marijuana brownies and were paying the price for their poor judgment.

Then, the police brought in a screaming, naked nineteen-year-old male meth head, a person addicted to the illicit methamphetamine, who had been wielding a machete in the middle of the street. He was tased by the police so that they could gain control and disarm him. Still agitated when he arrived, the taser wires were dangling from his chest as the tips of the taser projectiles were embedded under his skin. He was in restraints.

While on patrol, our security guard heard a vehicle screech out of the ambulance driveway at a high rate of speed. He investigated the area and found a twenty-one-year-old male who was semi conscious with blood all over his shirt. He had a gunshot wound to his abdomen and was literally dropped off onto the pavement by his friends. Off the record, we call this mode of transportation a "homeboy ambulance."

Simultaneously, an ambulance brought in a forty-three-year-old male crying in agony, suffering from priapism for four hours after taking a sexual enhancement pill. Not becoming flaccid after intercourse, he made multiple failed attempts to quell the pain and discomfort of his prolonged erection by taking extremely cold showers. In desperation, he called 911.

Returning to the ER, I walked straight into this mayhem. All hell had broken loose during the ten minutes of my absence.

Standing there bewildered and shaking my head, I asked, "Ok, who said the Q word?"

Robbin, the charge nurse; Marla, the lab technician; my EMTs, Derrick and Michael; Jazz, the registration clerk; Roland, the security guard; and Rick, the x-ray technician, became stone-faced while pointing to a young acne-riddled EMT student who looked like he had barely passed puberty.

Looking at him, I asked, "Young man, did you jinx us, causing this mess?"

"Um…er…I dunno, miss."

"It's doctor," snapped Robbin.

Lowering his head in embarrassment, he responded remorsefully, "Oh, sorry, doctor. I didn't mean to say that it was quiet."

Patting him on the back, I remarked, "It's Ok, Mr. EMT student. What's your name?"

Barely audible, he said, "J-Jeff."

"Just don't say it again, Jeff. Back to the grind, everyone. C'mon, Jeff, you're going to be my assistant."

Raising his head, his spirits visibly lifted. "Sure thing, doc."

I worked nonstop during the remaining three hours of my shift.

My untouched tea grew cold.

During my next day off, I literally stayed in pajamas. I just wanted to vegetate in my home. My mantra was to eat, sleep, meditate, and repeat. Lounging on the sofa, I reminisced about how intense my career had become in LA versus in Washington. The LA culture after dark frequently consisted of people involved in violence or drugs. The grittiness of the criminal nightlife infiltrated the ER. Nightly, a barrage of overdose patients arrived by ambulance. Those who were awake normally exhibited extreme agitation and combative behavior, requiring restraints. The others were somnolent and near death. These patients don't arrive at noon but definitely at midnight. Just thinking about it made me exhausted. Oy vey!

After two nights off, I was mentally refreshed and rejuvenated, ready to tackle the ER madness. One of my first patients was a thirty-three-year-old male with right shoulder pain that occurred while he was playing night tennis. He felt a pop when he performed an overhead swing to hit the ball. Now, he was unable to lift his arm due to the intense discomfort.

When I examined him, I saw a noticeable deformity on his right shoulder. His muscles were spasming around the injury. X-rays confirmed that his shoulder was dislocated, out of the socket.

Deciding to use a less aggressive method than a manual reduction, or relocation, I ordered pain medication to decrease his discomfort and hopefully relax his muscles. Then, I had him lay in a prone position on the gurney, face down on his stomach, with his right arm and shoulder dangling off the mattress.

Within minutes, he had a brief outburst, saying, "It popped back in place!"

A repeat x-ray confirmed that his shoulder spontaneously slid back into place. A sling was applied to his right arm to minimize any movement. He was also given strict instructions to avoid stretching or engaging in vigorous activity with his right arm. He was required to follow up with an orthopedic physician in a couple of days.

Two hours later, another patient presented with a dislocated shoulder. This time, it was a sixty-three-year-old male who had stretched during his sleep. He had dislocated his left shoulder twice previously over the past couple of years. It isn't uncanny that multiple patients come into the ER with the same complaint during a shift.

This case was more complex than the previous patient. His spasms were more intense. I needed to place him in a conscious sedation state in order to replace his left arm in the shoulder socket. The medication that I had the nurse administer made him drowsy, but he easily awakened to my voice.

I had Derrick wrap a bed sheet around the patient's chest and upper back, holding the ends on the right side of the gurney. On my command, he exerted counter-contraction by pulling on the sheet, moving the patient's body toward him as I pulled and manipulated the left arm in the opposite direction.

I was unsuccessful in adjusting his shoulder, so I needed to be more aggressive. If my plan B didn't work, then the procedure would have to be performed in the operating room. He would be placed under general anesthesia, totally knocked out so that his arm could be forcibly manipulated.

Removing my right shoe, I placed my foot into the patient's left armpit. I told Derrick to hold the ends of the sheet firmly and pull. Pushing against the patient's body with my foot, I tugged and rotated his left arm, overcoming the resistance. I felt it pop into place after mere seconds. The patient remained in a medicinal stupor, feeling no pain.

"Whoa, where did you learn that maneuver, doc?" asked Derrick.

"In Afghanistan."

"You always amaze me, doc."

I chuckled as I placed my sneaker back on.

In the wake of an El Niño storm, local meteorologists warned LA County residents of impending flooding and a potential mudslide that was on the horizon. Even though concrete K-rail barricades had been strategically placed to contain moving bodies of water, debris, or boulder displacement, they were no match for the knee-deep rivers of water that penetrated the coastal cities as the storm slammed Southern California. Pedestrians were caught off guard as they waded through the flooded streets. Boats, thought to be securely docked in slips, were battered by the aggressive and massive swells. Beach city officials ordered bulldozers be used to construct sand berms along the shoreline in a last-ditch effort to control the surge.

As I got ready for work, I prepared myself for the gridlock amid the torrential downpour. Prompting flooding fears, the rain was going to wreak havoc throughout the county. I definitely had to leave earlier than usual. Traffic was bumper-to-bumper on the freeway, and drivers still wanted to speed. Damn Californians!

Most of the ER patients during the night were victims of minor car accidents. They weren't seriously injured, just banged up from fender benders. There weren't any shooting or stabbing victims either. Somehow, heavy rainfall deters criminals from engaging in violent activities.

The shift flew by as the precipitation continued throughout the night. When the morning sky was clearing, the rain decreased to a mere drizzle. I was ready to go home, mentally preparing myself to travel through the freeway slush. After giving my sign-off on my patients to my colleague, Dr. Eryn Gray, I quickly gathered my belongings. Picking up my backpack, I headed toward the exit, activating the motion sensors to open the ambulance bay doors. Before I could even step through, Dr. Thad Ritters called my name. *Oy vey, I was so close to freedom*, I thought.

Turning around, I gleefully said, "Yes, boss?"

"C.J., how much do you weigh?"

Perplexed, I answered, "A buck twenty-seven."

Talking into the phone, he replied, "She weighs 127 pounds. Awesome, that will be great!" Then he hung up.

"What's going on?" I questioned.

"Well, the people of LA need your expertise ASAP. A large mudslide occurred on Topanga Canyon Road in the exclusive Malibu region, and a vehicle is beneath the rubble. The driver's leg has been trapped for about eight hours. They found her vehicle thirty minutes ago."

Gesturing with his hands, he continued: "Early this morning on the 405, motorists were confronted with the effects of dense low-lying clouds that formed in the inclement weather. The wet, slippery asphalt triggered a massive chain reaction of accidents as vehicles careened into each other from multiple directions. Semi-trucks jackknifed then slammed into vehicles already at a standstill, adding to the catastrophe." He paused briefly, shaking his head. "Approximately fifty vehicles are involved. As you can imagine, there are multiple casualties, including fatalities. Some victims are still trapped in the wreckage. Trauma and orthopedic surgeons are overwhelmed."

"Oh no," I said in disbelief.

"I know, it's horrible. The Emergency Network System just sent an urgent message seeking a surgeon to perform a field amputation, and I responded that we could help. Well, actually, that you could help."

"Most definitely," I remarked, placing my backpack on the counter.

"You shouldn't have shared your war stories with me," he chuckled. "You're the best person for the job."

"Well, you know that I'm eager to help anyone in distress, boss."

"Good, because the ambulance is coming to pick you up in ten minutes. They'll drive you to the elementary school a mile away, where you'll board a helicopter waiting on the playground."

"So that's why you needed to know my weight."

He nodded yes. "The flight to the scene should be around twenty minutes. Now pack your medical bag and get ready to sedate, intubate, and amputate, Captain Johnston."

Smiling, I saluted him.

I summoned Derrick to assist me in obtaining some items.

"Hey, Derrick, please bring me five large packages of sterile gauze; three packages of Kerlix; two rolls of six-inch-wide ace wrap; three packages of sterile gloves, size 6 1/2; a bottle of betadine solution; two number 11 blades with handles; an assortment of sutures with large needles; two laceration trays; and an intubation tray. After obtaining those items, please go to the operating room and get the portable bone saw."

"What do you need all of this for?

"I'm packing a bag for a field amputation in Malibu. I'm boarding a helicopter in a few minutes."

Enthusiastically, he said, "Can I go too? You'll need an assistant! I can also pack the IV solutions and medications that you'll need."

"Sorry, Derrick," interjected Dr. Ritter, "but a county flight nurse will be on board to assist her and is bringing the medications and IV solutions."

"Bummer." Disappointed, he left to retrieve the supplies.

Entering the chopper, I sat in the front seat next to the pilot, and it brought back memories of war. The pilot dropped his metal clipboard, startling me to the point that I jumped.

"Are you all right, doc?" asked the concerned pilot.

Embarrassed, I said, "Um, yes. I'm fine, just a bit tired." *Keep it together, C.J.,* I told myself. At least this will be a safe helicopter flight. No one will be shooting at us. My PTSD had raised its ugly head.

The pilot extended his hand, introducing himself. "Welcome aboard! I'm Pilot Greene, but you may call me by my first name. It's Ever."

We shook hands.

"Hello, Pilot Greene! I'm Dr. Johnston, but everyone calls me Dr. C.J." Curious, I asked, "So your name is really Ever Greene?"

"Yup! My parents are eccentric," he said with a mysterious grin. "I heard that you've been in a helicopter a few times, and you even flew one, right?"

"True, during the war. I was even shot down in Afghanistan."

"Whoa, I didn't know that. Well, this should be an uneventful flight."

"I'm counting on that."

The journey was quite pleasant. We landed on Topanga Canyon Road. All traffic had been diverted. We tackled a short, muddy hike to reach the patient. Due to the previously burned hillside, evidence of natural erosion on the cliff had been monitored, but the torrential rainfall exacerbated an already compromised landscape. With the downpour of blinding rain, the driver's visibility had been obscured. For safety, she had pulled onto the right shoulder under a precipice. The landslide was swift and powerful, submerging and crushing her compact car under the excessive weight of the mud and an accumulation of solid and loose fragments of rock.

Her right leg was now wedged beneath the dashboard, preventing her from escaping. With the car encased in wet soil, cell service was interrupted, preventing her from calling for help. The crippled vehicle held her captive. The twisted metal compressed her leg until it was completely numb. As the fierce precipitation retracted at sunrise, turbulent winds infiltrated the scene and shifted the fog out of view, revealing a corner portion of her auto.

A passerby called 911.

The fire department used their mechanical equipment, aptly named the Jaws of Life, to remove the driver's door. Once the area was deemed safe, I approached the vehicle with caution. Poking my head in, I introduced myself. My new patient awkwardly lay across the comminuted front passenger seat in an unsuccessful attempt to wiggle her right leg free.

Her name was Phoebe Woods, a thirty-year-old divorced mother of a five-year-old girl. Calming her nerves, I held her hand and informed her that the amputation of her leg was necessary to extricate her and save her life. I channeled the same emotions that I did with Timothy Tuggle, allowing her to cry.

After a few minutes, I lightly touched her shoulder. "It's time, Phoebe."

Tearfully, she responded, "OK."

The room inside the vehicle was limited and cramped due to the weight and force of the boulder debris crushing the right passenger side while creating limited space on the driver's side. Besides the patient, only one of us could occupy the car at a time.

I exited, allowing the flight nurse, Richard Bodeen, to start an IV in the left arm. As the IV fluid was flowing into her vein, medications were given to sedate her. Placing myself in cumbersome positions, I performed the intubation, then amputation. This was quite a contrast to the first amputation I executed while surrounded by the calamity of war.

Attached to a portable transport respirator, Phoebe remained unconscious and stable. Decluttering my mind from the sounds of war enabled me to relax and genuinely enjoy flying over LA, as I found it peaceful. As we approached the elementary school, the waiting ambulance and a police unit came into view. Upon landing, we transferred Phoebe into the ambulance.

The rain ceased, and the clouds dissipated, revealing the brightest, largest, and most beautiful rainbow I'd ever seen. Once the patient was secured in the rig, we initiated Protocol Code 1 to transport her. En route to the ER, lights and sirens were engaged.

Most of my night shift staff stayed over and gathered outside as we drove up to the hospital's ambulance bay. The applause greeted me as I walked behind the gurney and entered the ER.

Indeed, I was blushing.

Met Zack

Occasionally, a primary care physician would visit the ER to see their patient. One night, around 10:30 p.m., a general practitioner came in to evaluate his patient. I'd spoken to him several times on the phone, but we'd never met. I was immediately captivated when this young, tall, dark, and handsome Black man entered my office. He introduced himself as Dr. Zack Cayman. I attempted to introduce myself but only stuttered nervously. Feeling awkward, I just smiled.

He wore an impeccably tailored designer suit that complemented his swag. He was the caliber of a man that made my heart go wild. We briefly spoke about his patient, then engaged in small talk. He welcomed me to the hospital and then mentioned hearing about a new ER physician who had performed a harrowing field amputation during the El Niño storm.

"Was that you?" he questioned.

Shyly, I responded, "Guilty. But the rain had diminished to a trickle by the time I reached the patient."

"That's incredible that you volunteered for such an arduous task."

"I performed it twice in Afghanistan," I said proudly.

"So, you're a war veteran?"

"Yes, yes, I am."

He offered to show me around LA. Playing hard to get, I told him I would think about it.

Dr. Cayman returned two nights later, but not to see a patient—to see me! We set a dinner date for the upcoming Saturday night.

Even though I had many beautiful dresses, this was an excuse to buy a new one. I went to my favorite boutique in Beverly Hills. Spending a small fortune was worth it!

I preferred to meet him at the restaurant. The evening was magical. We talked, laughed, and talked some more. Zack was five years older than me and quite established, having a private practice at thirty-four. We did have some things in common, including a love for traveling and sports. A night of dancing was on the future agenda.

The evening was special.

I had just begun my Friday night shift. Sometimes, I wondered if taking weekend night shifts in the ER was a sign that I really didn't like myself. Mentally, I was preparing for the onslaught of overdoses, intentional and accidental, and the parade of victims of senseless violent attacks committed with the use of guns and knives—victims of murder, domestic disputes, and police scuffles—all raw and gritty inner-city incidents that I was sheltered from while in the stateside military ER.

Let the show begin!

The paramedics contacted the ER via the red emergency phone to inform us that we would be receiving a forty-five-year-old female who had ingested pesticide in a suicide attempt. Her vital signs were stable, and she had been given IV fluids. Their arrival would be in 5–8 minutes.

My mind ran through the gamut of symptoms this patient could present with, such as anxiety, fatigue, lethargy, cardiac issues, dizziness, gastric upset, shortness of breath, altered level of consciousness, renal failure, and death. The symptoms could occur suddenly or be delayed. Her condition was considered critical.

The patient arrived awake but confused and lethargic. She was unable to tell me how much of the poison she drank or when she drank it. White residue from the pesticide coated her lips.

The nurses placed her on the cardiac monitor and took her vital signs. While examining the patient, I experienced sudden chest tightness and shortness of breath. I backed away from her quickly, and as I stepped away, my symptoms dissipated.

Aloud, I ordered, "Everyone, listen up! Please step away from the patient now! This is an organophosphate poison that she ingested, and it's seeping through her pores. Fumes are emanating from her body, exposing us all to toxins. We could inhale or absorb it through our skin if we touch her. The exposure could manifest symptoms of chest pain or tightness and shortness of breath, which I experienced just now when I stood close to her.

"Everyone must don personal protective gear—N95 mask, gloves, and an isolation gown. The patient needs to be moved into the negative airflow room. The toxic fumes emitted will be carried through the special exhaust system." I briefly paused as the staff involved in her care gathered the equipment. "Once she's moved, administer an atropine IV push regardless of her heart rate. I'll put the order in."

"Really? Atropine?" asked Myndy, her primary nurse.

"Yes, atropine is primarily used to treat a slow heartbeat, but it's also an antidote to treat organophosphate poisoning. Hopefully, this will save her. Let's do this ASAP, people!"

As I gathered the personal protective equipment, I recalled my exposure to opened bags of fertilizers on display at a home improvement store last year. I had developed the same intense symptoms of chest tightness with shortness of breath. Avoiding calling 911 at the time, I immediately went outdoors and indulged in fresh air until the symptoms subsided.

Shaking my head in disbelief, I reflected that only on the weekend would I get poisoned by a patient who ingested poison.

Once again, the lives of healthcare professionals are placed at risk while attempting to save a patient's life.

Oy vey!

Clad in the protective gear, I entered her new room to reassess her. She was improving slightly.

Approaching my next patient, a twenty-one-year-old male with an ankle injury, I was stopped by a visitor outside his room door. He, too, was in his twenties and reeked of marijuana.

"Yo, are you guys making a movie?" questioned the inebriated man. He added, "Everyone is buzzing around."

Responding curtly, I said, "No, we are not making a movie. This is an extremely busy emergency room." Slightly irritated, I thought to myself, *The only one buzzing is you. Stay off the weed, bruh.*

After examining the ankle, I ordered x-rays.

Moving on to another patient, I stopped at a man sitting on a gurney in the hallway. He was disheveled, with long, tangled hair, a scraggly beard, and tattered clothes. He appeared to live a peripatetic lifestyle, but he wasn't malodorous, which I found peculiar. After introducing myself, I asked him what was wrong.

He whispered, "I need to speak to you."

I wasn't in the mood for shenanigans.

"Sir, I'm very busy. Are you in pain?"

"Yes, you broke my heart."

Sternly, I said, "Sir."

"I will always, always love you, C.J."

Startled, I said, "W-What?"

"It's me, Ramesh. I really need to speak to you," he continued to whisper.

"Why the disguise? Why are you in LA? How long have you been here? I have so many questions."

Placing his left index finger to his mouth, he said, "Shh, lower your voice. Some people are looking for me. I need to stay incognito."

"Oh shit, you're in danger," I whispered.

"Meet me at the diner down the street when you get off in the morning."

"Ok, I will."

Being his typical annoying self, he left the ER in a disturbance.

Suddenly, Ramesh stood up and yelled, "Why won't you help me, doctor? I want Dilaudid!"

"You are such an asshole," I muttered under my breath.

He winked at me, then chanted, "Give me Dilaudid! Give me Dilaudid! Give me Dilaudid!" Fully animated, he aggressively pumped his right fist in the air as he continued to chant and stomp his feet.

With a look of disgust, I stood there shaking my head and crossed my arms across my chest. Two drunken patients down the hall joined in. Now, there was a chanting choir. I had security escort Ramesh out of the ER.

"Damn, Ramesh," I seethed.

As I was dictating a patient's chart, Ketra complained about a male patient yelling profanity and racial slurs at the nurses. Unable to insert an IV in him, they were subjected to being called niggas and bitches. Irritated, I told her that I would speak to him. I didn't have the patience, nor did I condone such behavior. I was already in military mode and not in the mood to be messed with. Upon reaching the verbally abusive patient's bedside, I immediately put the side rail down, gesturing that he was free to leave.

He looked perplexed.

I addressed him sternly. "Mr. Diller, it's not Ok for you to come in here and verbally abuse my staff. You've been shooting heroin in your arms for years, damaging your veins, and you know this.

We're here to help you, not to be the target of your anger. So, you are free to leave."

"What the hell—"

Interrupting him, I continued: "If you decide to stay, then you must be respectful. It's your choice, got it?"

He rolled his eyes. "Yeah, sure. Whatever! Damn!"

He consented to stay and be respectful. The nurse successfully placed a small needle as an IV in his right thumb.

During a rare appearance in the ER lobby, I was speaking to Jazz at the registration desk when a forty-ish-year-old woman frantically entered with her tongue protruding and her neck distortedly positioned to the left. Her speech was garbled since she couldn't open her mouth to articulate. Her tongue was trapped, wedged between her upper and lower teeth. Her jaw was involuntarily clenched closed, locked in place.

I escorted my new patient to an exam room. Asking her to nod her head to my questions, I began my examination.

"Did you injure your face or jaw?"

She shook her head no.

"Did you take any medication prior to this condition occurring?"

She nodded yes.

Touching her shoulder in reassurance, I said, "You're having what's known as a dystonic reaction to that medication. Your facial and neck muscles are in an intense spasm. I will order IV medications to break the reaction and also relax your muscles. These medications will make you sleepy but will make you as good as new."

She tearfully garbled, "Tank ooh, octor."

The nurse inserted an IV in her right arm so that she could be administered the antihistamine and muscle relaxant medications. I held her hand until she fell asleep. Watching her neck and facial muscles relax, I saw her mouth slowly fall open, releasing her tongue. There were teeth impressions on her tongue but no open wounds. Allowing her to sleep undisturbed, I left the room. After a few hours, she awakened fully. I discharged her to go home with her friend to drive her.

I acquired a fifty-two-year-old male patient who had been brought in by an ambulance and accompanied by the police prior to my shift due to his public intoxication. Because he was unable to stand erect or walk upright, a trip to the police drunk tank was deferred. Instead, the police dropped him off with us, and he ended up in the ER as an ETOH patient. That's the widely used acronym for alcohol, an integral part of ER lingo.

Making my rounds at the beginning of the shift, I found him asleep but easily arousable. The stench of stale alcohol hovered around him like a dust cloud. He briefly spoke to me. Although his speech was slurred and boisterous, I could make out some of his words as he asked me to marry him. Laughter ensued from the staff at the nurses' station. Letting him sleep off his drunken stupor, I planned to discharge him when he fully awakened.

His total time in the ER had been ten hours, and I was ready to get him out. I had had him under my watch for the past six. Surely, we could arouse him enough to stand and walk around the room, known as a "road test." Unsuccessful in waking him by calling his name, I resorted to shaking him. He briefly opened his eyes and spoke incoherently. His somnolence baffled me. Suddenly, I realized that the scent of alcohol was stronger than when I spoke to him several hours ago.

When an EMT searched his backpack, he found a practically empty whiskey bottle. The bottle cap was clenched in his right hand. Believing that he continued to drink booze while tucked away in this isolated room, I ordered a repeat blood alcohol level. His initial level was 0.24 percent. A level of 0.08 percent is considered legally drunk by California's drunk driving standards. When he arrived, he was three times the limit. Now, his level was 0.42 percent, over five times the limit.

Shaking my head, I muttered, "Oy vey."

I admitted him to the Medical Unit for Alcohol Poisoning.

After my shift, I met Ramesh for breakfast at the diner around 7:30 a.m. No longer in disguise, he wore a T-shirt, jeans, and a baseball cap to cover his freshly groomed shoulder-length dark blond hair. Like we were taught in spy school, he intentionally sat facing the restaurant's door, always being aware of who was entering and leaving. I sat down and called him a jerk. He laughed hysterically.

"It wasn't funny, you brat," I said while playfully hitting him.

"I'm going on an assignment, and I need your assistance. I hacked into your hospital's physicians' work calendar and noticed you have the next five days off. Wouldn't you like to spend it working as a spy with me?"

"Ramesh, why are you hacking into my work schedule?"

"I needed to know when you were off."

"Oy vey! All you had to do was ask me. By the way, who's after you?"

"I don't really know. I believe they're people involved in a previous case of mine. I'm not paranoid, just extremely cautious."

"Please be careful, Ramesh."

"Aww, you do care." He blew me a kiss.

"Can you be serious just for a minute?"

"OK, OK. Let's change the subject. Are you dating anyone?"

"Yes, I'm casually dating a doctor."

"What's his name?"

"You don't need his name. Let's talk about your assignment. I appreciate the offer, but I've given up the spy world."

"You're missing all the fun."

I solemnly responded, "Yes, I know."

We ate and laughed about our previous cases. During my drive home, I thought about how elusive Ramesh had become. It'd been months since we'd communicated. My gut feeling was that he was in some sort of trouble. Rumor had it that he had recalled his kidnappers—his deceased kidnappers. But he never admitted to it.

Code Silver

It was Friday, the thirtieth, a sultry night with a full moon radiating brightly in the dark sky. It was weird how my superstitions heightened only when I was at work. A defiant sixteen-year-old female had been ordered by her parents to clean the bathroom. In anger, she collected all the household cleaning products, shut the bathroom door, and sprayed, sprinkled, and squirted the products everywhere on the sink, tub, and floor. Within minutes, she was overcome by the accumulation of toxic fumes. Experiencing acute shortness of breath, she ran to her parents.

En route to the ER, she received an injection of adrenaline and a breathing treatment by the paramedics. Her respiratory status was compromised due to the toxic mix of fumes released in a small, enclosed area. She was still wheezing when I examined her, so I ordered an additional breathing treatment.

Half an hour later, an armed fifty-ish-year-old man entered the ER. This is known as a Code Silver, a person with a weapon. A silent alarm was initiated by one of the staff, prompting the hospital operator to call the Los Angeles Police Department.

Michael, an EMT, came to my office in a panic to inform me of the situation. He told me the police were en route, then abruptly exited and closed my door. Refusing to shelter in place, I channeled my military persona, leaving my office with the intent of confronting the gunman. A crowd of staff quickly passed me, headed in the opposite direction toward the rear door that led to the parking lot.

Entering the nurses' station, I noticed a large, intimidating man wildly waving a.45-caliber handgun at my crew. I approached him.

"Hello, sir, I'm Dr. Johnston, the emergency room physician. How may I help you?"

Apparently distraught, he was agitated, pacing, rubbing the back of his neck with his free hand, and aiming his gun with the other.

The tension in the room was thick and escalating.

Turning to me and speaking in a flat, monotone voice, he said, "My wife died this morning. I couldn't wake her up. She was cold, so I called 911. The paramedics came, but they said they couldn't save her because she died hours earlier."

With direct eye contact, I solemnly responded, "You have my sincere condolences, but this isn't the way to deal with her death." Placing my hands on my hips, I firmly added, "No one in my ER is responsible for your loss. Please lower your weapon!"

"SHUT YOUR DAMN MOUTH!" he screamed. "Since you're the doctor here, I will shoot you first. She went to her doctor yesterday and today she's dead! You all suck!"

I stood stone-faced, unfazed by his outburst. His demeanor changed from distraught to determined. Taking two steps closer to me and placing the barrel of the gun on my forehead, he was creating an atmosphere of terror. Audible gasps from the staff penetrated the silence.

In seconds, my sympathy transformed into apathy. He pissed me off. I entered a fight or flight mode, an autonomic nervous system response to a threat. My heart rate increased, my pupils dilated, my nostrils flared, and I balled my fists. Discreetly moving into a boxer's stance, I repositioned myself. Slightly rotating my body, I separated my legs to shoulder width, flexed my knees, and shifted my right leg back for balance to prepare for any imminent attack.

When I raised my arms as a gesture of submission, he slowly and methodically slid his right index finger from the barrel of the gun to the trigger.

Swiftly moving my head downward, I yelled, "EVERY-ONE DUCK!"

Pushing my left arm against his right arm, I knocked the gun out of his hand a nanosecond too late. The hot, stinging sensation pierced my left upper arm, making me grimace. The bullet seared through my skin at the average speed of 2,500 feet per second, traveling onward to the wall clock, crashing it to the floor.

My pain aside, I focused on maintaining my stance. Following through with a rapid and powerful right uppercut punch to his chin, I snapped his head back, dazing him. Before he could react, I quickly pivoted to the left, initiating a 360-degree martial arts maneuver spin. Gaining fierce momentum, I sprung high into the air. The force and height of the rotation lifted my white lab coat, flailing behind me, resembling a superhero's cape. Airborne and continuing to turn, I violently kicked him on the left side of his face with my left foot. Rendered unconscious, he fell to the floor.

I subdued him in less than ten seconds.

Although the threat was neutralized, the chaotic aftermath ensued. An emotional climate of hysteria, screaming, crying, and shock radiated from the traumatized staff. Some stood motionless, mouths gaping open in awe of the takedown. They saw me differently, not as a young, mild-mannered physician but as a highly trained lethal weapon.

Oy vey.

"Everyone Ok?" I asked, bending over to catch my breath.

Instinctively placing my right hand over the gunshot wound to apply pressure, I saw blood run down my arm, seep through my fingers, and drip onto the floor.

"Doc is shot!" shrieked Derrick as he and Ketra ran to my aid.

Reassuring them, I stoically said, "I'm OK. The bullet grazed my arm. It's just a flesh wound."

"You're going to need stitches," he remarked, concerned.

"That will have to wait until later. Could you please put a pressure dressing on it to control the bleeding?"

"Most definitely, Dr. C.J."

I removed my bloodstained lab coat. As my arm was being bandaged, I barked out orders. "Guys, put a cervical collar on the assailant to support his neck. Then, place him on a gurney and apply leather restraints to his arms and legs quickly before he regains consciousness. Afterward, attach him to the cardiac monitor and take his vital signs. Have Jazz register him as a patient. Security needs to stand by and guard his weapon until the police arrive. I don't want anyone to touch it. Thanks for the bandage, Derrick."

"No problem, doc. C'mon guys, let's do this."

A few minutes later, LAPD swarmed the ER with guns drawn.

Pointing to the restrained gunman, I calmly stated, "I took him down. His.45-caliber gun is over there next to security. He shot and killed the clock."

"Doc whooped his ass!" said an animated Derrick.

They holstered their weapons.

Suppressing my anger, I instructed Ketra to call the nursing supervisor and inform her to notify the emergency system of this incident. They needed to place the ER on Internal Disaster status because it was a crime scene.

The police sergeant approached me and stated that he needed my statement. "I'll give you a statement in about ten minutes," I commented.

"Doctor, I really need it now," he demanded.

"I understand, but it will still be in ten minutes."

Walking between him and me, my cop friend, Detective Julie Bellows, chimed in.

"That will be just fine, Dr. C.J."

With my mouth perched in a pout, I walked away from them. Bellows tapped the sergeant's arm.

"Let's give her some time to process this," she insisted. Shrugging his shoulders, he responded, "Sure, whatever."

I was so damn angry that this idiot gunman thought he could come in here and terrorize everyone; I needed to compose myself before I spoke to anyone. With tears in their eyes, my staff approached me to express their gratitude and embrace me. But I couldn't hug anyone, not yet. I didn't want anyone to touch me. I wanted to be alone for a few minutes, so I asked them to give me some time.

Intractable images resurfaced. My mind raced back to the sandbox, to the carnage of war, to the men I killed. No one goes to the battlefield and returns unscathed. I entered my office and slammed the door. I'd been deployed, looked evil in the face as I fought in Afghanistan, and was an undercover agent eradicating terrorist cells worldwide. I felt like a fool thinking that I left the life-and-death situations behind. What happened to my mundane civilian life?

"I don't have the patience for this domestic homicidal bullshit!" I fumed aloud. "How dare he put a gun to my head. How dare he shoot me! Damn him!"

Fighting the urge to crawl into a ball and cry, I swallowed hard as a single silent tear rolled down my cheek. My emotions were all over the place.

The previously hostage staff assembled in the break room, away from patients. They comforted each other with hugs as they wept. Most of them called their families. Derrick couldn't contain himself.

"Damn! Did you see that? Dr. C.J. threw down some professional ass whooping."

"She was in the Army," said Ketra.

Wide-eyed and unable to stand still, he continued to babble. "That wasn't routine Army training. It was some kind of special forces shit, like Navy SEALs training. I mean, I know that she wasn't in the Navy, but she was a stealth fighter performing hand-to-hand combat. He had a gun to her head, and she didn't even blink or flinch. I was about to pee my pants! She actually effed-up home dude right before our eyes!" Shaking his head, he continued: "She's fearless! I'm gonna have her walk me to my car at night just in case a gangbanger is after me. She would jack them up!"

Everyone laughed.

"Shut up, fool," scolded Ketra.

"I'm serious! I'm a small-framed man."

"And she's a petite woman," interjected Ketra.

"Yes, but she has skills. Anyone messes with me, and I'm gonna tell them that my doc will righteously kick their ass!"

I'd already used up my ten minutes, so I needed to decompress quickly. I retreated to a few minutes of meditation.

I grabbed my bottle of OJ from the compact fridge and heard a knock on the door. "Come in," I commanded as I opened the bottle.

Ketra walked in. "Hey, doc, just checking on my sistah. That was beyond scary, a harrowing experience." She noisily exhaled. Looking at her hands, she said, "I'm still shaking. Are you OK, C.J.?"

"I will be. I'm vexed! That idiot didn't know that I had special training. I could have killed him, sistah. He picked a gunfight with the wrong Black woman. I need to put my mind in a happy place—too many negative memories."

"I don't need details, but I must ask: You've done a lot of things for America's freedom, haven't you?"

"Yes, yes, I have."

"You look like you need a hug from your older sistah."

Calmer and more receptive, I was ready to be touched. "Yah, mon," I whimpered. We hugged.

Leaving the office, I remorsefully said, "Hopefully, I didn't hurt him too badly. Now, he's my patient. Ironic, isn't it?"

Enraged, she responded, "Good Lawd! To hell with him! He was going to blow your precious brains out!" Closing her eyes briefly, she took a deep breath, exhaling slowly. "He actually pulled the trigger as you knocked the gun out of his hand."

"Yes, you're right."

I checked on my patient, the one that almost killed me. He was awake, alert, oriented—and in police custody. He was handcuffed to the gurney with two police officers at his side. Now, we could consider him an "Ok to Book," a patient requiring medical clearance before going to jail. Once treated, he'd be imprisoned for the attempted murder of me.

It was a conflict of interest for me to treat him, but I didn't have a choice since I was the only physician in the emergency room. My boss would assume his care when he arrived.

Assessing the villain, I noticed dried blood on the left corner of his mouth. Exploring further, I saw a laceration on the inner aspect of his lower lip, a result of his lip being forcibly pushed against his teeth when I kicked him. He required stitches. My boss would have the pleasure of sewing him back together. I ordered lab tests and CT scans of his head, neck, chest, and abdomen and a full trauma panel. Because I'd inflicted severe blows on him, I needed to make sure he didn't have internal bleeding or fractures. Derrick placed an ice pack on his face for comfort.

The nursing supervisor confirmed that we had been placed on Internal Disaster, so all ambulances were diverted to other hospitals. She also informed me that the ER medical director, chief executive officer, chief operating officer, and chief nursing officer were en route. I instructed the lead security guard to contact his manager because the police needed a copy of the video ASAP. He was the only one with access to it.

Three police officers interviewed me, and they requested that my bandage be removed so they could take pictures of my wound. Each one of them praised me for my bravery.

Bellows updated me. "His gun was fully loaded, and he had two full magazine clips in his pocket."

"Oh my God! He came to the ER prepared to orchestrate a massacre!"

"Yes, he did, and you stopped him. This could have been a blood bath. Everyone is indebted to you, doc."

Caressing my dreads, I sighed loudly. As the police accompanied the custody patient to radiology, the security guard informed me that the video would be available in two days, on Monday, when the manager returned to work. I felt the rage rising as my muscles tensed. Glaring at this young man, I instructed him to call his manager again so that I could speak to him. I had little respect for the supervisor of security. We'd clashed in the past.

"He's on the phone, Dr. C.J.," announced the guard.

I placed the receiver to my ear and answered, "Hello, Larren, this is Dr. Johnston. It's imperative that the police obtain a copy of the video ASAP, not in two days. It would behoove you to get down here now! I'm not in the mood for your shenanigans. Come here now and provide them with everything they need or come in on Monday to pick up your last check. I'm sure HR would agree with me."

"Ok," he said, cowardly. He arrived within the hour.

I continued to treat all the patients who arrived before the gunman's nefarious agenda. Nolan, the primary nurse assigned to the custody patient, informed me that he was complaining of a headache. Since all lab and radiology tests were normal, I ordered the nurse to administer 650 mg of acetaminophen orally to relive his discomfort.

By midnight, hospital administrators had arrived in solidarity to support and comfort the staff. Some were still visibly upset. While I was dictating in my office, they approached me. Each one thanked me for diverting the diabolical plan and acknowledged my bravery. Soon after, they corralled us to write our individual accounts of what happened.

My boss, Thad, arrived and gave me the biggest bear hug. "Thank God you're alright, C.J.! You know that you're my favorite, right?"

"Aw, thanks, surrogate Dad!"

"Come on, let me suture your wound."

Once he patched me up, he took over my assignments, relieving me of duty.

"C.J., what you've done tonight is nothing less than heroic. Go home and relax with a glass of wine. Take the next three days off. If you need more time, just let me know," he insisted.

The media got wind of the shooting and flooded the entrance to the ER. Detective Bellows escorted me to my car from a side exit to elude them. I was adamant about not holding a press conference. I quickly started my newly restored, vintage 1957 cobalt blue Porsche 356 A convertible. I sped off with the top down, the full moon glowing larger and brighter than ever. Listening to reggae music, I recalled the night's events. Subconsciously, I began to nervously wiggle my jaw. Anger stifled me as I drove home, and then I became despondent. Concerned that depression was going to consume me, and I had to get a handle on it. I'd done so much for so many. I hoped this didn't stain my reputation.

I went to bed but wasn't able to sleep. I decided to watch the news that catered to insomniacs, but little did I know I was the news. I was going to be cast in a fluorescent light that wouldn't dim anytime soon.

"Breaking news! This just in from our news affiliate in Los Angeles, California," announced the male TV commentator from New York as he shuffled sheets of colored paper. He continued: "A distraught male gunman entered the emergency room at Wiltern Medical Center, holding the staff hostage. The on-duty physician, Dr. Chanel Johnston, bravely approached him and single-handedly subdued the assailant as he held a loaded gun directly to her head. Here's the video."

Reluctantly, I watched myself disarm and attack that maniac. "Oy vey!" I protested.

After the news video, the commentator added, "Luckily for the staff, the doctor is a veteran, a decorated Army officer who served two years in Afghanistan combating the Taliban face-to-face.

"Here at the station, we say kudos to Dr. Chanel Johnston, a true American hero. We've just been told that movie director Dru Benedict has expressed interest in creating a movie adaptation of this event and Dr. Johnston's life."

Suddenly, the station unveiled my official military photo. Donned in full Army dress uniform with an array of shiny medals meticulously displayed on my chest, I became a muse for the world to see.

Lowering my head, I turned the TV off. "SHIT!"

I was appalled that my privacy had been compromised. I lay in bed, awake in darkness for the rest of the night. I loathed the attention. Since I thwarted a massacre in the ER, I was thrust into the media spotlight. By early morning, every TV news station and daytime talk show nationwide was broadcasting a clip of the video. They dubbed me "The No-Nonsense Physician." Ramesh sent me a text. "So much for a quiet civilian life." He followed up with a phone call.

"How's my girl?"

"I'm irritated!"

"I bet! I taught you that maneuver. Your form was impressive. You gained a lot of height in your spin, making your kick more effective."

"That guy was huge! I practically had to jump up to connect my right uppercut punch to his chin. Well, thank you! The Ramesh maneuver came in handy."

"Serves him right! Such an asshole!"

"Yup. I have to go. I'll talk to you later."

"Okay."

After a long sigh, I scratched my head in disappointment. He was still a narcissistic prick. I was surprised that he needed to take credit for my disarming the assailant. Some things never changed.

Jewel called. "Is Dr. Fighter available, or is she beating someone up right now? Oy vey, girl!"

"Oh, be quiet. I'm trying to live a nice, peaceful, normal life. I thought I'd left all that action behind. But no!"

"How are you holding up? I know that you don't like all of this attention, but I don't want you to get depressed and ostracize everyone. Let me take you away. We'll go to Santa Barbara later today. The ambiance up there is therapeutic. We can stay for a couple of days. I can take time off. Surely, you're off for a few days, too."

"Sounds nice, but the residents of Santa Barbara watch TV. Thanks, girl, but I just want to maintain a low profile despite the 310 million people in America who have watched the video. I want to crawl under a rock! Maybe I should go to Jamaica and chill out for a while. I can blend in better over there."

"Oh, hell yes! You should definitely go! I don't want you to hide in the house indefinitely. You need to get away. You almost died— again! He had a gun to your head! I can hardly fathom this."

"Well, if he had had his way and shot me in the head, there would have been serious brain blowback in his face."

"You're disgusting!"

"No, I'm an ER physician. My career thrives on blood and guts."

"And mayhem."

"Definitely mayhem."

"I couldn't stand the ER rotation as a resident. That's why I'm a family practice physician. Hardly any drama. Speaking of drama, has your ex-boyfriend called you?"

"Yes, he actually gloated because he taught me the martial art spin that I used to take down that idiot. I vaguely believe that he's concerned about me."

"I can't believe you were with him for 2 1/2 years."

"In the beginning, he was very nice to me and actually charming. He was always cocky but suppressed that trait when we were together." Unable to tell her the truth, revealing that we were spies, I added, "After his major car accident, he was angry at the world. I watched his character decay. That's when I left him. I couldn't take it anymore."

"I don't like him! I never did. He's a schmuck!"

"I know."

"I'll check on you later. Book your vacation to Jamaica. That's an order!" She ended the call.

By noon, my phone was ringing off the hook. Family and friends back east saw the video and wanted to ensure I was all right. I told them I was fine, but they should see the other guy. News traveled far and fast.

Shelley even called me from London after the video was displayed on the news there. On a conference call from New York, friends teased me.

"Obviously, he didn't know who he was messing with," said Marie. Jeanette added, "He picked a gunfight with a Jamerican war hero!"

"Yeah, man! What a dumbass," remarked Cantrice.

They cracked me up. I needed that.

Later that day, social media was abuzz with my historical feats. Somehow, they confiscated photographs of me on the summit of Mount Everest; in Afghanistan, carrying my medical bag and a fully automatic assault rifle slung over my shoulders; riding my motorcycle around Los Angeles; and even as I flew a helicopter around the county. I was plastered all over the web.

Refusing to enhance the media frenzy, I politely declined their email request for an on-air interview.

Later that afternoon, Zack called.

"I just heard about your ordeal last night. Are you OK?"

"Yes, I'm fine, just irritated that it occurred. I wasn't going to sit back and let him slaughter my staff."

"You're the bravest woman I've ever met."

"I just happened to be at the right place at the right time."

"How about dinner tonight?"

"That's so sweet, but I just can't. I'm actually hiding from the paparazzi."

"Well then, I'll bring dinner to you. Just a relaxing evening to distract you from all of this."

Caving in, I gave him my address.

I wore a sleeveless summer dress and a pair of wedge sandals. To create a relaxing ambiance, I played a Moroccan CD and lit Jamaican incense.

Zack arrived meticulously dressed in a tan linen suit and brown silk shirt without a tie.

I assumed this was considered casual attire for him.

Standing on the stoop of my townhouse, he gave me the warmest smile. A bag with dinner occupied his left hand, and a bouquet of flowers was in his right. Noticing the bandage on my arm, his pleasantry turned into anger.

"Oh no, that maniac hurt you! Are you alright?"

Lightly stroking my left arm, I replied, "Yes, I'm OK. He shot me as I knocked the gun out of his hand, but it's a flesh wound. I required just a few stitches."

"He needs to spend the rest of his life in prison for this," he seethed.

Changing the subject, I focused on the flowers. "Thank you for the beautiful bouquet. That's so thoughtful. They smell wonderful."

"You're welcome. It's the least I could do to placate the trauma you experienced last night. I decided on Chinese food. I hope that suits your palate."

"That's perfect! Let's eat!" I said enthusiastically.

I placed the flowers in a vase and then on the table. We devoured the brown rice, broccoli beef, steamed vegetables, and egg rolls over small talk. He was also impressed when I exchanged the disposable generic wooden takeout cutlery that required manual separation with my private collection of non-disposable customized ivory chopsticks. Once we were satiated, we relocated to the living room and continued talking over wine.

"That was delicious! I'm glad that you came over, Zack."

"My pleasure. I love this music. It has a wicked beat. What is it?"

"It's a Moroccan group. I call it Moroccan jazz. I listen to it for hours. It reminds me of my travels there."

"I don't want to intrude, but your profile popped up on a social media site. I believe you're now known as Dr. Badass. Such a colorful moniker."

Covering my face in embarrassment, I said, "Oh my goodness! Please tell me that you're joking."

"It's true," he smiled. "I think it's cute."

Tilting my head slightly and boasting a mischievous grin, I teased, "I can't believe my secret powers were revealed."

Sitting forward on the sofa, he questioned, "So, who is Chanel Johnston?"

Picking up the bottle of wine and refilling his glass, I chuckled. "You're going to need more wine."

"Is it that bad?"

"No, it's not bad at all. I can describe myself in two words: Jamerican Anomaly."

"I know what anomaly means, but I've never heard the word Jamerican."

"I'm a Jamaican-American. My parents were born and raised in Jamaica, but I was born over here." Slightly anxious, I played with my hair, twisting my locs. "I'm just different, one could say unique, but I wouldn't change anything about myself. I'm proud to be an anomaly. Normally, I don't toot my own horn, but you insist, so I will tell you." For liquid courage, I took a sip from my glass. "Here's the CliffsNotes version. I march to the beat of my own drum. I'm honest, kind, giving, and extremely private. For that, I'm an enigma to most. I'm also fluent in six languages, a war hero, an elite mountaineer, a scuba diver, a yoga fanatic, a motorcyclist, a licensed helicopter pilot, and, as you know, a certified emergency room physician. That's it—that's me!"

With the broadest grin, he gently grasped my right hand. His fingers toyed with my bangles. "You're an exceptional woman. Don't ever change."

Leaning in, he kissed me.

Shyly, I lightly bit my lower lip as I gazed into his eyes.

He chuckled, continuing to stroke my hand. "Rumor has it that you climbed Mount Everest. Now you tell me that you ride a motorcycle and fly helicopters. I would never have guessed. When can I hear the stories of your escapades?"

"I tend to live on the edge of an adventure." In a flirtatious tone, I said, "In time, I'll tell you my stories."

"Oh, I can't wait." He winked, then took a sip.

"Are you afraid of heights?"

"No, I don't believe so. Why?"

"Flying relaxes me. I normally fly solo a few times a month. I would like to have you join me tomorrow afternoon. Lunch is on me."

"That would be great. I'm in!"

"OK, we'll meet here at noon. I admire that you dress so sharp but tomorrow is a T-shirt and jeans kind of day," I giggled.

"Duly noted, pilot Johnston."

Before he departed, we kissed again.

Smiling as I closed the door behind him, I felt vulnerable. I couldn't wait until the next day.

Jewel called to check on me. I gave her an update on my evening. She was ecstatic. Even though she never met Ramesh, she hated him. She was my best friend, and I told her everything. Well, almost.

Zack arrived promptly at noon. Compliant with my advice, he wore a navy blue polo shirt, jeans, and spotless lily-white sneakers. Even dressed casually, he looked like a model. He was so sharp, muscular, and confident—such a handsome Black man.

I flaunted a cute pink top, jeans, sandals, and a pink baseball cap.

I drove to the Long Beach airport with my convertible top down. He admired my classic baby.

When we signed in at the airport counter to retrieve the key to the rental helicopter, the flight coordinator inquired, "Hello, pilot C.J.! Was that you on the news?"

"Yes, it was. I need to decompress. That's why I'm flying today."

"I understand. Well, I just want to say that you're my hero." Handing me the key, he added, "Have an awesome flight. It's a beautiful SoCal day!"

"Thanks, Bob!"

Approaching the five-seater R44 chopper, Zack took a deep breath. He whimpered, "I have butterflies in my stomach."

Touching his back, I reassured him. "You'll be okay."

I walked around the aircraft to perform an external check. Entering the cabin, I gave Zack a safety briefing. I instructed him not to touch the cyclic stick in front, the collective lever at the side, or the foot pedals on the floor. He acknowledged with a nod.

We donned the headsets, and then I ran through the internal safety checklist. After communicating with the tower, I waited a few minutes for clearance to take off, then ascended into the friendly skies.

Distracting Zack, I pointed out Long Beach's iconic images that appeared below us. I watched his anxiety dissipate as his posture relaxed, and he smiled randomly.

"This is awesome," he exclaimed.

"It's spiritual up here," I rejoiced.

The flight was flawless. Thirty minutes later, I landed on Catalina Island.

Toting our picnic lunch, we ate on the beach. We strolled along the shore hand in hand, swinging our joined hands ever so slightly. Since I typically fly solo, I usually rent the helicopter for an hour. But that day was special, so I reserved it for two hours. It was an expensive $1,000 lunch date!

I trailed a pod of playful dolphins in the Pacific Ocean during the return flight. That was definitely the epitome of the day. We were both jubilant about the sighting. As a thrill, I decided to spruce up the easygoing, mundane flight. I maneuvered a steep U-turn, rolling the chopper sideways.

"Whoa," blurted Zack. Unsuccessful in finding a comfort railing or handle to grasp, he resorted to curling his fingers on his seat cushion, holding on tightly. "Why aren't there armrests or handles on this aircraft?"

Laughing, I said, "I don't know. That's just how they're made. Are you okay?"

"Barely. I think my heart stopped briefly," he joked.

Before we knew it, I was descending onto the helipad at the airport.

"This was exciting," he admitted, gesturing with his hands. "Today was absolutely perfect. You are absolutely perfect." The corners of his mouth turned upward into a silly little smirk.

"I'm hardly perfect, but yes, today was perfect. Glad you enjoyed our date. I enjoyed it immensely."

We walked off the tarmac with his arm around me.

The drive home was filled with banter as we recounted our fun afternoon. The date ended on an upbeat note. When I arrived home, I told Zack I was leaving for Jamaica in the morning.

I landed at the Sangster International Airport in Montego Bay, Jamaica, the following afternoon. My cousins were overjoyed when they saw me pass through customs. We engaged in hugs, laughter, and more hugs. When I arrived at Aunt Alvita and Uncle Glenmore's house, the aroma of Caribbean food traveled beyond the block.

"Hi, Auntie and Uncle. I missed you both."

"Lawd, pickney, you still look like a likkle girl (Lord child, you still look like a little girl)," said Auntie Alvita.

"Wah gwaan, doctor? (How are you, doctor?)" said Uncle.

"Mi hear dat yu lick up ah mon (I heard that you beat up a man)," said Auntie.

"Yah, mon. (Yes.)"

"Yu tuh likkle tuh lick up ah mon (You're too small to beat up a man)," said Uncle.

I flexed my muscles. Everyone laughed.

Aunt Alvita provided a feast in my honor. She took pride in preparing my plate. It consisted of rice and peas, jerk chicken, and callaloo. Famished, I ate all of it.

After spending three days with my family, I had my cousin Arnie drive me to the resort on Negril Beach, where I would stay for a couple of days. The drive took a little over an hour.

Negril Beach is the island's iconic coastal scene, possessing seven long miles of white powdery sand alongside the warm and clear azure sea. Admiring its eye-appealing eclectic landscape, I strolled along the shoreline. I needed to spend time alone to soul search, so I went swimming in the open waters. As an added treat, I indulged in a double scuba dive excursion. Immersed within the depths of the ocean, peacefully floating alongside an array of fish, accompanied by the beauty of sculptured multicolored corals, I was engulfed in silence. Well, except for the sound of my exhaled breath bubbles underwater. This was exactly what the doctor ordered.

Being back in Jamaica allowed me to nurture myself. It was the distraction that I needed to get out of the psychological funk that the shooter had tossed me into.

There was another family party on the eve of my departure. This one was bittersweet because I didn't want to leave.

The Diagnosis

On day three of my coma. Dr. Drummond, the ophthalmologist, arrived to examine my bloodshot eyes. He spoke to me as if I were awake—such a gentle, mild-mannered man. I could hear every word but couldn't respond. I was still trapped in my body.

Please help me.

At his request, my nurse, Fiona, dimmed the lights as he shone a penlight into each eye to check my pupil reactions. The response was normal: equally reactive at three millimeters in diameter. He then used an ophthalmoscope to examine my pupils and the inner aspect of my eyes. No abnormalities were found. Last, he instilled fluorescein stain into each eye, turning my sclera, the white portion of my eye, a bright orange. Darkening the room completely, he cast an ultraviolet (UV) light into my eyes, enabling him to visualize any external abnormalities. Immediately, he noticed abrasions across both corneas, the colored portion of my eyes.

While conversing with Fiona in the darkened room, he kept his hands by his side, still holding the illuminated UV light.

"I will prescribe antibiotic ointments that need to be instilled into her eyes twice daily," he instructed. "Both of her eyes sustained injuries from a scratchy object, or she may have vigorously rubbed them, causing the corneal abrasions."

A trail of vibrant purple light shone on the urine collection bag that hung on the bed railing, causing my urine to produce an eerie neon glow in the dark.

"Look at that," she remarked, pointing to the bag.

"Oh my," blurted Dr. Drummond. "This woman has been poisoned with ethylene glycol! Call the police ASAP!"

Ethylene glycol is found in automotive solvents. Its properties are undetectable to the naked eye. It has an extremely sweet taste and is fatal when swallowed. My hair follicle drug test result coincidentally was just released and confirmed ethylene glycol poisoning, resulting in multiorgan failure and crystallization of my heart and kidneys. Finally, I knew why I experienced irregular heartbeats and kidney failure. The crystals that accumulated in my kidneys had sloughed off, shedding into my urine. Contact with the ultraviolet light caused the crystals to glow.

The mystery had been solved—someone wanted me dead! The physicians were pleased to know what ailed me but despondent because there wasn't a cure for ethylene glycol poisoning. All they could do was treat my symptoms and pray.

Police Detective Daniel Rockwell, a.k.a. Rocky, was assigned to my case because my fingerprints were unobtainable. The officer who initially retrieved my prints a couple of days ago submitted them to AFIS, the Automated Fingerprint Identification System. This sophisticated system uses digital imaging to obtain, store, and analyze over 100 million fingerprints. Commonly used by the police nationwide, it has become an essential crime-fighting asset. Due to my high-security status, my prints had been concealed and shielded from the local police.

Responding to the call initiated by Dr. Drummond, the detective arrived promptly and was in my room conversing with Fiona. He inquired if I was able to communicate, and she said no.

Wedged between small talk and flirting, he mentioned that the police couldn't identify me because my fingerprints had been blocked. He speculated that I was either a secret agent or in the WSP—Witness Security Program.

"Someone tried to kill her, but she's safe here," he said confidently.

"Whoa!" she exclaimed.

"I must take her clothes and belongings to the police lab."

She returned the belongings bag containing my clothes and handed it to him. "Here's everything she had on her. Unfortunately, she didn't have a purse or wallet. No identification at all. The bag contains her blouse, pants, underclothes, shoes, socks, and Jamaican bangles."

Rummaging through the bag, the detective found something in my pants pocket. It was a folded, tattered picture of me standing on the summit of Mount Everest. He asked the nurse to move the tubes from my face and then took a picture of me. After receiving Fiona's phone number, he left.

The detective went to the hospital's security office to view the video of the ER entrance three days earlier. On the grainy video, he watched me stagger into the waiting room and collapse. Rewinding the tape, he paused the video when he noticed the taxi that dropped me off. It was from the Red Cab Company, and the medallion identifier on the roof was 5555.

"Bingo," he jubilantly remarked. He received a copy of the video and began his mission to find the taxi driver.

After he ate lunch, Rocky went to the taxi company. He spoke to the manager, a thin man with a handlebar mustache and a nasty cough whose breath exuded an ashtray's stench. The taxi driver was summoned to return to the office. He arrived in twenty minutes.

As the detective showed him my picture from his phone, he blurted out, "I know her! I picked her up from the Elliott Convention Center on Monday morning. I was parked in front of the main entrance when she entered my cab and requested that I take her to the hospital. I offered to call 911, but she declined, stating that I would be faster. Later that day, I realized she left her purse in the back seat. Actually, I found it on the floorboard. I've been waiting for her to claim it. Is she OK?"

"No, she's very ill. Where's her purse?"

"In my locker."

Receiving my purse, the detective pulled out my wallet and driver's license. "Bingo!"

Hit and Run

Zack and I dated for a month before we became lovers. He was a true gentleman, a funny companion, and he was mine. On my nights off, he would spend time at my condo in LA. My dog, Roscoe, adored him. I had never given much thought to getting married, but I would definitely marry him.

My colleagues didn't know that we were dating. Although I was often criticized for being secretive, I kept my private life private and was frequently ridiculed for doing so. It's just that I didn't share every aspect of my life with everyone. For this, I've been ridiculed. Just another anomaly, I thought.

I occasionally worked with Mark Pelligrano, a Certified Physician Assistant. Having PAs in the ER to assist with the high volume of patients was a blessing. Pelli, as we all called him, was exceptional. He was smart, knowledgeable, and so handsome. He possessed movie-star good looks. The nurses referred to him as the Italian Stallion. They were falling all over him, but he politely brushed them off. To my surprise, he asked me out a few times. Preferring to maintain a platonic friendship, I gently rejected his advances. Unknown to everyone, including myself, I was falling in love with Zack.

Pelli and I developed a strong relationship. I was his yin, and he was my yang. We could always make each other laugh at the drop of a hat and complete each other's sentences. Six months later, he left the ER to partner with a friend in opening an urgent care center in downtown LA. I missed him, especially our banter.

Before I knew it, I had fallen for Zack hard and fast. I was no longer in denial and realized I was deeply in love with him. He was kind and loving like Hans, the polar opposite of Ramesh. We spent a lot of time together at my home. Our conversations were always light and pleasant. He was only a few years older than me, but so accomplished, starting a private practice at the age of thirty, three years ago. As he was notably the most eligible bachelor in town, I would tease him that his mother was probably pressuring him to get married. He said that he repeatedly told her that he wasn't ready.

Having him at my condo made it feel cozy. From sipping wine in the Jacuzzi, eating popcorn while watching suspense movies on TV, and admiring him cooking dinner, he was the perfect boyfriend. I often fantasize about being his wife. He would sometimes visit me in the ER if I worked during the weekend and he was on call. Some of the staff were suspicious of our friendship.

Since my right ankle had become stronger, I decided to start jogging. For added support, I consistently applied an ace wrap. Mapping out a two-mile course, I planned on gradually advancing to five miles. I ran only if I was off the previous night. I noticed the same familiar faces on my route and gave my anonymous running mates a moniker. First was a thirty-something-year-old Caucasian woman, whom I affectionately called the soccer mom. Next was a tall, lean Caucasian male in his mid-twenties who resembled a marathon runner. The last member was a fortyish, attractive Black female with a toned body to die for. She looked like an Olympian or at least a gymnast. While on the street, we graciously acknowledged each other with a nod, remaining anonymous.

Elated that my right ankle was getting accustomed to jogging, I progressed to the five-mile course. I found myself running parallel to the Olympian, who was across the street. The other joggers were probably on the original route. With the lights on the same circuit, I jogged in place as she did her signature backflips.

We waved at each other as the traffic signals prepared to give the synchronized instruction to cross. She proceeded across the street when a large black Hummer suddenly peeled away from the curb with extreme acceleration, blowing through the red light—striking her!

Startled by the sound of the impact, I stepped back onto the sidewalk. The driver ran over her entire body without braking or even caring. As he passed me at a high speed, I saw his face and the tattoo on the left side of his neck. Once he fled the scene, I ran to help her.

Mangled and motionless, she lay with her extremities extended in unnatural positions. Removing my T-shirt, I balled it up and used it to apply manual pressure to a gaping wound on her abdomen while simultaneously calling 911 with my free hand. Because she wasn't breathing and didn't have a pulse, I made a futile attempt to resuscitate her by initiating CPR. Her rib cage collapsed beneath my hands with every chest compression as a large amount of blood spewed from her sides. With her mouth partially opened, her natural pink gums faded into pallor. The Olympian's contorted body lay bathed in a pool of crimson-colored fluid.

Reluctantly, I aborted CPR, then watched helplessly as she quickly exsanguinated—bled to death. Looking at my watch, I pronounced her time of passing at 6:32 a.m. I prayed for her soul.

The paramedics arrived within minutes. Recognizing me from the emergency room, they concurred with my decision to terminate life saving efforts. The medical examiner was contacted. She became a coroner's case, pending an autopsy.

Standing over her body in disbelief, I noticed a tear in a concealed pocket in the right upper thigh of her leggings, revealing an ID holder. Usually, I wouldn't remove a victim's personal effects without the coroner present, but I was determined to know who she was.

She was no longer anonymous: Her name was Rochelle Dupont, an FBI agent.

I relinquished her ID card to the LAPD officer. Once she was identified as a federal agent, the FBI encroached on the scene with a vengeance. After repeatedly being interviewed by both law enforcement agencies, I offered to draw a composite sketch of the perpetrator.

Recalling his distinctive appearance, I verbally recounted his face as I drew. "He's a white male, in his early thirties, with a cornrow hairstyle and a large spider web tattoo on his left lateral neck." Handing the sketch to the officer nearest me, I added, "He drove a black late-model Hummer with the license plate number two-Bravo-November-Papa-Oscar-fifty-six. That's 2-B-N-P-O-5-6."

"Thank you, Dr. Johnston. You're the best witness I have ever interviewed," claimed the rookie cop.

"Glad I could help. She didn't deserve this; no one does."

I overheard the homicide detective remark, "Boy, she's damn good!"

Yes, I am. I'm a retired spy.

My composite of the perpetrator was splashed all over the televised news stations. Someone had to recognize this guy. The FBI immediately offered a $25,000 reward leading to the arrest and conviction of the hit-and-run killer.

The phones lit up.

Distraught and too distracted to work that night, I switched shifts with Dr. Michael Watson. Being preoccupied with the senseless death of my anonymous acquaintance, I wasn't fit for duty. Zack came over that evening to comfort me. He spent the night, but I couldn't sleep. My head was pounding, and relentless pressure penetrated my forehead. Over-the-counter analgesics couldn't ease my pain. It was built-up tension.

The following day, at 8 a.m., I received a call from homicide Detective Ricardo Jaurequi. He needed me to view a lineup of the alleged killer. Elated, I knew that he would be easy to identify.

I was quite impressed that they apprehended the creep within twenty-four hours. The detective also informed me that the perpetrator's vehicle was reported stolen and found torched near an abandoned warehouse.

I went to the LAPD headquarters around noon to do my civic duty. An officer placed me in a room with a two-way mirror, like the FBI office in Colorado. I could view the perpetrator in the adjacent room, but he couldn't see me. The officers escorted only two men into the other room.

They were twins, identical!

My spirit deflated as I could not detect which one was the driver. Both men possessed freshly cropped hair with the same spiderweb tattoo on their left lateral neck.

Perplexed, I turned to the detective, "I honestly can't choose."

"I understand." He let out a deep sigh. "Unfortunately, we can't arrest them both. Only one was the alleged driver. They will be released immediately due to a technicality. I'm sorry, doctor."

Oy vey! Unbelievable! I left disappointed; I wasn't able to think straight. Identical twins? Seriously? What were the damn odds of such a twist of fate? Determined not to give up, I vowed to find out which twin had turned Rochelle into roadkill.

I called Zack and left a message for him to call me when he had a chance. He called within fifteen minutes. I gave him an update.

"How is that possible?" he fumed. "Oh my gosh!"

"I know! I'm in disbelief myself. I'm not giving up, babe. She deserves justice."

"Look, honey, I know how headstrong you are, but please be careful. Remember, you are still the sole witness, and we don't know what other nefarious acts those guys are capable of. I love you, Chanel, and I don't know what I would do if anything happened to you," he cautioned.

"You—you love me?"

"Yes, I do! Please, promise me that you will be careful."

"I will." The call ended, but somehow, I was prompted to say, "I love you more."

Zack called again in the afternoon. "Let's get away this weekend, honey. The fresh mountain air will do you good, away from the chaos."

"I agree. I'll reserve a cabin. We'll talk later when you're off work."

"OK."

I knew that I would never forget the gruesome images of Rochelle Dupont. I never jogged again.

Zack and I planned to drive to the mountains in a few days. Staying in a cabin, surrounded by nature, would do us both good. The days flew by. I packed quickly, and my dog, Roscoe, and I were ready to inhale the fresh mountain air. I was supposed to meet Zack at his house at noon but decided to surprise him with breakfast at 8 a.m. He answered the door with a shocked expression. Roscoe ran to his feet, wagging his tail for attention.

"Surprise, babe!" I gleefully barged in, playfully pushing past him as I held a cardboard tray with breakfast bagels, gourmet coffee for him, and OJ for myself.

As I placed the food on the table, a partially clad white female exited his bedroom. Instantly, my demeanor escalated from calm to rage. Too angry to cry, I began to tremble.

"Please, let me explain," he begged.

I squinted my eyes, and my face hardened into a glare. "Don't bother!" I muttered under my breath.

I picked up Roscoe and left, slamming the door behind me. During all of this, the other woman stood deathly still, never saying a word.

I made it into my vehicle before falling apart. Resting my head on the steering wheel, I sobbed uncontrollably. My heart actually ached. How could I have been so damn wrong? He was nothing like Hans. I felt like such a fool. My cell phone rang. I didn't want to speak to anyone, so I reached for it and prepared to turn it off. Realizing it was Ramesh, I decided to answer.

In a weakened, monotone voice, I said, "He-hello!"

"What's wrong, C.J.?" he demanded.

Crying, I managed to speak only in short intervals. "You were right…he's not for me…he hurt me…he's a liar…a cheat."

Returning my head to the steering wheel, I continued to cry.

"OK, babe, take a breath. He'll pay for hurting you. I'm coming over. I'm in LA."

Ramesh had always doubted Zack's sincerity. He didn't believe that he was committed to me. Sniffling, I managed to say, "We were supposed to go to the mountains this afternoon and spend the weekend in a cabin. You know what? I'm still going. I need to go away."

"I'll go with you. Be there in an hour."

Wiping the tears from my eyes, I muttered, "Okay."

I mustered up the energy to stop crying and drive home.

Concealing my red, puffy eyes behind sunglasses, I headed to Big Bear Mountain with Ramesh and Roscoe. The three-hour drive was sometimes entertaining as we reminisced about our days at QA. Whenever I became quiet, my mind drifted to thoughts of Zack. Unable to escape my emotions, my chin trembled. Ramesh was a true gentleman. Our relationship was platonic—well, for me anyway. I knew that he was still in love with me.

Arriving at the cabin, we unloaded our bags and hit the trails. The cool air was medicinal, and my mind was calm and clear, even though my heart was broken. Hiking and photographing the landscape was cathartic. Ramesh treated me like a princess. He did all the cooking and retired to the sofa to sleep without my suggestion.

During our return drive a couple of days later, I told him about Rochelle Dupont and the twins. He was genuinely interested but told me not to get involved further.

Annoyed, I told him, "You know that I just can't let this slide. She deserves justice! Could you please use your connections at QA to help?"

"I'll see what I can do."

Zack had called repeatedly since I left his home. I didn't answer, and I had no intention of speaking to him. I even considered blocking his number. We returned home by midday Sunday, and Ramesh stayed a while to watch a spy movie with me. He stated that he was in LA on business but wouldn't elaborate. I respected his privacy. Entering work on Monday night, I noticed an extravagant floral arrangement of red roses on my desk.

I was relieving Dr. Watson of his shift. As I walked into the office, he curiously said, "Someone loves you. This is at least a $400 bouquet."

After reading the card from Zack, I tore it into a billion pieces. I picked up the flowers, stepped on the foot lever to open the trash can lid, and discarded them.

Turning to Watson, I snapped, "Please give me your report on the patients."

Timidly, he replied, "Oh, okay."

After giving me his report, he quickly left. The shift seemed to fly by. I was glad when it was over. I just wanted to be home alone. And then I found Zack standing at my condo door.

"Please don't leave me, C.J.," he pleaded. "I love you! Please give me ten minutes to explain."

Crossing my arms over my chest, I snapped, "You get five!"

"I should've been upfront with you about being married, um, separated. Falling in love with you took me by surprise," he said tearfully.

Just when I thought it couldn't get any worse, it did!

"Everything you told me was a lie! For a man who was never married, now you tell me you have a wife. Somehow, you're not making me feel better."

The more he talked, the more I hated him. "You need to leave now," I demanded.

He left. I cried in the shower, then went to bed. When I woke up to get ready for work, I called Zack and told him he needed to pick up his belongings and return my house key. I insisted that he arrive and leave the key while I was at work because I didn't want to see him. We needed to remain professional at work, but our intimate relationship was over.

Ramesh called me while I was on my way to work. He wanted to make sure that I was OK. I told him I wasn't but would be in time. He was angry to know that Zack was married. I also told him that Zack would arrive at night to pick up his things and leave my key. I placed his items in a gym bag, put it on the dining table, and left for work. I thought Zack would text me after picking up the bag, but he didn't. It was better that way, anyhow. I really didn't want to hear from him.

I arrived home in the morning to find my key on the table and the gym bag gone. Distracted by thoughts that our relationship was officially over, I didn't realize that Roscoe hadn't greeted me at the door like he usually did. The only true love was the unconditional love from my dog.

"Roscoe, come here, pup-pup." No response.

I entered the kitchen and saw bloody paw prints on the floor. I was concerned: Somehow, Roscoe must have injured himself. I scoured every part of my condo but couldn't find him. I called Zack, but his phone went directly to voicemail. I called multiple times, leaving numerous messages. None of my calls were returned. Around 10 a.m., I called his office, sounding like this was professional business. I was informed that he was two hours late, but they hadn't heard from him.

Worried, I called the police.

Two officers arrived to take my report. They summoned CSI, Crime Scene Investigations, to collect samples from the blood-soaked rag I had used to clean my kitchen floor. The presumptive result indicated that it wasn't canine blood but human!

Baffled, I said aloud, "What the hell happened here?"

My home was now a crime scene. I was asked to vacate for a few days. Before departing for a hotel, I gave the police Zack's address. I didn't have a key to his residence. The officer initiated a welfare check on him. Officers forcefully gained entry into his house, but no one was there.

Fab Four

Two months later, I bought a cute three-bedroom bungalow on a cul-de-sac in Long Beach. The neighborhood was quaint and picturesque. The park-like setting created a welcoming ambiance. Tall palm trees and shrubbery that bore colorful flowers accentuated the single-family dwellings. Changing from my previous basic decor, I spent a lot of time designing my new home in an African and Jamaican motif. Dealing directly with furniture consultants in Kenya and Montego Bay, I ordered uniquely eclectic and stylish furnishings. I turned the second bedroom into a guest room, and the third became my yoga studio/exercise room with high-tech equipment.

Burying myself in work by picking up extra shifts, I noticed a pattern with three homeless men. Over the past month, I treated them at least three times, and I was directed to have them admitted to the hospital under the service of a new group of physicians. When their names were presented on the tracker board during my shift, I felt something peculiar. They had returned with vague, generic ailments like abdominal pain and low back pain. I arranged to speak to them separately. They were Army veterans, very nice men who had lost their way.

I did not call the medical group this time; I didn't sense the need to have them admitted. I am sure my unilateral decision probably irritated the hospital corporation, but I felt I could help my veteran brothers. They were Michael Cragg, Richard Ford, and Thomas Matthews. The men admitted to staying in homeless shelters periodically but didn't like the people there. Avoiding the dark rabbit hole of addiction, they had bonded together as brothers, protecting each other as they stayed on the street. Some veterans suffer from the horror of war, unable to adjust to civilian life. I spoke to them with respect and showed sincere concern.

I graciously invited them to join me for breakfast at the diner down the street at 7 a.m.

They were there when I arrived.

Over breakfast, we talked about our military tours and shared stories of grief, despair, and an impenetrable brotherhood. My mind was made up; these were my new friends—my extended family. Their postwar stories were parallel to mine. Even though their journey had been different, yet the same, all three of them ended up on the street. Feeling inadequate and having difficulty adjusting to civilian life, they turned toward the street, which they felt was forgiving. I was determined to change their way of thinking and bring them back to a working-class society. I offered them a proposition if they were willing to have gainful employment.

They all nodded, "Yes."

I set them up in a respectable motel, assigning them individual rooms. I took them shopping for new clothes and toiletries, then to the barbershop. Then, it was time to see Timothy. He arranged temporary jobs that could possibly transform into permanent positions for them. They were jubilant, and so was I. It was an enlightening but exhausting day. I'd been up for about twenty hours. I'm glad I was off that night.

My new friends elevated my spirit as I elevated theirs. I considered the three men and Timothy my band of brothers—the Fab Four. Over time, as our relationship blossomed, their role changed. They all fussed over me like I was their kid sister (well, they *were* older than me by ten years). Concerned about whether I ate enough, rested enough, and received adequate sleep, they formed my West Coast family, especially since Jewel moved back to New York to partner in a family practice clinic.

During my nights off, we ate dinner together at my house. Timothy joined us when he could. The guys couldn't believe the story behind our friendship. I shared my pain and anguish surrounding the disappearance of Zack and the murder of Rochelle Dupont. They were flabbergasted. They voiced their concerns about me becoming a target.

Without divulging my life as a spy, I briefly spoke about my ex-boyfriend, Ramesh. My stories about climbing Mount Everest intrigued them. I teared up talking about Hans. He remained my true love.

On a motorcycle ride heading home from Torrance, I noticed a massive, heavily tinted truck tailing me. There was a silhouette of two large occupants. I didn't want to speed on the street, attracting the attention of the police. The truck was on my heels as I entered the freeway on-ramp. With its intimidating size, cars changed lanes to let the vehicle pass. Being creative, I used my defensive riding as a last resort to elude them.

I rode on the shoulder, then leaped onto the retaining wall—a daring balancing act. The width of the surface was barely five inches wider than my tires on each side.

Unable to keep up with me, the truck fell behind.

I felt a jolt, then a sting to my left side, before hearing the echo of a gunshot.

My grip on the handlebars jerked the front tire, and my rear tire fishtailed. I nearly fell off the wall, plunging twenty feet to the street below. Mind over matter: I had to mitigate the pain of being shot again.

The truck-to-motorcycle shooting went unnoticed by the motorists. Focused and more daring, I increased my speed, placing more distance between me and them. They drove recklessly, an unsuccessful attempt to keep up with me. My blouse became wet, sticking to my skin, soaked by my blood. Exiting the retaining wall, I joined the plethora of commuters.

I needed help.

I tapped the helmet shield three times to activate the facial recognition feature, which connected me to QA. After hearing three tones, I said hastily, "This is CJ2210. I've been shot in California and am trying to elude the perp. I'm on the 405 Southbound, leaving Torrance, heading toward Long Beach. They're on my tail. Please, help!"

"Agent Johnston, this is Agent Phillips. I just assigned a vehicle from the Long Beach airport to assist. It's two miles away from the Spring Street exit. How long will it take you to get there?"

"Eight to ten minutes. I initially rode on the retaining wall, but now I've blended in with traffic."

"Do you have smoke grenades on your bike?"

"Yes."

"Okay, listen carefully."

Exiting on Spring Street, I continued east. The tunnel was two blocks ahead. At the entrance was a commercial box truck with the hazard lights illuminated, the rear door opened, and its ramp extended. Approaching the truck, I initiated the smoke grenades to conceal my escape. I rode up the ramp and into the vehicle. Laying the bike on its side, I secured it to the wall straps. The driver quickly retracted the ramp and closed the doors. He drove off as the smoke began to dissipate.

I was safe but needed medical attention.

Frustrated by losing sight of my motorcycle, the twins decided to retreat to their warehouse. Confident that I'd been shot gave them joy.

The truck driver drove me to Pelli's urgent care clinic. I called him while we were en route. He waited for me at the back door.

Hospitals and clinics are mandated to report victims of violence, especially gunshot wounds. Due to our friendship, I was an exception to the rule and was treated without a chart.

The bullet had penetrated my left side. After an extensive visual examination, including an ultrasound, he was ready to break the news to me.

"Well, I've got bad news and good news. The bad news is that you've been shot. The good news is that there are no internal injuries. The bullet is lodged in the surface aspect of the external abdominal oblique muscle. I'm going to remove it."

I nodded in agreement.

After administering an injection of a local anesthetic, he cleansed the wound with betadine. Using a scalpel, he made an incision, extending the depth and length of the wound to reveal the bullet. After extracting the metal fragment from my side with forceps, he then sutured the wound. He applied a sterile bandage and gave me an antibiotic injection.

Then came the lecture.

"Here's food for thought: You left the war overseas; please stay away from the war in America, C.J."

I gave him a hug and a kiss on the cheek. "Thank you, Pelli."

I went home and submitted a request for a one-month leave of absence from work.

My life was in danger.

The next morning, my doorbell rang. Peeking through the blinds, I saw a package delivery truck in the driveway.

As I approached the front door, I asked, "Who is it?"

"I have a package for Chanel Johnston. It's from New York," said the muffled male voice.

I opened the door, and suddenly, the twins entered, aggressively pushing me down. I gasped as the sudden movement pulled at my stitches. I was ready to jump up, but they aimed their weapons at me. Consenting to their nonverbal command, I cooperated and sat back down on the floor.

Holding my wrists together in front of my body, they applied zip ties and then covered my hands with a towel. Gripping my arms firmly, they escorted me to the delivery truck. Once inside, they zip-tied my feet. Before driving off, they placed a black hood on my head.

Once we arrived, the hood was removed. I was placed in a chair in the center of a large room in what appeared to be a warehouse.

I glared at my kidnappers.

They anxiously paced. It was apparent that they were waiting for someone. The door opened.

Ramesh walked in.

He was impeccably dressed.

"Nice suit!" I commented. "What the hell is going on, Ramesh?" I asked angrily.

"Settle down, C.J.," he snapped.

"No! Untie me!"

"I told you to leave the hit-and-run case alone. These guys work for me. The victim was an FBI agent who was investigating me!"

"So, it is true! You did go rogue! I didn't want to believe the rumors about you. I wouldn't vilify you! Why did you change? What happened to you?"

"I wanted more! I was offered more from the other side. Now, I'm rich! You know what that's like. Remember, you taught me how to dress like a gentleman."

"You became an outlaw for money? I see your lips moving, but I don't hear anything that makes sense."

"Initially, I wanted to impress you. Unfortunately, you rejected me and fell in love with that—that man whore! I would never have hurt you like that and cheated on you. He didn't deserve you. Now, he has no one!"

"You, you kidnapped him? Bring him back, Ramesh!" I scolded.

"I can do many things, but bringing back the dead is a trick I haven't mastered yet," he said arrogantly.

"He's dead? You killed the man I loved? How could you be so callous? You have a blatant disregard for life! DAMN YOU!"

Pointing his finger at me, Ramesh responded. "He hurt you! He didn't deserve you! He didn't love you like I did!"

"Where is his body?"

"He'll never be found. Screw him!"

Bringing my tied hands up to my face to wipe my tears, I barely managed to speak. "I'll never forgive you. I don't know you anymore. You've lost your moral compass and your mind. I don't know how I ever loved a man like you."

"Whatever."

"Where's my dog? Where did you bury Roscoe?"

"I'm not the monster that you think I am. I could never harm Roscoe. He wouldn't stop barking at me. He wanted to play and jump around. Somehow, Zack's blood was all over him, so I took him with me. After bathing him, I gave him away."

I took a deep breath. "Untie me," I pleaded. "Please."

"No! I told you to leave the twins alone, but you kept questioning the police about them. I told you to live your civilian life in comfort. But no, you're like a dog with a damn bone!"

"Woof woof!" I sarcastically responded. "I witnessed a senseless murder, and you want me to dismiss the images that infiltrated my dreams. Unlike you, my moral compass is always in check. It's my obligation to avenge her death!"

Unleashing his rage, his face reddened. "SHE WAS A STRANGER TO YOU," he screamed, staring at me with contempt.

My chin trembled.

It was then that I remembered the ruse used during the murder of Akbar Abar was a delivery man at his door. The twins at my door impersonating delivery men wasn't a coincidence. Ramesh had them track Rochelle's daily activities. Southern California is notorious for being the "hit-and-run" capital of America. I'm sure he thought her death would be just another statistic. Most witnesses of such an act wouldn't recall much. Fortunately for her, I was the witness and able to provide meticulous detail.

Ramesh is a cold-blooded murderer, a serial killer. Once again, I was afraid of him. Pacing back and forth, he stopped and stood in front of me.

"You're so damn honorable, always trying to save the world."

"You used to be like that, too! Now, you're distorted, morphed into the monsters we were eradicating. You can't eliminate everyone that you don't like." Shaking my head, I added, "Go to hell, Ramesh!"

"YOU FIRST!"

Opening the door, he turned toward the twins and yelled, "KILL HER!" Exiting, he slammed the door behind him.

The aggressive twin pulled out his gun. Smiling, he pointed it at me.

Slumping my shoulders, I lowered my head and muttered, "Oh shit."

In Jeopardy

The sun's rays peeked through the blinds, landing on my face. Opening my eyes, I found myself in a suite at the five-star Le Rue Hotel in downtown LA. I had awakened fully clothed on the high thread count Egyptian bedding. Every muscle was tight and tense, especially my head. Rumbling through my purse, I found a bottle of an over-the-counter analgesic. After taking two tablets of acetaminophen, I lay back down with a moist washcloth on my forehead and then dozed off. For the first time ever, I didn't have the desire to stretch, do yoga, or even meditate.

Famished, I awoke two hours later and picked up the phone to call room service. With my credit card in hand, I was prepared to charge my meal when I remembered Timothy's advice: "Don't use your credit card for anything in this hotel because it will leave a digital fingerprint of your location, alerting the twins. Charge whatever you need to the room—to my account."

Although I was already aware of this fact, I didn't want to add more expense to Timothy's credit card. He'd reserved this swanky hotel room in his name as my temporary hideout. Recounting the dismal events of the previous night, I gripped the pillow firmly.

The twins had argued after Ramesh ordered them to kill me. The less aggressive, minutes-younger twin refused to have me killed in their warehouse. He had actually stepped in front of his brother's gun, which was aimed at me.

The older twin had protested. "What does it matter where she dies?"

"It matters! I don't want our warehouse turned into a place of horror."

"All right! I don't need you whining about it all night."

"I have an idea. We'll take her to her house, make her death look like an accident."

Now with my hands restrained in zip ties behind my back, they laid me on my kitchen floor. After ransacking my house and gathering all my candles, they placed them on the kitchen table, lighting each one. After turning on all the burners and the oven on my gas stove, the grand finale of their wicked plan was initiated when they extinguished the stove flames. The unburned gas escaped, permeating the air. Then, they left.

It was inevitable. I would die in the house explosion when the gas fumes collided with the flames of the candles. My neighbors were also in jeopardy. They would be annihilated, too.

I became nauseous, then dizzy, overcome by the noxious gas fumes.

Fuel that doesn't burn fully emits an odorless, colorless, and tasteless gas known as carbon monoxide, which is deadly. Inhaling the fumes in large quantities manifests symptoms of nausea, vomiting, headaches, abdominal pain, dizziness, lethargy, shortness of breath, and death. As the blood replaces oxygen with carbon monoxide, the skin becomes flushed, producing a ruddy complexion.

I hoped, at least, that I would pass out before I blew up.

The Fab Four were worried about me. They had been unsuccessful in contacting me since the afternoon. After getting no response to their calls, they had finally gone to my home. Since I wasn't there, they decided to return later to warn me about Ramesh's connection with the twins. In my absence, they staked out the warehouse that the twins were known to frequent. The guys photographed them speaking to a well-dressed man in the parking lot and then left immediately to go to the VA Center to show Timothy the photo on their phone. He recognized Ramesh as the well-dressed mystery man.

During their second trip to my home, they noticed that the wires to my alarm were severed.

"It wasn't that way earlier today," remarked Thomas.

The guys walked around the perimeter of my house, peeking in all the windows. The flickering flames illuminated the kitchen floor.

"I see her legs! She's on the kitchen floor," yelled Timothy.

To gain entry, they had broken through the sliding glass door on the patio. Noticing a pungent odor of gas as they entered, Timothy abruptly stopped moving.

"Don't turn on the lights! Open all the windows. There's a gas leak. Any spark occurs, and the house will blow," he ordered. Running to my aid, Timothy found me breathing but lethargic.

The other guys immediately extinguished the flames and turned the burners and stove off. With the windows open, the relentless Santa Ana winds that were indigenous to SoCal assisted in aerating the house, eradicating the accumulation of noxious, lethal gas.

Carrying me to the backyard for fresh air, they cut off the zip ties.

"She looks weird. Her face is red. She needs a doctor," urged Richard.

"I have a plan," replied Timothy. "Grab her phone and purse. Let's get out of here before someone calls the police." He wiped his moist eyes and continued: "Place her in the front seat and turn the AC on high. She needs to breathe clean air."

"What's the name of her PA friend?" asked Michael.

"Nelli," said Thomas.

"I think it's Relli," interjected Richard.

"No, it's Pelli," affirmed Timothy.

Scrolling through my phone, Richard found Pelligrano's number and called him. When I arrived at the urgent care, Pelli noticed that I was lethargic and my skin cast a red hue. With just a glance, he knew that I suffered from carbon monoxide poisoning. With time working against me, Pelli immediately placed a non-rebreather oxygen mask on my face, cranking the tank to full blast.

Barricading me from his staff, he treated me in his office. As I lay on his recliner, he inserted an IV into my arm and attached a bag of normal saline to infuse wide open, flushing my bloodstream.

Turning his attention to the men, he sternly said, "She needs to stop doing whatever the hell she's doing because she's always in danger. Yesterday, she was shot in her side, and I removed a bullet."

"W-WHAT?" exclaimed Timothy. "We didn't know that." Angrily, he added, "She witnessed a crime, and now she's a target in someone's crosshairs. She's a threat to them, a liability!"

When I awakened fully, there were five pairs of eyes staring at me. Perplexed, I asked, "Am I dead?"

They chuckled.

"No, you're very much alive," Timothy reassured me with a smile.

After monitoring my condition for four hours, Pelli agreed to let me leave.

"Tomorrow, you will feel stiff and sore. " Drink plenty of water, C.J.," my personal medical provider advised.

"I promise." Hugging him, I said, "Thank you. I owe you my life."

Timothy reserved a suite for me at the Le Rue Hotel in his name. No one would know that I was there.

"It's the least I could do for you, Captain," he explained.

The guys informed me about my patio door and stated that they would cover the repair expenses. My objection was futile; they insisted.

"Let us take care of you," said Michael.

Ramesh approached the twins in the warehouse the following morning. He demanded detailed information pertaining to my death. They told him that they had booby-trapped my house to explode last night.

"Huh, seriously? I religiously listen to the police scanners, making sure that my businesses aren't raided. There was no mention of an explosion in Long Beach," said Ramesh as he ran his right hand through his hair. Pulling out his cell phone, he viewed a live satellite feed of my neighborhood, zooming in on my intact house.

Shaking his head, he placed his phone back in his pocket. "Well, C.J. is alive, and you two worthless assholes are dead!"

With a swift and smooth move, Ramesh pulled his semiautomatic weapon from the waistband in his back. Rapidly releasing two rounds, he struck each twin with a bullet between their eyes.

They fell dead.

Instead of reporting my abduction to the local police, I called the general, who stated that he would consult the FBI. Two days later, he updated me.

"The FBI are looking for Ramesh and the twins. They're nowhere to be found, presumably on the run. You're safe to resurface."

I seriously considered leaving California, severing my brief tenure, since my life was in jeopardy. But since the general assured me that Ramesh and the twins were on the run, I decided to stay. I was supposed to be safe here. How did my civilian life become more dangerous than being in the Army? I just wanted a mundane life. That wasn't too much to ask for. I rescinded the remainder of my leave of absence and was scheduled to return to work. My house alarm was upgraded. Driving with my eyes focused on the rearview mirror, I never drove home the same way twice.

I signed up for an upcoming medical conference in LA. Enrolling online, I was unaware that my registration was automatically sent to the physicians' work calendar website.

The weeks flew by. My vacation rapidly approached.

The Dead Patient

Upon the start of my last shift before I left for my birthday vacation, paramedics arrived unannounced with a murdered male patient. He had been pronounced dead by the medics in the field fifteen minutes earlier. The explanation for this unusual occurrence was that the crime scene was a nightclub, and the atmosphere had become hostile, so it was unsafe for them to wait for the coroner. They just needed a location for the coroner to pick up the body. Since the patient was already pronounced dead, there was nothing for the ER to do. Actually, the police didn't want anyone to touch the body. It was considered a hands-off situation.

The patient was transported with a towel draped around his head, obscuring his identity. Bullet holes were prominent on his bloody shirt. A couple of LAPD officers accompanied the paramedic team. Everyone denied knowing his name. I was in a heightened sense of suspicion about this ordeal. I had Ketra meet me in my office. She entered five minutes later, finding me reclining and vigorously tapping my fingers on the desk.

"Something's up with this case," I fretted. "I smell something fishy, and it isn't the decomp, sistah! I think we're being played."

Nodding her head, she replied, "Mm-hmm."

Taking a stance, I made an executive decision. "He might be the cop's murder victim, but now he's my murder victim, too." I stopped tapping.

Our mystery patient was registered as John Doe, an unidentified male. Ketra wrote the triage note that read as follows:

Paramedics brought in an unidentified male, dead on arrival, pronounced in the field. Patient sustained multiple gunshot wounds to his chest. The crime scene was hostile, unsafe for the medics to wait for the coroner. LAPD officers O. Smith and E. Grant escorted the body. Awaiting arrival of the coroner to transport the remains. No intervention from the ER will occur. End of note.

Determined to find out who he was, I entered room 17, passing the two police officers who were diligently writing in their tiny notepads outside the doorway. I approached the draped corpse in the center of the room. Unnoticed, I discreetly pressed his right thumb on the touchscreen cover of my newly cleaned cell phone, preserving his fingerprint.

His right forearm bore a unique tattoo that jarred my memory.

"Interesting tat," I acknowledged to the cop who was now standing next to me.

"Yeah, if you're into that kind of thing," he said flippantly as he loosely pulled the sheet over the arm, concealing the tattoo.

I activated QA's fingerprint scanner on my phone. Almost in an instant, I had feedback. An audible tone was generated, indicating that he had been identified.

Speaking to no one in particular, I said, "Excuse me, I have to take this call."

I headed to my office to view the message that stated, "Match found." A facial image appeared on the screen. My dead patient was no longer John Doe; he was Theodore Michael Rodgers, the mayor's son.

A squadron of LAPD officers, maintaining their blue code of silence, encroached upon the ER. They provided no information and answered no questions. After an hour, the band of blue brothers dispersed, leaving a sole rookie behind to guard the body.

Making pleasantries, I brought him a bottle of my orange juice. "Hi, you look thirsty. I can get you a bottle of water if you prefer."

"Thank you, doc. This will be fine."

"How long do they plan on having you here?"

Shrugging his shoulders, he said, "I don't know. This is really boring, but part of the job."

"I get it! This brings back memories of when I was standing guard while in Afghanistan. I hated it! I preferred to be where the action was, making a difference."

"Air Force or Army?"

"Army."

"Me too!" He abruptly stood up. "I should be out there with them chasing down the lead on this high-profile murder."

High-profile indeed, I thought.

"Well, that sucks! You could be on scene at the nightclub in Brentwood."

"No, it was Hollywood. It's the club Rocket Launcher."

GOTCHA! "Oh, I see."

He chugged down some OJ, then continued: "But no, thanks to my almighty supervisor, the infamous Sergeant Maverick Crayon, I'm stuck here."

"Crayon. Is he related to Harrison Crayon, LAPD's chief of police?"

"Yup, his son, the prick! There should be a law against nepotism within the LAPD. That guy thinks he can get away with anything and everything. He's running the lead on this case."

"Interesting," I whispered to myself. "Well, I better get back to the grind. If you need anything, officer, let me know."

"Sure. Hey, doc, I'm Logan."

Yielding a flirtatious grin, I responded, "Hello, Logan. My friends call me Dr. C.J."

Logan stared me down until I vanished in the hallway among a sea of inquisitive ER staff wanting to know about the infamous dead guy.

Reassuring them with an edge of cockiness, I asserted, "I don't have all the answers yet, guys, but I will. You know I will."

"Damn straight, doc! We got your back," said an invigorated Derrick. "We're not going to let them jam you up over the dead man walking in room 17."

Remaining in the room with the corpse, Logan performed a little dance while grinning widely.

"Hot damn! She's the doctor who was on the news," he marveled to himself.

After examining other patients, I retreated to the office to contact QA. I requested a deep dive on LAPD Sergeant Maverick Crayon. There was something hinky going on, and I was determined to find out what it was. I was involuntarily drawn into a deception, and I didn't like that.

The body had been in the ER for four hours when the squadron returned. Pointing to me, Logan alerted Sergeant Crayon.

"She needs to talk to you."

Turning his head, the sergeant asked, "Who? The young nurse?"

"She's the ER doctor."

Raising his eyebrows in disbelief, he said, "Seriously?"

I entered the room. "Hello, everyone. Who's in charge?"

"I am," announced a plainclothes officer extending his arm. "Sergeant Crayon here." Accepting his gesture, I shook his hand. "I'm Dr. Johnston."

"Thanks for assisting us with this situation. The crime scene became quite hostile. We had to move him."

"So I hear. I'm glad to help, but unfortunately, we're getting busy, and this room is prime realty. You've already occupied it for four hours."

"OK. Let me see what I can do to expedite things." Nonchalantly, he added, "The coroner should be arriving soon."

"Great." I turned to walk away, then quickly turned back around, facing him. "Oh, I had your mystery dead victim registered into the ER as a John Doe. You don't happen to know his name, do you, Sergeant?"

"Well, not really, no." Running his left hand through his hair, he asked, "So, he's signed in?"

"Yes, this is my ER and my staff. Every patient, dead or alive, must have a paper trail. You understand, right?"

Grimacing, he nodded yes.

I returned to my office, allowing him to accept who was really in charge.

Obviously upset, the sergeant was pacing while rubbing the back of his neck. "Damn it," he blurted out. "Who does she think she is, having him registered?"

"She's the one they call Dr. Badass. Remember the doctor who beat up the guy who placed a gun to her head? Well, that was her," gloated the rookie.

"She looks like a damn kid."

"That's because she's young, in her twenties." Rapidly patting the left side of his chest with his right hand, the rookie surmised, "I think I'm in love."

Everyone in the squadron laughed except the sergeant.

Two additional hours passed. Finally, I received a message from the night administrator at QA. Reading an encrypted dossier on Maverick Lee Crayon on my cell phone, I saw that his police career profile was less than stellar, yet he was promoted to sergeant—surely a perk for being the son of the chief of police.

LAPD, with 10,000 officers, is the third largest police department in the nation compared with the New York Police Department, which has 35,000 officers, and the Chicago police force, which has 11,000. Multiple accusations of possible corruption, excessive force, and drug abuse were unsealed by QA. This guy was dirty to the core. Now, he's covering up the murder of the mayor's son.

I sent another message to QA. This time, I inquired about a shooting at the Rocket Launcher club. I continued to see and treat patients as I simultaneously indulged in activities of my former life as a spy.

The nightclub possessed several video cameras, but only those that were directed toward the bar and cashiers were capable of recording. The remaining cameras were limited to only a live feed. Fortunately, a shopping warehouse across the street maintained a high-definition recording system, including night vision capability. QA sent me their video.

The murder was captured and recorded. The murderer was in my ER!

Once again, I entered room 17. The squadron of police had left, but the sergeant and rookie remained. I addressed them both.

"Any word on the coroner?"

"No, not yet, but he should be here soon, Dr. C.J.," stated Logan. "These things take time."

"And sometimes, things just aren't what they appear to be," I interjected. "For instance, this patient, John Doe, sustained multiple gunshot wounds to his left chest. Since you, the LAPD, have forbidden me to examine him, I performed a preliminary visual assessment. The three holes in his shirt are of a tight grouping, almost touching each other. That's the work of a sharpshooter, a trained killer, possibly a cop!"

The men stood speechless.

I continued: "You, the LAPD, went to great lengths to obscure his identity, but I have already had our registration clerk change his alias, John Doe, to Theodore Michael Rodgers, the son of LA Mayor Titan Rodgers."

Wide-eyed and with their mouths agape, they looked like they were going to faint.

Crossing my arms across my chest, I concluded my ranting. "Looks like I've blown you both away with my—let's say—superpowers. I recognized the red star-shaped birthmark on his right deltoid and the tattoo of a hundred-dollar bill with his initials TR defacing Ben Franklin's right cheek. As a renowned LA DJ, he's known for wearing only white wife-beater-type shirts, exposing his distinctively masculine deltoids and arms. I watched an interview with him last week on late-night television while I was enjoying a night off.

"Now for the grand finale. Sergeant Crayon, you have a checkered past with the LAPD. You're young, tenacious, and should be a role model to others. Instead, you're narcissistic and despised by most of the rank and your colleagues. Do better! Officer Logan Williams, you, too, are young and tenacious, but unlike your supervisor here, you're warm and gregarious. Your LAPD record is unblemished. It would be great if you could maintain that record throughout your career. Unfortunately, after tonight, that won't be possible because you're going to be charged with the murder of Theodore Rodgers that occurred in the parking lot of the Rocket Launcher nightclub in Hollywood. Next time, smile for the cameras."

"What the hell," he objected.

Turning toward the door, I called out, "Gentlemen, you may come in now."

The police squadron entered—this time, with their guns drawn and aimed at the rookie. He retreated without resistance. As the chief of police walked in, the sergeant handed his personal handcuffs to him, giving him the honor of arresting the murderer.

After the rookie was escorted out of the ER, the chief approached me.

"It's a pleasure to meet you, Dr. Johnston. We have a few of the same friends in high places. The general said to tell you hello."

I snickered, "He's a great mentor. Glad you were able to view the crime scene video I forwarded to him."

"Thanks for your assistance. I apologize for the inconvenience and disruption we've caused tonight."

"Chief, my ER was used as a conduit, a channel to divert awareness from a murder. My staff and my patients were technically placed in harm's way."

"Understood. Again, my apologies, doctor."

Derrick came to the doorway. "Dr. C.J., the coroner is here."

Despite the intense events of the evening, the ER couldn't rest. A thirty-two-year-old female model presented with bilateral breast pain and swelling after an active day of surfing and snowboarding. While snowboarding, she fell hard onto her chest.

One of the many perks in Southern California during the winter months is the ability to surf the coast in the morning and ski or snowboard in the mountains during the afternoon, all on the same day.

Unable to sleep due to the discomfort, she decided to seek medical attention during the wee hours of the morning. I informed her that the fall she had endured had ruptured both of her breast implants, leaking the saline fluid into the surrounding tissues and causing her breasts to deflate, sag, and misshape. My visual observation, along with a CAT scan of her chest, confirmed the findings.

I called my good friend on her cell phone, waking her up. Dr. Bree Palmer, a renowned plastic surgeon who is recognized for her expertise in breast augmentation and reconstruction, answered on the second ring. She accepted the case and wanted to schedule a breast implant exchange.

It was 7 a.m., and she was my last patient for the shift. My ten-day thirtieth-birthday vacation officially began.

I headed to the morning conference.

Attending the early breakfast option before the conference, I enjoyed a delicious meal. The orange juice was a bit too sweet, but I indulged in a second glass when the rotund, red-haired waiter offered it to me. I was thirsty. He was slowly caressing his hand but abruptly stopped when I took notice. After finishing the second glass, I felt ill. My tongue became numb, and I had a brief dizziness episode.

The juice was tainted!

Grabbing my empty water glass and the full saltshaker, I clumsily ran into the bathroom. Filling the glass with tap water, I added all of the salt, then drank it to induce vomiting. Even after expelling the contents of my stomach, I still felt drugged.

Frantically running out of the building, I jumped into the first taxi parked in the driveway. I told the driver that I needed to go to the hospital emergency room immediately.

During the ride, my mind flashed back to the waiter who had given me the second glass of OJ. Something seemed familiar about him. Was it his eyes? Was he hanging around, waiting for me to drink the poison? Was it my imagination, or did he rub his hands together? I felt like I knew him. Was he wearing a fat suit?

I also felt like I was going to die.

The taxi ride seemed like an eternity as my health was deteriorating in the back seat, but in reality, it was only eight minutes.

My Birthday

It was my birthday week, and I had missed my flight to New York three days ago. Genesis called Jewel in a panic.

"It's been four days since we've heard from Chanel. I'm really worried! Her birthday is tomorrow, Veterans Day. Where the hell is she? I called her and was told that she's on vacation."

"I'm worried, too," Jewel responded. "That's not like her."

"I want you to meet me at Franklin National Bank in an hour."

"Why?"

"Chanel told me that if anything ever happened to her, then I would need to read a ledger in her safe deposit box. She called it the Duppy File. I'm on her account, and I have the key. I thought she was being paranoid, but now I feel compelled to get it. I'm too nervous to go alone."

"Duppy. Doesn't that mean ghost in Jamaican Patois?"

"Yes, it does. Very good!"

"So, this is some kind of ghost file? What the hell does that mean?"

"Secrets. The Duppy File is a ghost book or ledger that shouldn't exist, but it does," Genesis replied solemnly.

Keeping her curiosity in check, Jewel said, "I'm on my way to pick you up!"

The women were anxious as they stood in the bank vault. Genesis was actually shaking when she accompanied the bank manager to open the box with the two-key system—hers and the bank's. The manager removed the elongated metal box from its assigned housing space within the vault and placed it on the adjacent table. Pulling the curtain around them, the manager maintained a perimeter of privacy. Genesis stood frozen, absolutely still.

"We can't stand here all day," Jewel said, comforting her by rubbing her arm.

Taking a deep breath, Genesis opened the box. Methodically, she retrieved the items and placed them on the table. A ledger titled The Duppy File, a large manila envelope, and a business envelope with an attorney's name on it were displayed before them. She opened the white business envelope and found a copy of Chanel's will. Genesis was appointed the sole beneficiary of $3 million in an offshore account in the Cayman Islands.

Next, she flipped through the ledger with Jewel peeking over her shoulder. "Damn!" Shaking her head, Genesis slammed the open ledger down in disgust.

"What's that?" said an inquisitive Jewel. "It looks like weird doodling with all these lines and swirls across the pages."

It isn't doodling. Her notes are written in shorthand, a system of symbols and abbreviations for words or common phrases. She did this to deter prying eyes. When she was a teenager, she caught me reading her diary. She learned shorthand to prevent me from reading her deep, dark secrets. But that didn't deter me or keep me from being nosy. My friend's mom was a stenographer, and she taught me how to read and write it. I'm quite rusty, as that was over thirteen years ago.

Scanning the pages, Genesis was able to recognize a familiar word or phrase here and there. Jewel picked up the bulky parcel, opening the metal clip.

With wide eyes, Genesis gasped as she raised her head from behind the ledger. Making direct eye contact with Jewel, she said, "Oh my God! She's a spy!"

Jewel tilted the open tan-colored package, spilling its contents on the table. There was a pink gun and two passports, one French and the other Italian, bearing Chanel's picture and fictitious names. The formal, government-issued documents were heavily marked with European travel stamps. Dislodged from the bottom of the packet, a mound of foreign currency piled up in front of them. Perplexed, the two women looked at each other in disbelief with tear-streaked faces.

After spending the morning outside my Long Beach home, Detective Rockwell decided to leave and wedged his business card in the front door jamb. Later that afternoon, he went to the FBI field office in Los Angeles to gather information. He received my file, but everything was blacked out, except the fact that I was an Army officer in Afghanistan. My duties, missions, and even the medals I acquired were obscured. The word "CLASSIFIED" was boldly written in red across the top of each page. The file was useless; it was practically an official stack of papers with just my name on them, a redacted dossier.

The following day, Veterans Day, was a working holiday for the detective. He spent most of his time trying to track down relatives for this infamous ICU patient—me. He'd been ignoring the incoming calls on his burner phone. He knew who was desperately trying to reach him.

He'd looked at my photo on his phone at least 100 times during the past two days. Then, suddenly, it clicked. He recognized me as the woman in the video that went viral when I was fighting the ER gunman. *Why would someone want to kill her*, he thought? Looking at his watch, he realized that he was running late for a clandestine meeting.

At 7 p.m., he met a trim, athletic-looking, well-dressed yet unsavory character under the Elm Street bridge. Bypassing the homeless encampment, they met in the unlit corner of a well-worn path.

"Rocky, Rocky, Rocky. Why have you been ignoring me?" said the man in disgust.

"I haven't! I've been up to my neck on an attempted murder case. My supervisors are on my ass about this one."

Displaying an irritated expression, the man bowed his head and shook it back and forth a few times, staring at the ground.

"I'm curious," said Rocky. "Why do we always meet here, in the armpit of LA? There are used condoms and needles all around. This place creeps me out! I feel like I need a tetanus shot and a hepatitis vaccination."

"Quit whining! The people here have badge phobia, scared of cops. They won't snitch about our little meetings," he said with confidence.

"Did you ever see the video of the cute Black female ER doctor kicking a gunman's ass? You know, the war hero they call Dr. Badass."

The unsavory man paused before responding. "Yes, why?"

"Well, someone tried to kill her and almost succeeded. She actually died and was brought back to life. She's been in the hospital for several days as a Jane Doe, and I just identified her. I initially didn't recognize her with all of the tubes going in and out of her body. I should have noticed her hair, the afro twist style."

"They're called dreadlocks or just locs."

"Yup, that."

The man in the shadows became uneasy, pacing and rubbing his hands together. "Tell me more about this case."

And he did.

"She was poisoned and has been in a coma at Shepherd Medical Center's ICU. I finally received phone numbers for her family in

New York. I'm calling them in the morning. I expect they will take the first flight to California."

"Interesting!"

"I know! Oh, I almost forgot, I've got intel for you. The FBI is looking for the twins."

"They are lying low, real low right now."

"Good! Tell them to stay put."

"I'm sure they will." Handing Rocky an envelope containing $2,000 cash, the man commented, "You've been very resourceful tonight."

"Glad to do business with you."

They parted ways, driving off in opposite directions.

A ruggedly handsome man parked his car two blocks away from Shepherd Medical Center. Dressed in blue hospital scrubs, a white lab coat, and wearing white tennis shoes, he braved November's nighttime chill to walk to the hospital. Lingering around the employees' entrance, he placed his phone to his left ear, actually to speak to no one.

A young male nurse returned from making a coffee run to the local café down the street. Holding a cardboard tray with six large Styrofoam cups of gourmet brew, he struggled to avoid spilling the hot beverages as he approached the door.

The man ended his fictitious call by saying, "Nurse, administer the pain medication as I ordered. I'm entering the hospital as we speak. Goodbye."

Turning toward the nurse, he said, "Let me help you."

"Thank you, doctor."

Intentionally missing a step, he stumbled on the stairs, gently bumping into the nurse.

"So sorry."

"No problem. I didn't spill a drop."

Rapidly swiping a hospital badge against the door sensor, the man held the door open and gestured for the nurse to enter first. Inside the hospital, the nurse waited for the elevator. The man took the stairs, heading to the ICU on the third floor. At the entrance of his locked unit on the second floor, the nurse frantically patted his clothes, searching for his staff ID card to activate the door.

Somehow, he lost his hospital badge.

While the man ascended the stairs, a hospital-wide overhead page echoed.

"Code Gray ICU room 14. Code Gray ICU room 14. Code Gray ICU room 14," announced the operator.

That dispatch alerted the hospital staff that a patient was threatening or projecting violence toward employees or other patients. With a sinister grin, he acknowledged that this was a distraction to his advantage. Suddenly, he heard multiple fast-paced footsteps from people running up the stairs a flight below him. He hastened his gait. Making his way to the secure doors leading into the ICU, he quickly swiped a hospital badge for entry. A large group of staff congregated around room 14.

He stood among them.

A deranged male patient was standing next to his bed, yelling profanity and swinging an IV pole as a weapon. The hearsay within the crowd was that he was high on street drugs. A burly male nurse was holding a syringe that was surely filled with some kind of sedative. Unfortunately, he couldn't get close enough to the patient to administer it.

With his hospital badge intentionally turned backward, he struck up a brief conversation with that nurse. "I'm a new senior resident. Does this sort of thing occur frequently here?"

Shaking his head in disgust, he replied, "Nope, not really."

Overhearing their conversation, a bleached-blond, curvaceous nurse in extremely tight scrubs commented, "This is my first time witnessing something this crazy,"

The security officers entered the room and surrounded the highly agitated patient. They threatened to use nonlethal weapons and tase him if he didn't drop the IV pole. With everyone attentively watching the commotion, the staff impostor took this opportunity to wander away from the crowd, surreptitiously entering room 16—my room.

He approached my bed.

"Happy birthday, C.J.!" whispered the trim and fit red-haired stranger.

His eerily familiar voice penetrated my brain. My eyes spontaneously opened for the first time in four days. Through my blurred vision, he wasn't initially recognizable.

Lowering himself close to my ear, he continued to whisper. "It's time you went back to sleep—permanently."

I grimaced as I recalled who he was. Evil has many faces—and his was one of them!

Taking a 10 cc syringe filled with potassium chloride out of his white lab coat pocket, he connected it to the IV tubing in my arm.

"This will sting a bit," he warned.

As he administered the drug, excruciating pain traveled up my left arm. My cephalic vein felt like it was on fire. I frantically flapped my restrained arms wildly but remained speechless—I was still intubated, and my screams were silent!

With the injection completed, he placed the empty syringe back in his pocket and left the room to rejoin the spectators. Hearing my ventilator alarm, my bleached-blond nurse walked in to find me awake and extremely agitated. My constant thrashing around set off the alarms.

BEEP…BEEP…BEEP…BEEP…BEEP!

I had severe palpitations. My heart was racing as if it were preparing to jump out of my chest. This was different from any anxiety I had previously experienced. My entire body felt so weird and indescribable. This tachycardia was induced by the drug that the unfamiliar, yet familiar, stranger had injected into my bloodstream. My heart rate accelerated to 150…160…180. I shook my arms fiercely but wasn't able to free myself from the clutches of the restraints. Unsuccessful in verbally consoling me, my nurse decided to get a sedative.

BEEP…BEEP…BEEP…BEEP…BEEP…BEEP!

The cardiac monitor alarm belted out as my heart rate accelerated into a dangerous category: 188…232! As the nurse entered the medication room to obtain the drug, "CODE BLUE TO ICU ROOM 16" was announced overhead. Prior to running to my room, the impostor gestured for the husky male nurse to assist him. I was unresponsive, and the cardiac monitor showed a graph display of ventricular fibrillation, an irregular and chaotic fatal heart rhythm.

I didn't have a pulse!

As a backboard was placed under my body and CPR was initiated, the mysterious fake doctor with the familiar voice re-entered the room, taking charge of my code. Ironically, he had put me in this precarious situation. He ordered the muscular male nurse to defibrillate me at 200 joules. He charged the machine.

Ready to deliver its electrical current, he instructed, "Clear, stand clear!"

Everyone backed away from my bed to avoid being electrocuted. My body jerked as the electrical bolt ran through me in a futile attempt to correct my fatal heart rhythm. Although it changed— my heart was no longer quivering—it wasn't for the better. Now, it was at a standstill, not moving at all. The cardiac monitor revealed that I was in asystole, flatlined.

"Resume compressions and administer epinephrine 1 milligram IV push," ordered Dr. Evil. My bleached-blond nurse rapidly pushed the medication into the IV. As a group of staff, physicians, and nurses converged at the door, he held his hand up to protest their entry. "We have enough staff here, thank you," he proclaimed.

Timidly, the group retreated, preferring to avoid a verbal confrontation. The cadence of the cardiac compressions could be heard in the background: "…thirteen, fourteen, fifteen…"

"Stop CPR for a rhythm check," demanded the evil physician.

I opened my eyes.

Through the darkness, a string of lights transformed into leading lines, enticing my eyes to follow. I sat up and then trailed the illuminated path that led to a beautiful sacred garden full of inflorescent rhododendrons. Colorful species—burgundy arboreum, yellow austrinum, white bureavii, orange calendulaceum, purple capitatum, pink and white accidentale, and red spinuliferum—adorned the landscape as their sweet scent permeated the air. My mother, father, and Hans stood in the midst of the field of flowers with outstretched arms—ready to embrace me.

A loud, steady hum emanated from the cardiac monitor, indicating the ominous, non-survivable rhythm. The graph portrayed a single linear horizontal line across the screen.

Looking at the monitor, my nurse announced, "She is still flatlined, doctor—asystole, no heart rhythm."

"OK, then," he replied, "I'm calling it! What's the time of death, nurse?"

"2210. It's 10:10 p.m., Doctor."

Under her breath, a junior resident remarked, "That's it? It's over? He really didn't give her much of a chance by administering just one medication."

Overhearing her comment, he responded, "This patient has gone through enough. Thank you, everyone."

He dismissed the staff, and they left the room. My primary nurse turned off the cardiac monitor before exiting to get the Code Blue paperwork. Left alone with me, Dr. Evil closed my eyes and stroked my locs.

Muttering to himself, he said, "On this day thirty years ago, you were born at 10:10 p.m., and today, you died at 10:10 p.m. It didn't have to come to this, C.J. I have always, always loved you."

Walking out of ICU room 16, the nurse tried to get his attention. With his hospital badge positioned backward, she was unaware of his name.

Waving a sheet of paper, she beckoned him. "Doctor, I need your name for the Code Blue report."

The End

Acknowledgement

I'm truly fortunate to have chosen the editing team at Cup and Quill. They provided expertise and insight, enabling my novel to come to fruition. After my conversation with the CEO, Founder, and Editor, Linda Tucker, PhD, I was excited. She explained her company's services, which included a typist, considering that my 80,000-word manuscript was handwritten.

Editors Heather Smyth, PhD, and Andy Malinski, BSEd, guided me through this extraordinary journey. Kirsten Taylor contributed to the final process by proofreading and preparing my writing for publication. After reading my manuscript, this quintessential team gave me the most uplifting feedback. Cinematic, breathtaking, exciting, outstanding, excellent, and fantastic are the words they used to describe my beloved debut novel.

The exquisite cover design, provided by my publisher, Mike Cameron, CEO of Inicio Press, captured the essence of the main character's historic journey to Mount Everest. It was the first option offered, and I had no desire to look any further. It was perfect!

Thanks to Cup and Quill and Inicio Press, my dreams have transformed into reality.

Today, I'm an author.